ANCIENT WARRIOR
ANCIENTS RISING SERIES
BOOK EIGHT

KATIE REUS

Cover Art by Sweet 'N Spicy Designs
Editor: Julia Ganis
Author Website: https://katiereus.com

Publisher's Note: This is a work of fiction. Names, characters, places, and incidents are either the products of the author's imagination or used fictitiously, and any resemblance to actual persons, living or dead, or business establishments, organizations or locales is completely coincidental.

Ancient Warrior/Katie Reus.—1st ed.

ISBN: 978-1-63556-286-6

PRAISE FOR THE NOVELS OF
KATIE REUS

"...a wild hot ride for readers. The story grabs you and doesn't let go."
—*New York Times* bestselling author, Cynthia Eden

"Has all the right ingredients: a hot couple, evil villains, and a killer action-filled plot. . . . [The] Moon Shifter series is what I call Grade-A entertainment!" —Joyfully Reviewed

"I could not put this book down. . . . Let me be clear that I am not saying that this was a good book *for* a paranormal genre; it was an excellent romance read, *period.*" —All About Romance

"Reus strikes just the right balance of steamy sexual tension and nail-biting action....This romantic thriller reliably hits every note that fans of the genre will expect." —*Publishers Weekly*

"Prepare yourself for the start of a great new series! . . . I'm excited about reading more about this great group of characters."
—Fresh Fiction

"Wow! This powerful, passionate hero sizzles with sheer deliciousness. I loved every sexy twist of this fun & exhilarating tale. Katie Reus delivers!" —Carolyn Crane, RITA award winning author

"A sexy, well-crafted paranormal romance that succeeds with smart characters and creative world building."—Kirkus Reviews

"You'll fall in love with Katie's heroes."
—*New York Times* bestselling author, Kaylea Cross

"Both romantic and suspenseful, a fast-paced sexy book full of high stakes action." —Heroes and Heartbreakers

"Katie Reus pulls the reader into a story line of second chances, betrayal, and the truth about forgotten lives and hidden pasts."
—The Reading Café

"Nonstop action, a solid plot, good pacing, and riveting suspense."
—RT Book Reviews

"Exciting in more ways than one, well-paced and smoothly written, I'd recommend *A Covert Affair* to any romantic suspense reader."
—Harlequin Junkie

"Sexy military romantic suspense." —USA Today

"Enough sexual tension to set the pages on fire."
—*New York Times* bestselling author, Alexandra Ivy

"*Avenger's Heat* hits the ground running...This is a story of strength, of partnership and healing, and it does it brilliantly."
—Vampire Book Club

"*Mating Instinct* was a great read with complex characters, serious political issues and a world I am looking forward to coming back to."
—All Things Urban Fantasy

For Kaylea Cross, best friend and rock star all in one.

CHAPTER ONE

S omething was happening.

For the first time in years, he felt a crack in the spell encasing him underneath this blasted fae dungeon.

Heat. Power. Not fae. *Dragon fire.*

Something was affecting the spell from outside. Somewhere...

Aodh shoved out with his own magic, felt a snap as the powerful spell that had been holding him hostage fractured. It was just a fissure, but that was all he needed. All he'd been waiting for.

He shoved out again like a battering ram with the brute strength of his dragon and his magic. Roaring out his rage as his own fire engulfed him, he pushed out harder and stronger now that the invisible chains binding him had finally weakened.

He might never get this chance again. Had to take advantage.

Had to get free.

Get revenge.

Now that the spell was weakened, he shoved up through the stone slab that had buried him alive in dragon form, ignoring everything as it crumbled away, fell beneath him into the pit he would never return to again.

He'd rather die than be imprisoned again.

As he flew upward into the fae's castle dungeon—the one above his own secret one—he saw night sky for the first time in… He'd lost track of the time. Maybe fifteen years.

Nothing, for an ancient as old as him.

Except it had been stolen from him. Everything had been stolen.

As he emerged fully, he saw that fire and destruction bathed where the fae castle in the Domincary realm had once been. Hundreds of other dragon shifters were high in the air, their colors shimmering against the starlight. He didn't recognize their clan colors or their scent.

A lone naked female in human form stood amongst the rubble, her bare feet coated in ash, her hands on her hips as she surveyed the destruction around her with…satisfaction.

That was when he felt her magic, as ancient as he was.

He had no idea who these dragons were, but they'd somehow set him free in their battle against the fae. And he'd be leaving now, thank you very much.

Ignoring them, he flew upward even higher, letting his dragon fire carry him as he called on magic he hadn't been able to touch in far too long. Not since he'd been poisoned, then trapped.

His dragon fire consumed him as he moved through time and space in the rare way his line of dragons could transport until he disappeared from the fae realm and ended up…

In the middle of a Chicago street. But not the one he remembered. In human form now, he kept his camouflage in place as he surveyed his surroundings.

All around him were high-rises that looked as if they'd been bombed. Most of the glass windows had been blown out of the high-rises, the tops of some of them completely ripped away. And that was only the buildings still standing—most weren't. Foliage had started to grow as it slowly overtook the once bustling human metropolis surrounding him.

He inhaled deeply. Scented life, but no humans.

A wolf howled in the distance, and when he saw a shadow move in the building nearest him he narrowed his gaze, then laughed lightly at himself.

A jaguar loped out of the bottom floor of a building, dragging a limp, dead deer. It paused and stared at him even though he was concealed.

Animals could always sense more. Unlike humans, they never questioned their sixth sense.

Aodh waited until the jaguar finally left, its meal leaving a bloody streak behind it, before he shifted to his dragon form. Still unsure of everything at this point, he kept his camouflage cloaked around him as he took to the skies and surveyed the destruction below.

This was not the city he remembered. Not the world he remembered.

And this destruction hadn't been done by humans. The scent of dragons was faint on the air as well as the distinctive remnants of dragon fire charring various buildings. He knew what bombs smelled like, knew what kind of destruction large ones could inflict. But this... had been done by supernaturals.

In that moment, his plans were merely altered, not cancelled.

He would find Harlow, wherever she was in this new world. And he would get his answers, find out why his fierce, deadly tiger abandoned him to rot in that prison.

Then he was going after the witch who'd imprisoned him. And he was going to kill her.

CHAPTER TWO

From a treetop, Flavia watched the flames lick high into the air as the destruction from the wretched dragons spread—ruining everything.

The castle of the Domincary realm no longer stood, and that weak, pathetic king was dead. Not that she cared about that. But her captive was free.

She'd gotten lucky years ago, so damn lucky—more than she could have imagined. But she'd seen an opportunity and had taken it, had used trickery to gain the most delicious prisoner ever. One of pure power. One she'd slowly been feeding off for years. It was every energy witch's dream.

Now, he was free.

And all because of bloody dragons. She loved and hated the powerful beasts. Their power was intoxicating, and now that she'd had years to drown in the taste of one, to siphon off energy whenever she desired, she could not settle for anything less again.

Human energy was too weak more often than not. Supernaturals in general had a slightly stronger energy, especially shifters. But dragons and other creatures of fire were like drinking raw power.

She wasn't sure what it was, but something about their life force worked exceptionally well with her own powers. And now she'd lost her main source of it.

As the fae ran through the forest, looking for shelter far away from what had once been their home, she remained in the shadows high up in one of the trees. From this point of view she could see that the dragons were starting to leave, one by one, their female leader directing them.

The two violet moons of the Domincary realm shone bright, illuminating a pile of rubble, ash, and a large cavern underneath the castle and dungeon.

The gaping hole yawned wide, the edges of it jagged from where her prisoner had broken free.

Flavia was briefly tempted to confront the female dragon, who was now in human form, surveying her destruction with what Flavia assumed was pride.

Flavia was too far away, her position on the edge of the forest giving her a wide view of everything, and she was up too high. And unlike shifters, she did not have the same eyesight. When she was at full capacity, glutted on her prisoner's energy, she had those same powers, but not now.

She'd been off in the human realm and had come back only to find this one invaded.

No, she could not face off with the dragon female with silvery hair. Her power pulsed in the air, the energy crackling like lightning. No one else would be able to see it, but Flavia could. She saw the little waves around the female, wanted to go to her, drive her athame through the female's chest and take everything.

But she was too weak, having waited too long to feed on her prisoner. Stupid, stupid, she silently berated herself.

She'd gotten complacent in the knowledge that he would be waiting for her when she needed a hit. And this female was at full capacity, would burn her to a crisp if she even approached. The only reason Flavia had even gotten a dragon in the first place was because they'd been in an enclosed basement and she'd managed to use a confusion spell. It had been so quick, then he'd been hers.

Now she would have to make a new plan, regroup. And that meant she needed power. Turning away from the temptation of the naked female dragon shifter, because she did not wish to die tonight, she quickly descended the tree, using her reserves to slow her descent.

Her feet touched the snow-covered earth, but she barely felt it. Using more of her magic, she called on a glamour spell, ensured that she would blend in with the fae of this realm.

Luckily she already had a willowy build and long blonde hair similar to many of the royal guard, but she made sure that her ears appeared the same and that her dress was comparable to everyone else's. The image she portrayed was of an elegant fae female wearing an embroidered tunic, loose pants, and thick boots. Over the top was a long fur coat that finished the ensemble.

Moving quickly, she hurried in the direction of the fae crowd who'd been running away. It would be easy enough to blend into the chaos and pick off a few stragglers.

People, regardless of race, often underestimated females. They never expected someone with such a pretty face and easy smile to stab them in the heart.

So she always used it to her advantage.

As she raced across the snow-covered forest, she heard the sound of hoofbeats in the distance, saw that she was coming up on a well-traveled road.

"Help!" she shouted as she stopped in the middle of the road, waving her hands wildly. She could see a rider on a horse in the distance so she started waving her hands even more. "Help, help!" she shouted again as the horse slowed.

The rider looked like one of the royal fae guard in full battle uniform. As he approached her, he slowed down and jumped off his horse, but kept a hold of the reins as he approached. "My lady, why are you out here alone?"

"I fled along with everyone else and got lost," she said on a cry, hurrying toward him, her hands clasped against her chest. "I'm so afraid and I got turned around."

He looked behind him, clearly agitated. "There are a handful of riders behind me. I cannot stay and help you, but they will—"

"But my sister has broken her leg. She was with me and I'm afraid I cannot carry her by myself. Please, I beg of you," she simpered as she got even closer.

Close enough to smell the male's cologne.

She feigned tripping on a rock and flew forward, stumbling into him. She clutched onto his biceps as she brushed up against him. He had on armor, but there were little slits she could easily slide her blade through.

So she did.

"My lady—" His eyes widened as he stared down at her, the receptors in his brain finally catching up to the pain in his chest.

Stupid male.

The tip of the blade was drenched in poison and it had already started coursing through his veins, paralyzing him almost immediately. This was her specialty. Poison.

She shoved deeper, unable to twist because of the shape of the armor, but it was no matter. Her venom was doing its job.

Then, because she was far stronger than she appeared, she hefted him up and tossed him over the seat of his horse. Grabbing the reins, she led beast and fae off the path, tossing a small spell over her shoulder that would clear away the hoofprints of the big animal. No one would know he'd come this way and she would have time to drain all of his energy.

Unfortunately she wouldn't be able to savor it, not when she needed to refill her strength.

And after she finished with him she'd find more targets, pick them off one by one. This realm was massive, and she'd seen the dragon leave it. He was gone, at least for now.

Which meant she could regain her strength and power before she hunted him down.

Or before he hunted her down.

Either way, because she knew one day he would come for her. Dragons could hold grudges for lifetimes and he would never let her go.

When they faced off again, she would be prepared.

7

CHAPTER THREE

Seven months later

Harlow shifted her pack against her back as she and Ace trekked through the forest. They'd been tracking rogue vampires for days and she was getting cranky.

Especially since they'd lost the scent a couple hours ago. These bastards were going down—but only if they could find them.

"All right, what's up with you?" Ace murmured as they reached a clearing and surveyed a long-abandoned neighborhood.

There were no manmade lights out here now, but the moon was full tonight, the stars a brilliant illumination.

The area was fairly rural, about twenty minutes by vehicle away from the closest town—also abandoned—with McMansion-style homes that had acre yards. But nature had started taking back most of it, the foliage overgrown in this area that humans and supernaturals alike had abandoned two years ago. It was one of the "in between" places, as she thought of them. Areas that no Alpha had claimed yet, usually because they were too far from any claimed territory to matter. But still good land, untouched by the dragon fire that had destroyed most of the big cities.

"What do you mean?" She inhaled deeply, trying to catch the scent of the vampires again. Her eyesight was just as good in human and tiger form, and so was her sense of smell. It was why she was such a good tracker—and why Ace had asked her to come with him on this little op.

"I get being quiet, but it's been three hours and you haven't said a damn word."

"Oh." She inwardly winced. She did that sometimes; just didn't talk. It made people crazy. "Sorry. I'm caught up in my head." She'd had a weird dream last night. Or nightmare, whatever. She'd been having them for months, as if something inside her had suddenly woken up. And she wanted to claw out of her own skin sometimes.

"Abouuut?" He stretched out the word.

"Why are you being so nosy?" She scanned the neighborhood, looking for anything that moved. Shadows that didn't belong.

"What the hell else are we going to do out here? Come on, I'll talk about the weather if you want. I can't stand this silence anymore."

"You're bordering on whining. I don't know why so many females in New Orleans think you're broody and mysterious."

Ace snickered as he ran a hand over his jaw. "It's because I'm so handsome."

"So something," she muttered as she tugged on her toque to make sure it was in place.

Ace's bronze skin was a natural camouflage and they'd both dressed in darker clothing to blend with the night. But she'd had to cover her auburn hair. It was a beacon no matter what.

"Moody tiger," he grumbled, but his tone was teasing.

"Fine, let's talk as we walk and hope we don't scare off the vamps."

"I think they're long gone," he muttered.

"Yeah, me too. So what do you want to do if we can't find them?" Realistically, they couldn't track them forever, especially since they were so far outside King's territory now.

"Track tonight and if we don't find them, head back."

"You're the boss."

He just snorted at that, but he was. He was basically King's second-in-command, one of his highest-ranked lieutenants. Harlow had never done rankings with her OG pack, but since assimilating into a large one she'd had to adapt to everything that went into being part of a vast community. She'd always worked in the shadows, as part of a smaller group for all her past jobs. And only with people she knew and trusted with her life.

"Have you considered King's offer?" he asked as they stalked down the hill toward a retention pond at the back of the abandoned neighborhood.

"Yeah. It's...enticing."

"What's holding you back?"

"I don't know."

"Yeah you do."

"All right, Doctor Ace. What's holding me back?" She jumped over a rotting log, her boots silent on the grass.

"Fear of change, maybe. But that's hard to believe since you've done a lot of cool shit over the years." He started lifting his fingers as he ticked things off. "Personal security for a world-famous singer, alleged supernatural black ops before that—"

"Oh, sweet goddess, Ace. Fine, I'm a little scared-ish. King wants me to run a small section in New Orleans—it's a huge responsibility. And I'd be living in a different area, away from my crew. It's...I don't know. A big change. I need time to think about it."

"Good things come from change. Also, it's like a fifteen-minute bike ride or run from your crew."

"You are so annoying when you're right."

He just grinned at her, and okay, she knew why so many females loved to gossip about Ace and wonder who he was dating. He was objectively good-looking. But he did nothing for her and she knew she did nothing for him. Thankfully. Because she loved patrolling with him; he was funny, if annoying, and he was tough as shit. She knew he'd have her back in any situation. And at the end of the day she knew he'd die for King and Aurora, the Alpha couple of their territory.

Since Harlow viewed Aurora as a little sister—always would—she loved him for that alone. Just not the romantic kind. That was reserved for one male from long ago.

Not that it mattered—he was still in her blood, in her bones, even if he was dead. No matter how hard she tried to forget him. Time was supposed to heal and all that crap. The male had tried to kill her and she'd had to kill him first—she shouldn't still think about him except with rage. But... She sighed. *But.*

When was the healing supposed to finally happen? Because when she went to sleep, more often than not, all she saw was his face. His gorgeous, harsh expression as he thrust inside her.

Gah! She'd gone years being able to compartmentalize and all of a sudden she just couldn't anymore. She'd shoved all her feelings for him down, locked them up so damn tight—they should have stayed buried!

"So when do your parents arrive?"

Glad for the change in subject, she kept alert as they reached the quiet winding street. Grass had grown through cracks in places, but without much use, the roads of the area weren't too bad. "A month, give or take." And she was excited to see them. "I'm hoping they'll decide to relocate. Brielle is too." She and her twin were often on the same page.

"I admit, I'm curious to meet the parents of two ferocious tigers."

She grinned. "You'll be surprised."

"Why?"

"Because they're hippie artists."

Ace blinked in surprise. "Seriously?"

"Yep. All our parents are artists of one kind or another. And they had no idea what to do with us when we formed our little 'fighting pack.'" She snickered at the memories of growing up in an artists' compound.

"*All of,* meaning..."

She withdrew one of her blades when the wind picked up, more out of habit than anything. She couldn't scent anything but she liked the heavy feel of a blade in her hand, always had. "Me, Brielle, Axel, Aurora, Bella, Lola, Marley and of course Star, Aurora, Kartini, Athena and Taya. We were like these little feral beasts just running wild, blowing shit up. Or tearing it up. I mean, we weren't malicious or anything, just wild shifters with very peaceful parents. And our parents all had us around the same time."

"Even Star and Aurora's parents?"

"Yeah, but they were definite fighters. Axel's too, though they chose the peaceful life. My parents, however, are just full-on vegetarian hippies."

"But they're tigers." He stared at her, confused.

"Oh, I know," she said on a laugh. "Probably the only vegetarian tiger shifters alive." She mock shuddered. "And it's not a coincidence that all of our parents lived together. They were all sort of misfits and never fit into any of their prides, clans or packs. So they created their own, and fit in among humans, who just thought they were a commune of human artists. They never expected all of us, but we were raised knowing we were loved for who we are."

"They never made you feel guilty or anything?"

"Nah. I don't think they'd know how. And when we went after the bastards who killed Star and Aurora's parents, they watched Aurora. Didn't try to talk us out of it or anything. Just packed us enough supplies so we wouldn't go hungry."

"That's awesome," he murmured, his gaze tracking over the quiet houses even as she did the same, looking for any movement, inhaling any odd scent.

Yeah, it had been awesome. Star had been the one to actually kill those dragons who'd killed her parents, but the entire crew had gone with her, been her backup. Harlow appreciated where she came from and knew she was lucky to have the parents she did. Hell, she was lucky about a lot of things because not everyone had the family she did.

But there was still a hole in her heart that even her family couldn't fill.

A giant, dragon-sized hole.

"Oof, I recognize that expression."

Harlow shot Ace a surprised look. "What?"

"You're thinking of someone. A male, perhaps?"

"Oh my goddess with the nosiness." She kicked out at him but he dodged out of the way, jumping up onto the sidewalk.

He simply grinned. "So who are you dating?"

No one. She wasn't ready. Couldn't seem to move on from the only male who had captured her heart. Then destroyed it. "I'll tell you if you tell me."

"Easy. No one."

She laughed lightly. "Same."

He shot her another surprised look.

"What?"

He lifted a shoulder. "You've seen a mirror."

"Yeah, well, *same*. Just...ugh, fine, but this shit better stay between us."

He mimed a zipper over his lips as they reached a crosswalk in the neighborhood. A penis had been spray-painted on one of the stop signs, and for some reason it struck her as hilarious. Someone had likely done it when the humans had evacuated the area. Because why not?

Ace grinned, nodding in approval. "Penis art, always a classic."

"Males are far too impressed with them. I would never have the urge to go around and spray-paint vaginas. Or...boobs or whatever. Males are weird."

"True enough. So, you're not dating anyone...but what about Axel?"

"Why? You interested?"

"Not my taste, but I might have placed a bet on when he'll get together with Christian. Or kill him. Or both."

"Wait...what?"

He winced only slightly, not really looking apologetic. "Some of the pack has bets on those two. But not just them. Tons of others."

"Oh, that makes it better," she murmured as they took a left on the deserted street. A few cars were outside along this street, though all were unused, the tires rotted out. "Any bets on me?"

"Hell no. Or your sister. Or...anyone in your house except Axel. My wolves are too scared of the females in your house."

She flexed her arms once jokingly. "That's right." Then she froze at the same moment he did.

The scent of blood tinged the air.

Close too.

Far too close... She pointed with her blade even as she withdrew her other one. She fought in both her forms, usually only shifting to her tiger when it was time to kill.

Because her seven-hundred-pound animal form was only conducive to some areas, and trying to sneak into a house as a tiger wasn't happening.

Ace nodded and they fell in step, hurrying toward the side of a two-story McMansion.

As they silently made their way along the side of the house, she looked up. So many humans and even some kinds of shifters never looked up for an attack. But she was a tiger who loved to climb.

No visible threat.

She touched her ear gently and Ace shook his head.

So he couldn't hear anything either.

But...there was too much blood nearby. Maybe an animal had been killed? Or maybe... She didn't like to think of the other maybes even though she'd seen them far too many times.

A scream tore through the air and she jumped into action, racing along with Ace toward the sound.

As they reached the overgrown backyard and the empty pool, she knew at once that it was the house behind this one.

A couple lights, like lamps, flickered in the distance.

She motioned to Ace that she'd loop around from the left while he motioned that he would come up on those lights from the right. They intrinsically knew the way each other moved. One of the many reasons she loved working with him.

Her boots were silent along the grass as she raced toward what had once been the property line, a falling-down privacy fence. As she reached it, she peered through the broken slats and her tiger roared to the surface as she saw a bleeding human limping across the yard, a male vampire stalking behind her, quiet malice in his expression.

Nope. Not tonight.

Harlow jumped the fence in one liquid move and hauled back, threw her blade with perfect accuracy across the yard, the swishing of it the only sound before—*thunk.*

The vampire burst into ash as he died and her blade fell to the grass.

Standing on unsteady feet, the young human finally processed her as Harlow continued racing across the yard, not breaking stride.

"Are there others like you?" Harlow demanded, hating that she couldn't be softer now.

The human who was perhaps in her twenties stared at her, her eye swollen, her lip split as she nodded.

"Hide. I'll save who I can. How many vampires?" They were all going down, but she wanted to know what she was up against.

"Five," she rasped out. "Maybe more. In the house."

Harlow nodded and grabbed her blade from the ground—from the pile of ash the vampire had turned into.

She spotted Ace by the edge of the house, disappearing toward the front. Knew he'd be taking a front entrance as she stepped through the slightly open back door.

Music played somewhere…a basement, maybe. It was faint, not loud enough to travel. She heard laughter, a scream, then more laughter.

Using instinct and years of training, she quickly found the door to the basement. She sheathed one blade and opened the door—and came face-to-face with a surprised-looking shirtless male.

His fangs descended and she stabbed him without pause, right through the chest.

He burst into ash before he could make a sound.

"Grab Ricky, see what the hell is taking so long!" a male voice called from down below. "Party's just getting started."

Harlow rolled her shoulders as she hurried down the basement stairs. It was clear this place had been renovated before The Fall, given the luxury wooden stairs and art still on the walls. But the bloody hand streaks told a story of horror.

She looked over her shoulder as Ace joined her, having already scented him.

He mouthed one word. *Go.*

She eased down the rest of the stairs, peered around the corner and saw red.

Three vampires lounged on couches, two young-looking human females passed out on the floor, teeth punctures all over their bodies.

They were clothed at least and didn't have any visible bruises. Two other vampires were currently having sex, moaning like adult film stars.

Harlow hurled a blade at the nearest vamp even as she raced toward another one.

He sprung up off the couch, hissing as he launched himself at her.

She was aware of Ace attacking the two vamps enjoying coitus while humans suffered.

Her claws extended on instinct and she slashed at the vamp's middle, enjoying his yelp of agony as she disemboweled him. He burst into ash before she could get in another good shot.

"What the—"

She turned toward another male voice on the stairs, narrowed her eyes as he raced back up and disappeared. "I'm going after him." Ace had everything covered down here and that human female outside wouldn't be fast enough to escape anyone.

Unable to hold back, she shifted to her tiger, the beast inside her giving in to the hunt as she quickly ate up the distance, pounced on the vampire as he reached the kitchen. One bite on the back of his neck and he was ash, though she'd already broken all his ribs with her seven-hundred-pound frame the moment she'd slammed him to the now cracked tile.

Scenting another runner, she raced out the back door and froze as she saw the vampire had a knife pressed to the throat of the human female she'd told to hide.

The human stared at her with big blue eyes, her jaw tight. Okay, this one was a fighter and Harlow would be damned if she didn't save her.

"Stay back!" the vampire screeched. "Just...keep your distance!"

Harlow crouched low, watched the vampire from roughly thirty-five feet away. A leap she could easily make, something this vamp might not realize. Normal tigers could jump about twenty feet, but she was more powerful, larger. Deadlier.

She snarled low in her throat, her gaze pinned to his as she scented his raw fear.

"I'm just going to leave and you're going to let me. I won't hurt the human if you don't move. Got it?" he screamed, the scent rolling off him so wrong. Fear, yes. But...he stunk, almost like how addicts smelled.

She sat up perfectly still and nodded, trying her best to look like a docile cat. Kinda hard, given her size and teeth, but she didn't bare them again. All she needed was one moment.

One quick moment—and she would take him down.

Because she could scent Ace nearby, but this was her kill.

"Okay, then," he breathed out, loosening his grip on the human, causing her to fall forward onto her knees.

And Harlow's cat smiled. Right before she pounced, sailing through the air with not just shifter speed, but tiger speed.

She slammed her paw across his head with enough force to break his neck even as she landed on him, breaking multiple bones. The quick kill was more than he deserved.

Ash burst into the air, making her sneeze even as she winced at the pinch of his damn knife.

She snarled as she shifted to human, looking down at the gash on her ribs that had already started to heal.

"You good?" Ace asked as he helped the human to her feet.

"Yeah. Stupid vampire," Harlow muttered, turning to the human. "I think we've killed them all, unless there are more at other houses around here?"

The human swallowed hard, stared at her in shock and a little awe. "No, that was it, I think. But I don't know for sure. We..." She glanced around the yard, almost as if looking for more danger, before she focused on Harlow again. "They hunted us. Toyed with us, I think. Tonight they caught a couple of us, brought us here."

"There are more of you?"

The human nodded. "Yeah, about fifteen of us. We...used to live around here. Not this neighborhood, but in a neighboring town. On a farm. A couple of our families banded together and we've been doing fine until...the vampires."

"Okay, well, first thing, we're going to check on your friends inside and get them on their feet." They hadn't been close to death, and all she'd have to do was give them some of her tiger blood and they'd rebound. "Then we'll meet up with the rest of your family. From there, we'll go over some options. Okay?"

The human's eyes were less glassy now as she nodded. "I wasn't abandoning them," she blurted, the scent of truth rolling off her.

"What?"

"My family, my friends." She indicated the house. "I was trying to escape, to find a weapon. Something to fight back," she growled.

"I understand," Harlow said gently. "You stay here with my friend Ace. I'll get your friends." And put on some clothes—and hopefully clean all this disgusting ash off her. Her wound had already knitted up, was just itchy now.

So she ignored it because they had work to do. While they wouldn't force the humans to come to New Orleans, she and Ace were certainly going to strongly suggest it. Otherwise, these humans would always be targets out here in the wilds, unprotected.

Harlow simply couldn't stand by and let them die when they had a safe haven to turn to.

CHAPTER FOUR

15 years ago
Undetermined black site, somewhere in Russia

Harlow broke off the doorknob with one quick twist, her supernatural strength coming in handy today. Like most days.

"This job is way too easy," Aodh murmured, a hulking presence next to her.

"Now you're complaining about how easy it is?" She eased open the reinforced metal door, then shoved back her annoyance when Aodh immediately moved in front of her, weapon drawn.

Not that he needed the pistol. None of them did, but this undercover job was supposed to be quick and quiet. So they were using human weapons with silencers instead of claws, teeth and fire.

"I'm just saying, shutting off the security cameras was too easy. Too quick."

She moved up next to him, her own pistol drawn—though she still had her blades strapped to her back like always. She eyed the interior of the seemingly deserted warehouse. "This is supposed to be an easy grab-and-bag job." Well, easy was relative, considering they'd had to actually get to this ice palace in Nowheresville, Russia by air, avoiding any radar, in the middle of a goddamn winter. Luckily they were all shifters, but if they'd been human, they'd have had to wear a lot more cold weather gear.

19

"Now you've done it, Red." He swept the place with a clinical eye and she did the same, not bothering with a flashlight.

With her tiger sight and his dragon sight, they no doubt saw the same thing. An empty, dusty warehouse. But...she could still sense something pulsing in the air. Like a buzz. As if there was a hidden beehive somewhere. "Done what?" She kept her voice subvocal so only he and the other two on their comm lines could hear—Brielle and Axel.

"Jinxed us."

"That's bullshit and you can suck it." Her boots were quiet as she took another step forward.

"I will definitely suck your breasts later."

She shot him a shocked look, instinctively slapped her free hand over his mouth. "Shut it." They were on a job, and her sister and Axel didn't know about them! What the hell was he playing at?

He licked her palm, a wicked glint in his eyes. "If you think the others can't smell me on you, you are definitely mistaken."

"Yeah, we've known for a while," Brielle murmured over the comm line. "So...what the hell? Was our intel bad? Because I'm seeing the same thing you are and it's a whole lot of nothing."

Harlow was going to go back later to Aodh outing them to the team. For now, she focused on their rescue mission, which was turning out to be a big dud. "Maybe. I can sense something though." Both she and Aodh had tiny cameras on their chests, giving the others the same view.

"Me too." Aodh's jaw was tight as he holstered his pistol, then—breathed fire into the vastness.

Oh shit!

His fire hit something—a force field. A purple dome appeared in the middle of the warehouse, revealing what had been there all along. An invisible prison.

Well, shit.

A big male was suspended inside it by magical chains, tethered to the force field. His eyes were closed, but she could see the rise and fall of his chest.

"Guys, movement coming in fast from about a mile away." Axel's voice was tight. "I see them on the radar."

Harlow didn't bother to ask how many because it didn't matter. They were in this shit, and they'd finish the damn job. Someone had captured this supernatural agent, and she and her crew had been tasked with busting him out. She didn't know the male, but that didn't matter. They weren't leaving one of their own to be tortured and killed. Or worse, turned into a weapon or a hundred other equally horrible options.

"Can you break this?" she asked Aodh as she slammed her sword against the glowing dome—and got blown back ten feet for her effort, electricity arcing through her. Fuuuuck. She blinked at the impact, but shoved to her feet.

"Yeah. You good?" His expression was dark as he looked her over.

She ignored his worry. "Of course."

He didn't shift, simply called on his fire and breathed a wild stream of raging hot flames at the dome. It was one of the most beautiful things she'd ever seen.

Just like the male himself.

Aodh. Old as hell, his body covered in scars, his silky dark hair pulled back into one of her hairbands as he pummeled the dome, his power raw, rolling over her skin like a lover's caress.

The only reason she was even standing here was because he'd somehow given her and the rest of the team some of his dragon's essence so they were immune to the power of his fire.

Above them, the roof started to blister away, even as the dome cracked, split.

"I got him!" she called out the moment it broke open, slamming her blade into it.

A frisson of electricity surged through her, but whatever magic had been holding this male was dying now. She jumped through the crack and hacked away at one of the magical chains.

It snapped, whipping wildly now that it was free.

She jumped up ten feet, avoiding the snap of it, and in the next moment it fizzled, disappeared completely.

"We're coming in hot. Be ready! I'm dropping cables." Brielle's voice was tight and Harlow could hear the gunfire in the distance, along with the sound of the chopper approaching. She knew her twin would be flying as close to the top of the burning warehouse as possible.

Aodh snapped the other chain free with his bare hands, his amber-orange eyes flashing. "I should just fly us out of here," he snapped.

"No, those aren't our orders." Harlow shook her head, not wanting him to catch any flak.

She hoisted the wounded prisoner up, slid her arm under his shoulders as she tried to keep the male upright. He was a complete dead weight and this was going to be awkward trying to hold him while climbing the cable.

Before she could contemplate anything, Aodh grabbed him, tossed him over his shoulder. "Fine," he gritted out. "But if it comes down to our safety, I'm doing things my way."

"Fine." They both looked upward as the sound of the chopper grew louder.

Relief punched through her as two cables suddenly appeared through the new holes in the ceiling.

She and Aodh each grabbed one, held on tight. "Go!" she shouted through the comm line, the chopper the only thing she could hear now.

As she gripped the cable tight with her gloved hands, they lifted off rapidly, breaching the roof. The icy wind battered them as they ascended—a bullet whizzed past her head, shouts of anger filling the air as they escaped.

"Forget this," Axel growled through the comm line.

She looked up, saw him hoist a handheld rocket launcher through the opening of the chopper—and moments later a huge explosion filled the air behind them.

Blistering wind whipped around them as Brielle flew them in the opposite direction, toward their exfil point twenty miles away.

Squinting against the gusts and the vast white landscape—and cursing the fact that her goggles were in her backpack—she glanced over at Aodh as she began climbing upward.

He moved just as quickly as her, as if he didn't have anything weighing him down, and she told herself not to be impressed. Not to want this arrogant male so badly.

She'd fallen hard and fast for him. Had never seen him coming.

Had never thought she'd meet someone who made her forget all reason. It was too late now. She was hooked on him and there was no way in hell she was walking away—

Harlow sat up with a start, her breathing labored.

"You good?"

She looked over to find Ace cooking sausage over their campfire.

The sun was peeking over the horizon, the forest around them waking up.

"Ah, yeah." *Just peachy.* She sucked in a breath, took stock of their surroundings as she tried to slow the wild beat of her heart. For the last seven months she'd had wildly vivid dreams about Aodh. Random memories: their missions together, lots of sexytimes, anything and everything. And it was making her nuts.

"You said it was too late." A frown pulled at his mouth.

"Oh, just talking in my sleep," she muttered, standing and stretching. Last night they'd managed to round up all the humans and camp out here instead of trying to start their trek back to New Orleans immediately.

Two of the humans had needed the sleep anyway, to recover from blood loss. And it had taken time for the others to pack up their belongings—not that they had much. Since The Fall they'd learned to travel light and live with the basics.

"Anyone else wake up yet?" she asked.

"Nah, but I figure they will soon enough. You mind starting some coffee?"

"Yeah, just give me a couple minutes." She needed to take care of business in the woods and use that time to simply breathe, remind herself that she wasn't back in that icy tundra with a male she'd loved more than life itself.

The male she'd had to kill because he'd been trying to kill her.

CHAPTER FIVE

A odh watched Harlow from the sky as she and the male wolf she was working with helped the injured humans on the trek back to New Orleans. It had been over fifteen years since he'd seen her and... watching her was pure torture.

Long, lean, strong as titanium, Harlow was walking power and sex. Her auburn hair was slightly longer than last time and she had it pulled back into a braid, falling down her back. She moved with that feline predatory grace that had always fascinated him, as if she was always ready to kill or attack. It was one of the reasons he'd fallen so hard for the warrior.

He'd almost intervened last night, had almost incinerated that vampire, but Harlow had kept things under control. And seeing her in her gorgeous tiger form had been... It had brought up too many memories.

Both perfect and painful.

Of a female who'd stolen his heart, every part of him, from practically the moment he'd met her. It had taken him an entire year from that first meeting to convince her to give him a chance.

Because her walls were up high, and they'd been reinforced.

But he was a patient dragon. And after she'd given in to her need, they'd been absolute fire together. She was the best teammate he'd ever had, on top of it. Because he'd been doing forms of "black ops," as the humans liked to say, for longer than he could remember.

And now Harlow was helping people who needed it in this new world. Because of course she was.

She'd always been like that; had a strong moral compass where she knew her limits and would kill or die for those she loved. And if someone screwed with the weak or bullied them, her blades or claws came out. Which was why it cut so deep that she'd abandoned him.

Just left him to rot in that lonely prison. Sure, maybe she'd searched for him initially, but it hadn't been for long.

Because here she was, guiding a group of needy humans instead of looking for him.

If it had been her who'd been imprisoned, if someone had taken her from him...he'd have destroyed the entire world to find her. He'd have never given up. Once upon a time, they'd been everything to each other.

Until they hadn't.

He shot upward, unable to watch her anymore, *smell* her. Because her wild sunflowers scent was a drug.

And he hated himself that he couldn't just turn away, just leave and start over, without knowing why the hell she'd left him. He should be out hunting the witch who'd imprisoned him, but instead he was chasing after a tiger who'd clearly never loved him the way he'd loved her.

Hours passed as he followed them. And to give the humans credit, they didn't complain as they walked back to their destination. Harlow and that annoyingly handsome male she seemed to laugh with far too often had a vehicle not too far away. But they'd left it during their hunt. Still, it would take the humans another few hours to get there and he didn't think they'd make it today.

If he was a betting dragon, he'd bet on them bunking down at the big creek-fed pond about a mile away.

When they started to unpack he landed and shifted out of sight, but tucked his pack of belongings away and kept his camouflage in place as he crept closer.

He should be thinking of all the ways he would make Harlow pay for her abandoning him, but instead... As she stripped down to shorts and a tank top and started setting up tents, he simply watched her lithe form work.

And fantasized, remembered exactly how she'd tasted, sounded, as he'd made her break apart in his arms. Over and over.

"I'm gonna hunt up some game," the male—Ace, he'd heard her call him—murmured to her. "You good?"

She nodded, smiled at the wolf. "Yeah, we'll hold down the fort."

Aodh wanted to burn that male to a crisp for being so close to her, for getting her smiles.

The humans, mostly females with a few teenage males, were working together to set up a couple fires and getting the young ones comfortable. Harlow had carried a couple of the kids on her back for a good portion of the trek, and so had that dumb wolf.

Harlow cared for people.

Just not him apparently.

He turned away from the scene, stalked back into the woods, needing distance. He made sure to go in the opposite direction of the wolf, flying high and scouring some fields he'd seen before.

There had been wild animals grazing, and picking off a deer and a few sheep was easy enough. Even though he knew it might give himself away, he didn't care.

Rational thought, when it came to Harlow, was a rarity.

Keeping his camouflage in place, he brought the dead game to the edge of the forest near their camp and rustled one of the trees loudly. He'd rolled around in so much foliage and dirt that she wouldn't be able to pick up his scent.

"Stay put," Harlow ordered, grabbing those familiar blades as she stalked in his direction.

They had a few hours until sunset so she'd have enough time to clean and cook everything.

From the shadows he watched as she stared in surprise. Then she called out for Ace.

"Huh," she murmured before jogging back to the group. She took the two oldest human women, the ones who were clearly in charge, and they grabbed knives for skinning and cleaning.

He left then, heading to the creek to swim and wash off while she and the others got their food ready. She would definitely wonder where it had come from when she realized that Ace hadn't brought the food back.

But he did not care. He simply couldn't have some other male feeding her.

Not rational, he reminded himself. Not one little bit.

Plenty rational, his beast purred. *Chain her to your bed, claim her, mate her.*

I will never mate her, he silently growled to his baser half. Or lock her up somewhere so she knew exactly what it was to be abandoned and left to die.

No, we will never do that. His dragon's roar was wild, fierce in his head.

So he dove underwater and screamed, letting out a fraction of the anger stewing inside him, ready to erupt.

LEAVING her clothing on the bank of the pond, Harlow waded into the icy water, rinsing off the sweat and grossness of the long-ass day. Most of the humans had opted to simply wipe themselves down but she could stand the colder water since she was a tiger. She hurriedly washed off, not bothering with her hair. Instead she left it in its braid and dove under the water, gasping as she came back up for air.

"You're braver than me," Jolie, a human in her fifties, called out as she sat on the edge of the bank, a blanket underneath her.

"Not braver, just run hotter."

The human snorted then stretched out, staring up at the sky. "Will you tell me more about New Orleans? About...your Alpha?" She hesitated on the word, no doubt because of how foreign it was.

"First, the Alpha couple, they're fair. More than. And they've managed to keep all sorts of different supernaturals in line and working together, which is a rarity. A lot of the territories around the world are fairly insular in the sense that they're run by dragons only or wolves, or whatever. You get it."

"What about tigers?"

Harlow laughed lightly as she got out of the water, shook off before grabbing a towel. "You mind if I lie here naked for a bit?" She'd planned to shift to her tiger form and relax but didn't want to be rude. Besides, she liked Jolie. The tough woman had kept all these humans together as a community, and while life had been hard on them, they were all survivors. That took a good leader.

"Nah. You do you, child."

Sighing, she stretched out under the moonlight, staring up at the sky through the trees, her tiger slumbering. "As far as I know, there aren't any tiger-run territories," she said, answering the earlier question. "My kind are rare anyway, and tigers are...well, we have small prides. Some of us anyway."

"You don't?"

"Well, not now. I ran with a small crew before The Fall." Before she'd assimilated into New Orleans. "But other than me and my twin, we're the only tigers in that group," she murmured, a smile curving her mouth.

"You're giving me hope for this move. I'm...grateful, for what you did." Jolie's voice grew tight. "For saving my daughter and the others. We've already lost so much and...I'm forever in your debt."

"You don't owe me anything. We just did what was right. Unfortunately, some vampires have been roaming wild throughout the world." And it pissed her off to no end. There needed to be a sort of...organized group that handled that shit. The only silver lining was that the females who'd been taken hadn't been sexually assaulted last night. But only because Harlow and Ace had gotten there in time, because she had no doubt that had been coming.

"Well, I still owe you, no matter what you say."

Grunting, Harlow sat up and pulled on her still dingy clothes. She'd shift to tiger later and dream about a real shower when they got back. "We won't have as much walking in the morning at least. Remind your group." Not that they'd been complaining. Not a single one of them had, not even the kids—who'd treated this more like an adventure, probably because they'd gotten to ride her like a horse.

"I will. And make sure you get more to eat. We saved you another couple plates. You did a lot today carrying the kids. You need to recharge all your energy." Jolie patted Harlow's shoulder gently in such a maternal way it made her chest ache as she thought of her own mother. Even the way Jolie politely told her that she needed to eat reminded her of her mother.

"You're sure everyone's eaten?"

"And then some. We're good. Thank you." Then she walked off toward the camp.

Harlow stayed where she was, trying to decide if she wanted to grab the food or just fall back and sleep. The way the dead animals had just been delivered to them was still bothering her. She'd assumed they'd been from Ace at first, but when he'd arrived later with his own kills and found they'd already cleaned and prepped everything, he'd been surprised.

And adamant that he wasn't screwing with her. So...who the hell had delivered the meat?

It hadn't been tainted or poisoned; she'd have smelled it. The kill had been fresh and just *given* to them.

Beyond weird, and while she wanted to figure out who the hell had done it, she shelved it because Ace was taking first watch and she was going to grab that food after all.

Then she was going to sleep. And not dream about a dragon with wings that actually turned to fire when he wanted. A dragon with amber-orange eyes the color of her stripes. A dragon she'd never gotten over.

And never would.

CHAPTER SIX

"Hello, Harlow. I need your help." Legend, the almost nine-year-old phoenix boy—also a twin like her—sat at the island top across from her, his expression somber.

Unlike his twin Enzo, Legend was serious and mature for his age. His brother was a wild thing, more like Harlow at that age, but she loved them both the same. Copper-haired, bronze-skinned, green-eyed little angels. Goddess, she loved the kids so much, was so glad they'd come into their lives. Of course she was a hundred times more obsessive about the property's security now because the thought of anything happening to them gave her cardiac stress.

"Okay, shoot. You hungry?" she asked as she made her turkey sandwich, held up the grainy bread in indication.

"No, thank you. I've already eaten this morning." Again with the serious, formal tone.

"Okay, then. What do you need, kid?"

"To set a trap."

She lifted an eyebrow. "For who? Enzo?"

He shot her a look that said he was questioning her brainpower. "No. I sleep in the same room with him. The payback would not be worth it."

"Ah." She suppressed a grin as she cut a thick tomato slice. Made sense. And also the reason she and her own twin hadn't messed with each other. They'd usually teamed up and messed with other shifters instead. Because Legend was right—don't screw with the person you share a room with. "So not your brother. Who, then?"

"In school we're learning about different minimal and maximum tensile strength and I want to test something."

Okay so the little booger wasn't answering her question—likely because she'd scent a lie. But she'd play along because she was a cat. Forever curious. "All right. I can probably help with that."

He nodded in approval and slid off his stool, eyeing her expectantly.

"You want help now?" She cut her sandwich in half and wrapped it up in a cloth to carry with her.

"I want to show you the location of what I'm thinking."

"Okay, give me a sec." She wiped up and put the condiments back in the fridge before heading out the front door with him.

To her surprise, they didn't go too far, just around the side of the house next to some azalea bushes on the east side of the mansion.

"This is where I'd like to set the trap, and it has to be invisible to the shifter's eye."

"Do you have any idea how you'd like to set it? Use magic or not?" He was a phoenix and had a little bit of magic.

"I'm open to all ideas but I think magic would be good."

"Is the intent to injure the being you trap?"

"Of course not," he said immediately, giving her a shocked look that she'd even asked.

She took another bite of her sandwich, grinned as she eyed the area. Well that was good at least. "Okay, we won't injure our prey, just trap them. When do you want to start work on it?"

Before he could answer, one of the windows from the third story above them opened and his almost sixteen-year-old sister popped her head out. Phoebe had the same copper-colored hair as he did, but hers was long and braided. "Hey bozo, what are you doing down there?"

"None of your business!" he shouted back, then looked at Harlow. "We'll talk later," he whispered before racing off.

What the heck? Harlow snickered and looked up at Phoebe, waved. "You staying out of trouble?"

"Heck no!"

Then she disappeared back inside, making Harlow laugh. Sounded about right. She glanced at her watch, saw that the kids should be leaving for school soon and decided she'd walk all of them.

School was different now than it had been before The Fall. It started a little later in the morning, and while they all learned basic stuff across the board, there were different schools with different focuses, starting around age twelve. Harlow hadn't gone to a regular human school so she didn't have anything to compare it to anyway.

As she headed back in the house, the back of her neck tingled, as if she was being watched. She didn't sense any danger but... She resisted the urge to itch her neck.

Nothing was there.

Once she was inside, she texted everyone in the house. *I'm walking the kids to school, then I'm going to shore up security around the property, test our wards. If anyone wants to help, let me know.*

She immediately got pings back from almost the entire crew, which eased the weird sensation buzzing inside her.

Ever since someone had left those killed animals yesterday for the party they'd rescued in the woods, she'd felt...off. Uneasy.

As if she was being watched. Or stalked.

HOURS LATER, Harlow tucked away the cleaning supplies under the sink and decided to go running since she'd finished cleaning the downstairs earlier than she'd thought.

"You taking my chores now?" Bella strolled into the kitchen, eyed her suspiciously. Wearing jeans and a bright red sweater, the petite snow leopard shifter looked stunning as always. Her jet-black hair was down today instead of pulled back at her nape.

Harlow shrugged. "You've been busy."

"Yeah, and so have you. I'd planned to clean tomorrow morning... So what do you want for this?"

Harlow snickered around the weird ache in her chest. "Uh, nothing. Just felt like doing something nice for you."

Bella watched her for a long moment. "Not that you don't do kind things, but...in the forty-plus years I've known you, you've never voluntarily cleaned. For anyone."

Harlow rolled her shoulders once, feeling as if she could crawl out of her skin. "So? I'm gonna go for a run if anyone needs me."

"Harlow!" Bella snapped in her "mom" tone she used to keep them in line. "What's wrong?" She moved suddenly in front of her, clasping Harlow's hands in hers gently. "Please talk to me."

The kindness in Bella's expression and tone nearly unraveled Harlow. She swallowed hard, shoved back tears. Actual tears, and she hadn't cried in almost sixteen years. Instead of answering her friend, she simply pulled her into a hug, kissed the top of her head, then hurried outside.

If she started telling any of them about the dreams she'd been having, they'd insist she go to therapy, to talk to one of the healers in the territory.

And that was a big fat hell no.

She didn't do that. Certainly didn't talk about her feelings. That wasn't how she and her twin handled things. Though normally she told Brielle everything—they were each other's therapists. But she'd been keeping her feelings to herself lately, not wanting to burden her twin with shit from their past.

After stripping and leaving her things in a pile by the front door, she raced off in her tiger form, stretching her legs as she headed for the local animal sanctuary.

After The Fall, they didn't really have a zoo in the sense that people came to see animals anymore. Now it was a sanctuary, and she loved visiting and playing with the older Malayan tiger.

Right about now she'd do anything to keep her mind off Aodh—because her mind was betraying her. She couldn't seem to keep anything compartmentalized anymore.

After years of handling shit just fine—or fine enough to survive—now, nothing helped. Not even sleep. Hell, especially not sleep. She used to be able to at least lose herself for a few hours but now when she closed her eyes, she saw him.

Every. Single. Night.

CHAPTER SEVEN

"What's up with your twin?" Bella shoved open Brielle's door to find her and Marley playing a video game.

"What?" Brielle turned her head in Bella's direction but didn't take her eyes off the screen.

"Ha! Eat it, sucker!" Marley shouted as...well, whatever, she won something on-screen.

Bella didn't understand any of this nonsense. Never had. "Harlow. Something's up with her. She's been off for months and now that she's back she's worrying me."

"What, why?" Brielle still didn't look at her fully. "She's been kinda moody but she gets like that sometimes. Just let her be. She'd have told me if anything was wrong. She's fine, trust me. We tell each other everything."

Bella resisted the urge to stomp her foot, mainly because she wasn't wearing heels and it would be a wasted effort.

"I don't know, Bella's never wrong," Marley said, in between shouting obscenities at the screen. "We should take her out this weekend."

"Yeah, all right," Brielle said. "We'll round up the crew, do a night out. I think everyone's off work too. It'll be good for all of us."

Bella rubbed a hand down her face, took a breath. "I don't think taking her out will do..." She trailed off as they shouted at the screen again. She'd lost them, and short of standing in front of them—and having them throw stuff at her like children to get out of the way—she decided to check in with some of the others.

At least Marley had gotten out of her funk since returning from Scotland. It had been months but she was back to her normal self after a bout of depression.

Maybe...that was what Harlow was dealing with? Bella wasn't a psychologist and she'd never really thought of Harlow as even capable of getting depressed. But that was nonsense, she realized.

Everyone could get depressed.

Downstairs, she found Axel and Lola in the living room, going over the household chore list as well as reviewing the online security they had for the house.

"Have either of you two noticed something off with Harlow?" she asked as she strode in, not bothering with small talk.

They were all the same age, had grown up in the same compound, then gone their separate ways for a few years before teaming up again. And she'd always taken on the maternal role with everyone.

"Ah...yeah, a bit." Axel leaned back, his expression thoughtful. "She mentioned she's been having weird dreams."

"What kind of dreams?"

He looked uncomfortable for a moment.

"Sexy dreams?" Lola asked.

"What? Ew, no. Or, I don't think they are. She's been, ah..." He cleared his throat once, twice, then stood. "I just remembered I've got tea with Prima in an hour. She needed to discuss something important with me." Then the big lying lion tried to run from the room.

As if Bella was letting that happen. She sprang like the snow leopard she was, jumping on his back and wrapping her arms and legs around him. He was just lucky she was still in her human form.

Lola howled in laughter behind her as Axel yelped. "What the hell, Bells?"

She wrapped an arm around his neck, tightened her legs around his middle and squeezed. "Talk or I start biting!"

Lola laughed even louder.

"Um, are we interrupting some sort of weird foreplay?" a female voice asked.

Bella turned at the sound of Dallas and Rhys, though she'd scented them not too long ago. They had permission to be on their property, their signatures allowed by the wards they kept around the house and yard. The couple had even stayed with them at one point, the sweet witch and her dragon mate good friends of theirs now. "Hey guys! No foreplay. Axel isn't that lucky." She nipped his shoulder once and he punched her leg.

"Let me go, you psycho!"

"So, we're here to see Harlow if she's around. Willow's with us."

Bella stopped attacking Axel and jumped off him. "Willow's here?" The little dragonling was the cutest thing and they all adored her.

"Yeah. In the back, terrorizing your chickens."

Bella snickered and punched Axel once in the shoulder. "You'll talk later."

He rubbed his arm, kissed Dallas on the cheek then ran out the front door before Rhys could punch him for kissing Dallas.

"I love coming here, but I always forget how wild you guys are," Dallas murmured, eyes a bit wide.

Bella simply grinned. "Harlow's not here...but did she ask you to bring Willow by?"

"Ah, not really. But I talked to Harlow a week ago and she was asking about her. I know how much she loves Willow and we had some time off. So." She had her arm wrapped around Rhys, her head on his shoulder.

Rhys was pretty quiet, as usual, and had his arm tight around Dallas.

"She should be back soon, and I know she'd love to see all of you." Bella glanced at her watch, saw that it was about four. The kids had all gone to friends' places after school and wouldn't be home for a bit. "You guys want to hang out while I start dinner?"

"We'd love to," Dallas said, smiling warmly. "We're staying with Avery tonight but she's not expecting us until late."

Dallas and Rhys helped run one of the farming communities on the outskirts of New Orleans and didn't often make it into the city proper.

"I'm going to visit Willow for a bit," Lola said, giving hugs to both of them before heading for the back.

Before the three of them had made it to the kitchen, Brielle and Marley came pounding down the stairs, racing to see Willow as well.

"I see how it is," Bella called out to them. "You'll stop playing for a dragonling, but not..." And they were out the back door already.

"So how are the kids?" Dallas asked as they headed to the kitchen.

"Exceptional," Bella said as she started to pull out all the foodstuffs. This was one of the rare nights they were all going to be home at the same time and she planned to make everyone dinner.

And figure out what was going on with Harlow.

She knew she couldn't fix anything if Harlow was depressed, but she could nudge her to talk to someone. That was what family did. They looked out for each other.

CHAPTER EIGHT

Harlow opened the front door, moving quietly, hoping to go unnoticed. She could hear the laughter when she was walking up the drive, knew that everyone was out back having dinner.

And she didn't want to be a buzzkill.

As she locked the door behind her, she smiled to see her twin on the stairs, a glass bottle of cider in hand—courtesy of one of the local bear clans. "Hey."

"Hey, yourself. We're all out back if you want to join."

"Yeah, of course." She kept her voice light, not wanting Brielle to realize anything was wrong. In a moment of weakness she'd admitted to Axel about her dreams, but she'd kept them from Brielle. Because deep down, if she admitted that she was hurting to her twin, she was terrified she'd break, would be unable to keep all that shit locked down anymore. "I need a shower because I stink."

Brielle snorted. "Always."

She rolled her eyes, snagged the bottle out of her twin's hand and raced up the stairs, ignoring the yelp of indignation. She chugged it as she started her shower, hoping it would take some of the edge off, but knowing it wouldn't. She would need to drink a lot of alcohol for that to happen. She would need...vodka.

Or tequila.

As the hot water pounded down around her, she flashed back on the first time she'd ever had tequila. Drinking wasn't a huge deal to shifters because of their metabolism, but that particular time had been after a mission.

With Aodh.

Because all she could ever think about lately was Aodh.

"Stupid female," she growled to herself, snagging the shampoo from the shelf.

She felt so weak and stupid and helpless right now because she couldn't get him off her mind. He was dead, gone.

What was wrong with her? Something had to give.

But as she started working conditioner into her thick hair, the memory overwhelmed her, made her chest constrict because she swore she could almost hear his voice right next to her ear.

"I'll bet you that I can hit the bull's-eye five times in a row. And if I win, I get to drink tequila out of your belly button." Aodh sat across from her at the high-top table in the hole-in-the-wall bar in Jacksonville, North Carolina.

Brielle and Axel were currently at the bar in a drinking contest with some Marines—who had no idea they were competing with supernaturals. Harlow and Aodh had been waiting for their turn at the dart boards.

"Why would you want to drink it out of my belly button?" She slid off her seat when the two human males playing tossed their darts into the bucket and nodded that they were done.

"I think the more important question is, why wouldn't I want to?" His voice was a low, dark whisper as he slid the coins into the machine.

She ignored the effect his words had on her, the sensation of his voice wrapping around her like a soft caress. Or she tried to. "What do I get if I win?"

He paused for only a moment. "You can drink it out of mine."

She barked out a laugh at the ridiculousness of him. "Does this ever actually work on females?"

He shrugged. "How would I know?"

She paused from grabbing her darts. Blue for her, red for him. She'd never actually smelled another female on him in the year she'd known him. But...he had to be hooking up with females, right? They had downtime in between missions. They were in a special branch of the Marine Corps and did top secret missions that always involved supernaturals, but they still had time off. Right now was a perfect example. They were stopped over in this little town for a night before they flew out in the morning to somewhere in California. "What does that mean?"

"I've never made this bet with another female before."

She narrowed her gaze at him. "I meant, does this sad attempt at flirting ever work with other females?"

He lifted a shoulder. "I am not...what's the word humans use? A whore? Or a player?"

Harlow glanced around, but knew no one was paying attention to them. The majority of the bargoers were watching some sports game on the televisions and the others were gathered around Brielle, Axel and the humans at the bar, cheering them on. "You're older than dirt. I know you're not a virgin," *she finally said.*

He grinned, a slow, wicked smile. "No, but it has been a very long time since I have been with anyone."

"I'm not asking and I don't care about your love life." *Liar, liar, her tiger purred in satisfaction. She didn't like the idea of another female touching him.*

He leaned in close, the dark, delicious scent of him intoxicating. "Well I'm telling you anyway. I haven't had a lover in decades. And I haven't wanted anyone the way I want you in...ever."

Oh. No. *He was being honest, she could scent it rolling off him sharp and true. Turning away from him, she tossed the dart at the machine.*

It lit up and made an annoying sound as she hit one of the outer rings.

Aodh frowned at it, then looked at her in surprise.

She'd never missed before, normally kicked everyone's ass. But...she wanted him drinking out of her belly button. Okay, she wanted his head between her legs while they were both naked.

He tossed his dart, hit the middle.

She tossed again, missed the board completely.

He sucked in a breath, threw his darts down on the table, his eyes molten. "Want to get out of here?"

"Yep." *Because she was not going another day or night without experiencing all of Aodh. She was obsessed, might as well admit it.*

Even if it ended in her heartbreak, he would be worth it. She had no doubt.

Harlow opened her eyes, hating the stupid tears streaming down her face as she remembered the *rest* of that night. He *had* broken her heart, but not until months later, and she still didn't know why.

Didn't understand why he'd tried to kill her.

And she'd never get her answers either. After everything had gone to hell on that fateful mission, they'd all left the Marine Corps. Honorably discharged, but they'd all been done in more ways than one.

He'd broken all of their hearts with his betrayal, and she'd tried to forget the past. Just erase it from her memory. Forget that she'd been forced to kill the male she loved.

"Get over it," she ordered herself, as if that would make it easier.

Annoyed and angry, she finished showering, determined to hang out with everyone tonight, have a good time and stay out as late as possible so that she passed out from exhaustion.

After braiding her damp hair, she headed to Brielle's room—because her twin had stolen her favorite pair of jeans.

When she couldn't find them in the drawers, she opened the trunk at the end of Brielle's bed, frowned as she opened a shoe box. "What the hell?" She pulled out a T-shirt that had belonged to *him*.

Aodh.

It was faded, didn't carry his scent anymore, but the green shade was familiar, as was the logo and words on it. The four of them had all had the same T-shirts made, much like human divisions in the Corps had. But this wasn't Brielle's or even Axel's. It was far too large.

"Hey..." Brielle stood in the doorway, her eyes wide. "Whatcha doing in there?"

"Why do you have his T-shirt? I told you to burn all of his shit!" Harlow slammed the trunk shut but clutched the shirt to her chest, then held it to her face and inhaled even though it just had a musty scent mixed with the pine of the trunk.

Brielle shut her door behind her with a click. "I figured you might regret that one day so I saved it. And some of his other things." And her twin didn't look sorry about it. At all.

"Are you kidding me? You had no right!"

"I had every right! He was my friend too! I didn't love him like you did, but I still loved him all the same. He was like a brother to me and Axel. And...I don't know what happened to make him turn on us but I still couldn't find it in my heart to simply cut him out of my memories!"

"Oh, like I did?" She wished she could have just sliced him out of her memories forever. It would have saved her so much pain and sadness. But that was a lie, she realized even as she thought it. Because then she'd have cut out someone who was a part of her, even if he'd betrayed her.

"I'm not saying that." Brielle stepped closer, her twin's eyes flashing tiger bright.

"You kind of are."

"What the hell is going on?" Axel moved into the room. "I could hear you both shouting from the kitchen."

"She kept some of Aodh's belongings and didn't tell me." Harlow held out the T-shirt as proof, shook it slightly, though she wasn't sure what the hell she expected Axel to do or say.

"Oh." Axel glanced between the two of them, looking like a lion caught in the headlights.

"Oh? That's all you have to say?" Harlow didn't know why she was pushing right now.

Okay, lies. She wanted to fight someone, had an energy buzzing inside her that she couldn't seem to extinguish.

"We all loved him, Harlow," Axel said, his tone cautious. "It's not like...she's betraying you by keeping it. She thought maybe one day you might want some of his things."

"Oh yeah, like I'd want the shit of the male who tried to kill me. The male I gave my heart to who tried to *kill* me!" She was full-on screaming now, knowing she'd lost it and unable to reel it back in. See, this was what happened when you tried to suppress your emotions. "Fuck you two and fuck all of this."

She tossed the shirt on the bed and raced out of the room, feeling possessed with the need to be anywhere but here.

Harlow yelped in surprise as she was tackled to the hard floor. "Son of a— Get off me!"

But her sister held her in a headlock as she pinned her to the ground. "You're not running out of here without talking, you big baby."

"Pretty sure that's exactly what I'm doing," she wheezed, half-ass punching Brielle in the ribs.

Her sister grunted, then she felt Axel wrapping his arms around her legs in a tight grip.

"Oh my goddess, you two, this is stupid! Let me go right this instant," Harlow demanded.

"Nope. You're both acting like assholes." Axel with his even tone again. Since when had he become the rational one of them?

"Hey!" Brielle was indignant and Harlow thought she might have an opening, but Brielle just tightened the grip on her neck and sat on her back.

If she wanted, she could get out of their hold. But she didn't want to hurt her family. "I promise to stay and talk if you let me go."

"You're such a liar," Axel grumbled. "And I'm not letting you up until you listen."

"Fine," she snarled, already plotting her revenge on Brielle. She was so gonna pay for this.

"And don't even think about trying to get back at your sister," Axel said, as if he'd read her mind.

"We'll see."

Brielle tightened her grip.

"Fine, fine, I won't. Jerk," she wheezed, reaching back and stabbing a claw into Brielle's thigh.

Her sister cried out, then laughed maniacally. "These are your jeans, dumbass."

Damn it.

"Children," Axel snapped. "We are going out tonight, the three of us, to get shit-faced."

Wait... "What?"

"Yeah, what?" Brielle asked, her grip loosening.

Axel loosened his grip on Harlow's legs too and Brielle slid off her.

Harlow turned over, sucked in a breath as she sat up, crossed her legs and stared at the two of them. "What good will that do?"

"We never dealt with…anything. And I know your grief was worse than ours but…I loved the guy too. And for the record, I saved some of his things too. I just couldn't bear to erase him from that part of our lives. It was a good chapter. Except the end."

Harlow hadn't gotten rid of all his stuff either. She had a box she'd kept hidden from everyone, even her twin.

"So let's go out tonight and allow ourselves to talk about everything, to grieve."

"Are you…in therapy or something?" Brielle asked cautiously.

"What?" Axel's voice took on an odd pitch, then he shrugged. "Yeah, maybe, so what."

"Oh." Harlow stared in surprise.

"Good for you, man." Brielle shoved to her feet, held out her hand for Harlow.

Grudgingly, she took it and resisted the urge to tackle her sister to the ground. Because she wasn't mad at either of them, not truly. "Yeah, good for you…and I could go for some drinks. Or whatever."

"Not whatever. We're going to actually express our emotions. And not try to kill each other. Or anyone else. Because we were there the last time…" Axel cleared his throat, looked at her pointedly.

Harlow was glad he didn't finish the sentence. Because she'd gone on a weeklong bender after she'd killed Aodh in self-defense, nearly gotten *herself* killed in a supernatural bar fight.

She hadn't cared about anything, and after that lapse in judgment she'd simply locked up everything tight and hadn't had an incident since.

Until recently when she'd felt herself starting to crack. "Okay, fine, let's go out tonight."

"I've gotta change now, jackass," Brielle grumbled, looking at her ripped, bloody jeans.

"That's what you get. So what else did you keep of his?" she asked after a moment, her curiosity clawing her up.

Brielle lifted a shoulder, nodded in the direction of her room. "Come see for yourself."

CHAPTER NINE

As Harlow tied the old Pearl Jam shirt at her waist right above her jeans, she eyed herself in the mirror. The shirt was too large but she didn't care. It had been one of Aodh's things she'd saved and never ever let herself think about.

But maybe Axel was right. Maybe they needed to just let all this crap out and talk about it.

Because they never had.

She'd been too broken back then, had been worried that if she talked about things, she'd break down. Especially after she'd acted like a total psycho in that bar, nearly getting herself and others killed. She never wanted to feel so out of control again, never wanted to give in to blood-lust like that.

It had terrified her, knowing she could have killed someone innocent in her rage.

And Axel and Brielle had never brought him up again so it had made compartmentalizing so much easier.

Her phone buzzed as she started unbraiding her hair, the compulsion to leave it down tonight strong. She didn't want to talk to anyone, but when she saw Star's name, she answered the video call.

"Hey!" Star was glowing—actually glowing a soft violet—as she smiled at her. "I've missed seeing your face. How was your last operation? Every time I called they said you were still gone."

Something settled in Harlow's chest as she looked at her original Alpha, the female she'd grown up following. "I've missed seeing your face too. And it went really well. We killed some vamps and saved some humans. All in a week's work." She grinned cheekily, shoving down the lingering sadness.

"Nice. So...I have news."

"You're pregnant," she breathed.

"What, no! Or I don't think so," she said on a laugh. "Kartini is officially mated and she hasn't told anyone because she's off on a mating frenzy for a while."

Harlow stared in pure shock. "Kartini got mated? That's like saying...goddess, I can't even think of a good analogy." Their lifelong friend had flitted about from relationship to relationship, not taking the many, many proposals she received seriously.

"Yep." Star's tone was dry, but her expression amused. "To two dragons and a wolf shifter. It's all anyone is talking about and I wanted to wait until you were all together to tell you. But no one else is answering their phone so I thought I'd take a chance with you."

Harlow laughed in delight, despite her own turmoil. "I'm so happy for her."

"I am too, and now you have the scoop before everyone else." Star cleared her voice. "And, I'm not trying to be nosy, but how's Aurora doing? I've been trying my best not to be an obsessive big sister and check in with her every day."

"Just every other day, right?"

"Ha ha."

"She's doing great. The territory has had some ups and downs but for the most part everything is steady and she's been handling things like a boss. Goddess, I love seeing her in this role, truly stepping into her power," Harlow said with pride in her voice. Aurora had been like a little sister to all of them, but she'd always had a wide Alpha streak, just like Star.

"You're making my heart sing. It helps me rest easier knowing she's so settled and happy. So. How's my Marley?"

Harlow wasn't surprised by the questions. Star had been their Alpha for a long time and Harlow figured part of her always would be. "So much better. It took a while but she's like her normal self again. Moving to New Orleans was the right decision."

"Thank the goddess," Star murmured. "I was so worried about her."

They talked for a few minutes more but Harlow paused at a knock on her door. "Hold on... Yeah?"

Axel popped his head in, looking as handsome as always. "You ready?"

"Yeah, give me a sec...I've got good gossip."

He grinned and shut the door behind him.

"Are you guys going out?"

"Yeah, just me, Axel and Brielle." She thought about telling Star what she'd been dealing with, but held back. Star was running an actual territory. She didn't need any extra crap heaped on her.

"If something was wrong, you'd tell me, right?" Star watched her with those bright violet eyes.

"Yep," she said with a grin, hoping Star believed her.

Star half smiled but Harlow wasn't so sure she'd been convincing.

After they disconnected, she found Axel and Brielle waiting in the hallway, all wearing something of Aodh's, which made her throat constrict.

Axel had his hair pulled back in one of Aodh's ridiculous neon green and pink scrunchies. Aodh had once insisted that he could pull off any fashion and she'd told him he couldn't pull off wearing scrunchies. He'd accepted the challenge and bought an array of them.

Brielle had a thin leather strap around her wrist she recognized as being another of his hair ties. He used to pull his hair back in all sorts of random things to keep it out of his face.

"You want to say hi to Willow before we head out?" Brielle asked.

"Oh yeah." She wanted to get some hugs and kisses in with the little dragonling before the three of them left.

Humans had therapy animals, so why couldn't she have a therapy dragon?

CHAPTER TEN

The Before

Aodh watched as Harlow held up the mini tequila bottle, drizzled a line down the middle of her chest and over her stomach.

In a hotel room off base, they had hours before their flight out in the morning. This wasn't how he'd seen his night going, but he was always hopeful when it came to a certain fierce redheaded tiger. His Red.

Every muscle in his body was pulled taut, his cock rock-hard against his jeans as he watched the confident, kick-ass female he knew was his mate.

Aodh crawled up her body, unable to stop his obsession with her. Not like he'd tried, not like he wanted to. From the moment he'd met her, he'd been ensnared by her smartass mouth. She was obviously gorgeous, but her twin did nothing for him.

Nope, it was Harlow for him all the way. Tall, strong, deadly.

All his.

She grabbed his hair and he groaned, until he realized she was ripping out the dumbass scrunchie he'd worn.

"You're ridiculous," she murmured as she tossed it off the side of the bed, her luscious mouth curving up in a smile.

"You like it."

49

She shrugged, lifted her hips and started to shove her panties down. The only thing she had left on.

But he took over, bending down and grabbing the thin red scrap of nothing with his teeth. For some reason the fact that she was wearing a sexy, lacy thong had surprised the hell out of him. He'd assumed she either wore nothing at all or something utilitarian. Because his female was practical.

But apparently he didn't know everything about her.

And he was glad for it, because he was sure they had a lifetime in front of them.

She wiggled her hips impatiently as he accidentally snapped the fabric with his teeth. Then she laughed, the sound deep and throaty as he cursed.

He was like an untried youth right now.

She slid her fingers through his hair, her touch surprisingly gentle. "You make me so damn crazy," she murmured, the words coming out like a confession.

He kissed her stomach, tasted the tequila. Moved higher, until he hovered over one full breast. "You've made me mad since the moment we met." And he was glad for it because he couldn't imagine his life now without her in it.

She arched up into him, and he didn't pause but took what she was offering, sucked one of her hard, brown nipples into his mouth.

The sound she made when he flicked his tongue over the hard bud, gently pressed it between his teeth, woke something deep and primal inside him.

A soft grayish smoke surrounded them, the bed, the whole damn room. Hopefully it didn't extend anywhere else and freak out humans, but he couldn't find it in him to care one iota. She was his mate, whether she understood that yet or not, and his mating manifestation just solidified what he'd already known.

Harlow slid her hands through his hair as if she was savoring the feel of it, of him. And he vowed to never cut his hair again.

"Your mouth is magic," she murmured as he moved to her other breast, taking his sweet time.

Though his beast was riding him hard, telling him to strip, to claim her, he was going to savor all of her. "We're just getting started."

Aodh shook himself out of the memory as he spotted movement at the front door of Harlow's mansion. He was across the street, high up in a neighbor's tree watching for her.

Like a stalker.

Might as well own what he was.

She strode out with...Brielle and Axel. The sight of all of them together was a punch to his senses.

The sharpest sense of betrayal, of *loneliness* overwhelmed him, the surge of it making him swallow hard. He was older than all of them, had been fighting in one form or another before his first Hibernation, and had continued after his third one.

Then he'd met them, been teamed up with them, and he'd realized there could be a different way to live life. For the first time in centuries the pull of sleep hadn't been strong. He hadn't been thinking about going into Hibernation again.

He'd enjoyed having friends...family.

Until they'd discarded him, forgotten him. Betrayed him with their apathy.

And he was just a masochist, determined to follow Harlow around until he figured out a way to approach her. Demand to know why she'd left him.

The answer would probably destroy him, but after he had it he could go after the witch who'd put him in that prison. He couldn't get revenge until he knew if Harlow and the others had played a role in it.

He...didn't think they could have. But he also had never thought they'd turn on and abandon a teammate. They'd been all about loyalty and family.

He took to the skies, following them at a distance even as he kept an eye out for other dragons. The little he'd gleaned about this territory was that dragons were supposed to fly without camouflage while in the city limits. But he didn't think all dragons followed that rule.

He certainly wasn't, but he also hadn't told the Alpha he was here. Aodh played by his own rules, always had.

Now was no different.

Besides, he wouldn't be staying long.

The sound of music and laughter trailed on the air, and at first he thought they were going to the Quarter. But instead they stopped at what appeared to be a street party.

Two blocks in a neighborhood had been roped off, and from his angle he could see tables set up in the streets, a DJ playing music on one end while people danced and laughed.

Against his better judgment, he landed a mile away in a quiet park since it was the only place big enough for him to easily land unseen, then shifted to his human form. Remaining naked, he hid his clothing pack high in a tree, then headed in the direction of the party.

He'd been imprisoned for so long that the thought of being around so many people, even without their knowledge, was a lot.

He'd never liked crowds, had always enjoyed covert work—sneaking into places, blowing things up. And doing all that with Harlow had been heaven.

Until she'd abandoned him to his own personal Hell.

CHAPTER ELEVEN

In the Domincary realm

Flavia strode down the street of the fae village, her glamour firmly in place. The fae were no strangers to glamour, at least the most powerful of them, and she had enough energy stored away to utilize that power.

There was a market going on this sunny, cold day and it was perfect for her to check out various targets she might come back for later. With the sun so bright, everyone was out, cheerful smiles on their faces.

This village was quaint, most of the homes looking like something out of a Swiss village in the human realm. Some of the royal guard had passed through on their trek to build a new kingdom. She'd been following them, slowly picking off easy targets, but once they'd tightened their ranks she'd decided to start picking off fae from the various villages around the realm.

There were so many, and it had been fun hunting them. She preferred to kill entire families. And she was doing them a favor anyway. Killing everyone left behind no one to grieve.

It also left behind no one else to hunt her down later out of vengeance.

Not that she was truly worried about that. She'd been around for a hundred years and would be so for a hundred more.

At one time she'd been paid quite handsomely by various governments around the world. Not all of them had supernatural divisions but some had, and she'd capitalized on that. Had become an assassin of sorts. Which was how she'd built up a beautiful nest egg and homes all over the world.

Until The Fall, when those goddamn dragons had ruined everything. Some of her homes actually still stood, but she'd retreated to this realm anyway. At the time she'd had that gorgeous dragon to feed off. But even once he'd escaped, she'd decided to remain here.

Especially if he decided to hunt her down. He wouldn't come back to this realm. No, he'd have assumed she'd left.

"My lady, is there anything in particular you're looking for today?" An older fae male wearing a tunic, thick pants and heavy work boots stood in front of his table of scarves and other little accessories.

She picked up one of the wool scarves, felt the fine quality. The male was too old and had too little power rolling off him to be of any use to her, but she did like the scarf. "I'll take this, thank you."

As he started bagging up her purchase, he said, "Where are you traveling from?"

She wasn't a local so of course she stood out in a town this size. It was why she'd adjusted her glamour so she would look as if she was from the original palace—right now she looked to be a lady of fine breeding wearing an expensive frock. The fae of this small village would automatically give her a sense of deference, make them less likely to question her. "My husband is out looking at land today. He thinks he'd like to settle closer to here than the mountain. We're camped a few miles outside town and I got bored waiting for him so decided to do some shopping. Your town is absolutely lovely. How long have you lived here?"

At that, he smiled broadly. "My whole life, my lady. If you and your husband make your home near here, I think you will be quite happy."

"I believe we will be," she said pleasantly.

They chatted for a few more moments, and once she'd bought the scarf she moved on to the next stall, looking at some of the jewelry but ultimately moving on again.

She was certain that word would spread among the various stalls that she was a rich lady just passing through, and most people wouldn't question it.

In her long life, she'd learned that most people only cared about themselves anyway. She wasn't harming anyone—that they knew of— and anyone she came in contact with would forget about her in a day or less.

As she reached another stall selling cheese and jams, she paused, picked up one of the jam jars.

"If there's anything I can help you with, please let me know." A girl who couldn't be more than thirteen approached, a shy smile on her face.

The blonde female was stunning, would grow into a beauty one day.

That alone annoyed Flavia. She gave her an icy smile. "Thank you."

A younger girl stalked up, wearing heavy boots that were two sizes too big at least. Her long, blonde hair was pulled back into two messy braids and her clothes were sloppy. She stared up at Flavia, a streak of purple jam on one of her cheeks. "Who are you?" she demanded.

Flavia lifted an eyebrow.

Her older sister nudged her. "Hush," she murmured.

But the little girl just kept staring, her eyes narrowing ever so slightly. "You smell weird."

Flavia blinked in shock. She knew she did not smell. She bathed every single day and used the finest bathing supplies. At one time she'd had all her soaps mailed in from Paris, but those days were gone.

The older girl gasped and nudged the younger one back more firmly. "Go see if Mama needs help. Now."

The younger girl shrugged, but kept watching Flavia in the most eerie way, her greenish eyes glinting in the sunlight. "Fine, but she still smells weird."

"I'm so sorry about her. She doesn't know what she's saying," the older girl stammered, grabbing a couple jars and putting them in a bag. "Please, accept my apologies and..." She trailed off as an adult male strode out, carrying the little girl on his shoulders.

Flavia eyed the huge male. He was broader than most fae she'd met and he was watching her in that eerie way his youngest had been. And there was no doubt he was their father. He had the same green eyes as both girls, though his hair was dark. And she'd bet money that he wasn't completely fae, not with his build. There was a certain type of energy rolling off him that was...similar to that of shifters.

His ears were softly pointed in the way of fae, but he was simply too broad. And that energy—he definitely had shifter blood in him. "Mave, why don't you go help your mother in the back?"

"Of course, Papa, but I think Keeva should come back with me. She's been rude and—"

The man winked at her. "Go now, please." He also didn't put the little girl down.

The oldest looked between them, sighed, then disappeared back behind the tented area and into a shop that clearly sold the same cheese, jam and other things displayed along the sidewalk.

"So where are you from?" the man asked casually as he peered into the bag his oldest daughter had started to put together for her.

"Your daughter was quite rude to me so I think I'll be moving on," she murmured, the need to get away from the both of them strong.

"Keeva, is there something you'd like to say?"

The little girl scrunched up her face, but then sighed. "I'm sorry I said you smell weird. Even if you do," she muttered under her breath.

Then Flavia watched as the male inhaled deeply, though he tried to be subtle about it. The way he did it reminded her of the way shifters scented people. *Ooooh. No.* She was right.

These were half-shifters, and they'd be able to pick up on her different scent even if they wouldn't know what it was. It certainly wasn't fae.

She was also aware of a few other shopkeepers watching their interaction. Which meant she would be remembered. Something she always tried to avoid.

She needed to move on fast. "Apology accepted. Have a lovely day." She strolled down to the next stall, but didn't pause as she felt eyes on the back of her head.

Power tickled at her fingertips, but if she blasted those two with anything, it would be stupid. Not in broad daylight. It would defeat the entire purpose of blending into this realm.

Unfortunately, now she couldn't hunt in this town. Not now, at least, but she was going to come back for that little brat one day. If she killed the family now, made them disappear, there was a chance the shopkeepers who had watched the strange interaction would remember her.

And there was definitely a chance one of those two would comment on her "strange" scent. The glamour she was using was powerful enough to fool even shifter eyes, but she couldn't hide her scent. Not without a surge of real power, and that usually wasn't worth the drain.

How could she have known there were half-breeds living here?

Annoyed that her day had been wasted, she made her way out of town only when she was sure no one had followed her.

She would move to the next town now, not wanting to risk that male getting curious. After this realm had been invaded by dragons, he might want to know more about her and hunt her down.

She wasn't going to give him, or anyone else, that chance.

Especially not when she hadn't fed in weeks. Goddess, she'd been so drunk on the power of the dragon for years that she'd forgotten what it was like to be without his powers.

She needed another dragon.

Needed that raw energy humming through her, feeding her. Soon, she promised herself. Very, very soon.

CHAPTER TWELVE

"Despite what people think of me, I don't like to be a buzzkill." Christian's delicious voice was formal in that snooty British way of his that Axel loved. "But this seems like it might turn bad at any moment."

Axel scrubbed a hand over his face as he watched Harlow and Brielle dancing on a table near where the DJ had set up. He also tried to ignore what Christian's mere presence did to him—namely, bring out his mating instinct. But Christian had made it clear that he wasn't interested. Axel knew he needed to move on, but his heart didn't want to listen.

He and Christian were on the edge of this particular dance party. The party was getting louder each second that ticked by. As far as he could tell there weren't many humans here. This was a full-on supernatural party and it was like it was a full moon or something. A couple blocks surrounding the area had been roped off and he'd seen more naked bodies than he cared to in the last hour. Whoever had decided to throw this thing had turned a regular neighborhood into a wild block party.

"Yeah," Axel grumbled. "You might be right." This was not how tonight was supposed to go.

"I'm sorry, can you repeat that?"

Axel shot the sexy male in the three-piece suit a sharp look. "Don't be smug."

Christian—tall, blond and everything Axel wanted but couldn't have —flicked imaginary lint off his sleeve, looking very feline in that moment, despite being a vampire. "It's hard not to be when I'm right so often."

Axel rolled his eyes, then looked back at the twins. Harlow had lost her pants at one point—which was nothing for the shifters here—and was wearing Aodh's old T-shirt like a dress. She was tall so the hem hit her mid-thigh. "I don't like all these assholes watching them," he growled.

Christian shot him a surprised glance. "That doesn't seem very modern of you."

"They're like my sisters, asshole."

Christian blinked.

And Axel winced. "Ah, sorry, didn't mean to be such a dick. I just... We came out tonight to deal with some heavy emotional shit and I didn't expect them to get all crazy. And I don't like lusty assholes watching my girls. I don't care if they can kick everyone's ass here."

"Ah." Christian nodded in understanding. "Do you wish to speak about whatever this is about, then? And perhaps tell me why you're wearing a neon-colored scrunchie in your hair?"

Axel let out a short laugh, then pulled out a stool as a round tabletop emptied out. Once Christian sat, he sat next to him, but kept his gaze on Harlow and Brielle even as Christian's deliciously dark scent wrapped around him.

Brielle looked like she always did—combat gear, her hair in a braid. Didn't matter that they were out to have a good time. She was always ready to kill.

Harlow, on the other hand, had let her hair down for the first time in ages, literally and figuratively.

"The three of us used to work with someone, who...died. This was his scrunchie," he said, motioning to it. "We all cared for him, but Harlow loved him." They would have mated too, if the damn dragon hadn't been a traitor. Something Axel still had difficulty processing. He was good at reading people, always had been, and Aodh's betrayal had struck so deep he'd never fully recovered.

"Is this the male she loved and had to kill?"

Okay, now he was really surprised. "She told you about that?"

"Not much, but yes. It was sort of an offhand comment."

Axel knew Harlow enough that she wouldn't have made the comment offhandedly. She'd told Christian because she liked and trusted him. Which made Axel's feelings for the male even more difficult—it was impossible to hate him when all his family loved him. When he was just a good male at his core. "Well, I don't know what the hell we thought to accomplish tonight. I thought maybe we could talk or some shit." He'd been talking to a therapist to deal with some things and she suggested being more "emotionally open" or whatever.

"Perhaps once they've gotten nice and drunk they'll want to talk."

Axel snorted a laugh out at that. "They're really trying hard to tie one on, huh?"

Christian snickered too, as Brielle passed a tequila bottle to Harlow, who tossed it back. It took a lot to get their kind drunk, but they were making a go of it. They might even have a slight buzz.

But Axel didn't want to be here right now. He'd rather be somewhere more private, a small pub, but Ace had invited Harlow so here they were.

A beefy-looking male climbed up on the table with the twins, and for a moment it looked as if Brielle would kick the guy off.

Instead Harlow grabbed the front of his collar and hauled him up.

The table wobbled under their weight, then steadied itself—and then the guy leaned in far too close to Harlow.

Axel shoved up from the stool. He knew Harlow could make her own decisions, but he wasn't going to let her do something she'd regret because she was teetering on depression. Or hell, maybe she was fully depressed, he couldn't tell.

As he approached the table, the male leaned in toward Harlow and then... Air whooshed by Axel as the male went flying through the air.

Harlow and Brielle both froze, looks of surprise on their faces.

Axel helped Harlow down while Christian did the same with Brielle.

"What the hell was that?" Harlow asked, pushing her hair back out of her face.

Before Axel could formulate any sort of answer, a very naked *Aodh* appeared out of thin air, picked up the guy who'd tried dancing with Harlow as if he weighed absolutely nothing and threw him down the street.

Harlow dug her claws into Axel's forearm, likely not even realizing what she was doing.

"You're seeing this too, right? I'm not losing my mind?" she whispered.

"Holy shit," was all he could get out.

Brielle screamed in rage, surprising both of them as she shifted to full-on tiger and launched herself at Aodh—or whoever the hell this was.

Axel and Harlow both lunged after her, with Harlow jumping on her back and tackling her as Aodh turned back to face the three of them.

It wasn't enough to stop Brielle.

She got free of Harlow and pinned Aodh against the concrete, and Axel was aware that things had gotten very, very quiet around them.

The music was off and people had gone ghost silent. Because if there was one thing supernaturals could sense, it was when blood was about to be spilled. And this wasn't some random brawl—the threat of violence hung thick in the air.

"Surprised to see me?" Aodh growled on the ground, Brielle's huge tiger body on top of him.

It said a lot for how strong he was, or maybe how gentle she was actually being, that he wasn't crushed under her weight.

"What the hell are you doing here?" Harlow snarled, horror, shock and something else etched onto her face as she stared down at the two of them.

"That shirt looks stupid on you," he snapped.

"Well, here, take it back then, asshole!" Harlow tore it over her head and threw it at his face.

Aaaand that was all it took for Aodh to shove Brielle off him and stand up to his full height of six-foot-plus stupidly tall.

Harlow should look ridiculous in just her boots and underclothing but...nope. She looked hot as hell, and it was clear that Aodh was noticing. Axel stared for a long moment at the male he'd thought was dead, tried to force a word out. Anything. What the hell was happening? He'd seen Harlow kill him, had seen Aodh come at her with that blade. Now the male was just standing in the middle of the road, naked and pissed off.

"So, gonna answer my question? Surprised to see me? How long did you actually search for me?" he snapped, looking between the three of them, his expression a mask of rage.

Um...what? Axel eased forward another step, not wanting to face off with the male, but he would if necessary. He wasn't dreaming or hallucinating. Nope. This was far too real.

"Look for you? What the hell are you talking about?" Brielle was human now, naked too, her clothes shredded on the ground, and more pissed than he'd ever seen her. "I should rip your head off for the way you hurt my sister!"

Harlow blanched, but Axel stepped forward, the reality of their surroundings setting in. Far too many people were watching. "Maybe we should take this somewhere else and—"

"Not now, Axel!" the three others snapped in unison, as if it was old times.

He scrubbed a hand over his face, shot Christian a worried look. What the hell should he do?

"How would we have looked for you?" Harlow asked, confusion and raw pain tingeing her voice as she stared at Aodh. Her dark eyes were filled with pain as she stared at the male who was supposed to be dead.

The male shoved his shirt back at her. "Put this on."

Oh, no. No, no, nooooooo. He should know better than to order her around.

Betrayal morphed to anger as she crossed her arms over her chest, pushing up her barely covered breasts. "Nah, I'm good, thanks," she snapped, ice dripping from her words.

Aodh took a menacing step forward, but everyone froze when a shrill whistle pierced the air and Ace strode up, looking between all of them.

Ace focused on Harlow first. "What's going on?"

"I honestly don't know. This bastard," she jerked an accusing thumb at Aodh, "tried to kill me years ago and I thought I killed him. Then he just showed up—"

"Kill you! What the hell are you talking about?" Aodh demanded. "Are you damaged, female?"

Harlow blinked, taken as off guard as Axel was.

Ace snapped his cold wolf gaze to Aodh. "Stop talking right now. You're in my Alpha's territory and I know for a fact you haven't announced yourself or asked for permission to be here."

"That's because I ask for permission from no one," he practically purred, clearly goading Ace. His hair was cut short, much shorter than it had been years ago, but everything about him was still the same. He wasn't handsome in any sort of sense, but he was pure power in a huge, muscular package—and right now the amber-orange-eyed dragon was staring at Ace as if he wanted to fight him.

Son of a... Axel moved swiftly, placing himself in between Aodh and Ace, keeping his back to Ace. Because he wasn't sure what the hell was going on. He looked at his old friend turned enemy, shoved down the emotions wanting to take over. Because the male had once been like a brother to him. "Now is not the time to go all asshole. We're going somewhere private to deal with...this. Like how the hell you're alive—and why you tried to kill us! We were like family! And you're going to behave for ten minutes because you owe us that." Axel could scent Harlow's pain and wanted to punch Aodh's stupid face in for that alone.

"I never tried to kill any of you. And you think I owe you assholes after you left me to rot in that prison?" he sneered, his eyes ice cold.

"Prison? I have no clue what you're talking about. Truly." Aodh had turned on them. And Harlow had been forced to defend them. To kill the male she loved. It had all happened so fast, but it had changed their lives forever.

Aodh stared down at him—because yeah, he was actually taller than Axel. "Wait…you're serious."

"Yeah, I'm serious. Think you can act semicivilized and not start a street brawl for, hmm, I don't know, ten minutes?" Since when had Axel turned into the calm one? *Ugh.*

"You guys can use my place to talk," Christian said quietly.

"That works for all of us, *right?*" Axel glared at Aodh even as he kept his back to everyone else. Something was seriously off right now. The scents rolling off Aodh right now were anger, but he also smelled like he was telling the truth.

"Fine," Aodh finally gritted out. "I know where the pretty vampire lives," he snapped before he backed up and shifted to his dragon form in a blast of fire and magic, taking to the air in a great whoosh.

Axel shoved out a breath, turned back to the others. And had no idea what the hell to say.

Harlow just stood there, trembling as she stared up at the sky, watching Aodh fly into the distance.

CHAPTER THIRTEEN

Harlow couldn't sit as they all stood in Christian's back patio area. No one else could either as they waited for Ace to return—and she tried not to stare at Aodh, who was just standing there like a statue, his thick arms crossed over his chest.

Seriously, what the hell was going on? She'd killed him.

Killed the male she loved.

Had mourned him. Was still mourning him to an extent. But here he was, denying everything, acting as if they'd abandoned him to some prison instead of the truth.

He wasn't emanating menace, and her shifter "radar" wasn't going off that he was about to attack...but she still kept her distance.

Unable to look at him anymore, she glanced over at her sister.

Brielle was back in her tiger form, pacing all around the backyard. Axel had his arms crossed over his chest as he leaned against the railing that encompassed the huge area. All the fancy furniture was unused—and...she was back to looking at Aodh, who hadn't moved an inch.

Because apparently she was a masochist and couldn't stop staring at him.

At least someone had given him pants so she wouldn't be tempted to look at what was between his legs—and salivate. Goddess, something was wrong with her.

Seeing him now, it was like the past had been wiped away. His hair was short instead of the longer, gorgeous dark hair she used to love running her fingers through. But of course it only showed off all the hard angles of his face, making him look even more dangerous. He'd never be called handsome, but he was...powerful. It was the only word she could think of to describe him.

That was what had attracted her in the first place. All that raw, animal power.

Then she remembered him coming at her, blade raised as he tried to stab her. The horror that had punched through her. The shock.

None of it had seemed real, still didn't.

She'd reacted on instinct, whipping out her own blade, shoving it straight into his chest, hitting his heart more by accident than anything else. Killing the man she'd loved, had wanted to mate. Had...wanted to start a family with. But it had all been gone in an instant.

Poof. Their future gone just like that.

He'd burst into flames, disappearing into ash, shocking her and the others, but it made sense given the type of dragon he was. One who could actually turn into flames.

Far too many emotions surged up and she was barely keeping a lid on any of them. He'd forced her hand to do the unthinkable. Now he was here, standing in front of her and acting angry. As if he had a right to be!

He was the one who'd betrayed them.

She turned away, scrubbed a hand over her face as she tried to banish the memory of stabbing him. It had nearly destroyed her.

If it hadn't been for the others, she wasn't sure where she'd be right now. Dead probably. She'd been on a dark path after he'd gone, had gotten into stupid supernatural fights, just trying to pick them all the time to let out her rage and anger.

"That's right, turn away," Aodh sneered. "Don't look at the male you abandoned to that hellhole. The one you claimed to love."

She spun around, opened her mouth to snap back, but Christian, all calm and elegant, stood in between them, palms raised.

"You've all agreed to wait until Ace returns with Everleigh. Clearly something is..." He trailed off as Ace and Everleigh appeared around the side of the house.

Everleigh, a beautiful female with choppy brown hair and glowing olive-hued skin, was a witch with an incredible truthsense magic.

As shifters, they could all scent when someone was lying to a certain extent, but that wasn't foolproof. Technically nothing was, but Everleigh was basically a walking lie detector. It was an incredible superpower.

Harlow found herself irrationally annoyed by how attractive Everleigh was in that moment—and she genuinely liked the witch. Had never been the jealous type, except when it came to Aodh.

She only ever wanted his eyes on her.

And...okay, they were on her now. Unfortunately, they were filled with rage and bitterness. Which just pissed her off. He was the one who'd turned on them. And she wanted answers, wanted to know why he'd betrayed them all. Money? Something else? They'd never been able to find a reason after... *After*.

"Glad to see you're all alive." Ace's tone was dry as he looked between them. "Clearly there's a huge misunderstanding or something, so I'm going to tell you what's going to happen. You," he said to Aodh, his jaw tight, "are going to speak with Everleigh, tell her about whatever brought you and your former team to this point." Ace looked at Harlow and the others. "Then you three will do the same. For the record, I know you're not a liar, Harlow." He then shot Aodh a dark look. "So if you think to come into my Alpha's territory and—"

"Save the threats," Aodh snapped. "I have nothing to hide." He had the T-shirt she'd thrown at him tucked neatly under his arm and she wanted to snatch it away from him as much as she wanted to punch the obnoxious look off his face.

Ace took a deep breath, clearly asking the goddess for patience. Then he motioned to Everleigh, who was calm as usual. She had on loose, bohemian-style pants, a flowy top and all sorts of sparkly rings on her fingers.

She motioned toward the seating area with big cushions and the lit firepit. "I think we should all sit first."

Christian murmured something about grabbing snacks, because of course he did. The male was like the perfect host. Harlow sat in a single lounge chair, only a long glass-topped table separating her and Aodh, who'd also sat in a single chair. Brielle stayed in her tiger form and flopped down next to Harlow by her feet.

Her twin far preferred to be in tiger form when she was angry.

Axel sat next to Everleigh on the couch and Ace stood sentry, arms over his chest as he watched all of them.

"So," Everleigh started, looking around at all of them. "It's my understanding that something happened years ago between all of you. Aodh, you seem to think that they left you in a prison—"

"They did!"

She cleared her throat. "No interrupting, please."

Harlow smirked at him while Everleigh continued.

"And you three say that Harlow killed him?"

Harlow nodded, her throat tight. She lived with it every day, the memory of it burned into her brain.

"So I want to hear everything in your own words," Everleigh continued. "We'll start with Harlow since I know you, and I have a good baseline already. Tell me simply, what happened between you two. Just speak your truth."

Harlow focused on Everleigh instead of Aodh. "We were working on a...job." She sighed, decided to just be completely honest. "I guess it doesn't matter anymore if it was classified. We used to do undercover ops for the human government. We were all Marines, but worked for a supernatural division."

Everleigh nodded, her expression gentle.

"We were hunting down a powerful, ah, witch." She cleared her throat, wincing slightly as a bit of guilt slid through her. It wasn't like they'd been hunting a random witch, but one who'd been pure evil.

Everleigh just smiled. "It's okay."

"So we were hunting this witch who'd been killing whole families. A serial killer. She'd been targeting military families, which is the only reason we were involved at all. She was targeting families where one member had a high ranking, and we always thought there was more to it. Like she'd been hired by Russia or something similar. But...that doesn't matter, I guess."

Harlow shoved out a sigh, looked at Axel, who nodded in support.

Then she turned back to Everleigh. "We'd tracked her into Canada, right across the Montana border actually, to this cabin and..."

She turned to Aodh then, unable to stop herself. She stared into his amber-orange eyes as she remembered his betrayal, how he might as well have cut her heart out that day. She wanted to launch herself at him and claw his face off, demand answers!

"We'd gone down into this basement and Aodh turned on us, attacked me with a knife. He said it wasn't personal, that this was just business, then struck. Just like that. It was so fast, happened so damn quickly, I just reacted in self-defense." To her horror, she felt tears pricking her eyes, but she blinked them back. She wouldn't cry in front of him. "I stabbed him straight through the heart with one of my blades. He burst into flames as he died and..." She couldn't go on, couldn't look at him anymore.

Aodh shoved up from his chair. "You never stabbed me! That's the biggest bunch of crap I've—"

"Shut it," Ace interjected. "It's not your turn."

Aodh sat back down but was gritting his teeth hard.

"We lost the witch's trail after that," Axel interjected. "But we saved the ashes, still scattered them even if you didn't deserve it," he snapped.

Aodh shoved to his feet again, a ball of energy. "That's bull—"

"You'll get your turn." Everleigh's tone was soft but sharp as she spoke before Ace could this time. "Sit. Down."

Aodh sat, scowling, so Harlow continued. "After that, we didn't last much longer in the Corps. We tried to figure out who'd hired Aodh to kill us, if he'd been involved with the witch or what, but we kept hitting dead ends. There'd been no money trail...nothing. Not even a hint of why he'd done it or who he could have been working for. And as Axel said, the trail for the witch we'd been hunting completely died. Eventually our commander shut everything down and we left the Corps."

Everleigh nodded slowly, then gave Ace a look Harlow couldn't decipher before she turned to Aodh. "I'm going to ask you a few questions. And they might seem silly but I need you to answer them honestly."

He nodded, his big body practically vibrating, and Harlow knew he hated sitting in that chair. He'd always been like that, unable to sit still for long, always had to be doing something.

"What is your full name?"

"Aodh of the Eiliason clan."

From there Everleigh finished getting her "baseline" for his truth, then said, "Okay, I want to hear in the simplest terms what happened between you and Harlow."

"Well I never stabbed her or tried to stab her," he snarled, looking at Harlow as if she was deranged. "I would have never tried to hurt you. I'd rather die."

Harlow wasn't sure what game he was playing but it smelled like he was telling the truth. Clearly she was wrong though. Had to be. Because if not... Her gut twisted. *No. Just no.*

He turned back to Everleigh, took a deep breath and seemed to calm a fraction. "Everything she said up until we hit that basement in Canada is true. Until the whole 'stabbing' thing," he muttered, using air quotes. "I would have just burned you to a crisp if I'd wanted to kill you. Which I never would have done," he added, glancing at her once before focusing on Everleigh again.

Harlow shifted uncomfortably.

"Something pierced my chest." His tone was darker now. "Certainly not from Harlow. I couldn't see it, but I could feel it. It was...dark, heavy, is the only way to describe it. And it paralyzed me. As if I'd been shot full of poison. The next thing I knew I was literally buried in an underground prison. I'd shifted to my dragon form but I was trapped, unable to shift back, or transport myself anywhere. I didn't know it at the time, but over the years I learned that I was underneath the dungeon in the Domincary fae realm. And I figured out that the witch we'd been hunting poisoned me. Whatever she used was fast acting, like a venom. And the bitch got lucky because once it paralyzed me she was able to lock me up, encase me and keep me weak."

Harlow sucked in a breath, unable to stop herself.

He ignored her and continued. "As far as I could tell, no one even knew I was under the dungeon. I could hear what went on in the castle so I gathered a lot of information while I was imprisoned. While I *stupidly* waited for my team to rescue me," he snarled, looking at Harlow and the others, his eyes accusing.

And she couldn't breathe, because what if he *was* telling the truth? But no, she'd been there, he'd...well, why *had* he tried to stab her instead of burn her?

"But they never came," he finished, his tone dripping with accusation. Betrayal.

"You said the witch imprisoned you?" Everleigh's question cut through the quiet.

"Yes, had to be. I mean, I never saw her, but—" Suddenly he turned to them, avoiding Harlow's gaze, focusing on Axel instead. "You said the trail went cold but did anyone ever find out anything about her?"

"No," Axel said on a growl. "The killings stopped though. We thought maybe..." He cleared his throat.

"You thought maybe I'd been involved in the killings?" Aodh looked disgusted, his gaze flashing to his dragon.

Harlow could barely breathe, let alone speak. She looked at Everleigh, waiting for the witch to say something.

Finally, Everleigh cleared her throat, looked at Ace once, then sighed. "Right now, you're both telling the truth. Which tells me that some kind of spellwork was involved. I could be off base, but it's believable that someone created an illusion that made you see Aodh attacking you."

"But...I felt the knife go in." Goddess, it hurt to remember it. "It was so real," she rasped out.

"That kind of magic is rare, but there are witches who wield that sort of power, specifically energy witches. And if you were in a heightened state of emotion, it's believable that someone was able to create a spell where you saw what they wanted you to."

Bile rose in Harlow's throat, but she swallowed hard and forced herself to look at Aodh. Goddess, had everything been a lie? An illusion? Oh...goddess. *No. No, no, no.* "I never would have abandoned you if...

any of this is true. If you were imprisoned, I never would have left you." She'd have torn up the world looking for him.

Brielle shifted to her human form then, took the T-shirt Axel gave her. "We wouldn't have left you to die," her sister added.

"Ever," Axel finished.

Aodh just glared at them, rage shining bright as he said, "And I've never tried to kill any of *you*. Of all people."

"How sure are you they're both telling the truth?" Ace asked Everleigh.

"Ninety-nine percent, because there is no one hundred percent anything. But they're not lying. Or at least they both believe the story they're telling."

Ace scrubbed a hand over his face. "Is there a way to find out if there was spellwork involved in what happened?"

Everleigh paused. "Perhaps. I'll need to speak to my coven members. And I believe the Magic Man might be able to help. We could theoretically recreate what happened that day, see it through their eyes sort of like a movie playing out. I've seen such a spell done once, but never attempted it myself."

"Is it dangerous?"

"No. But it's an intricate spell."

"Could Dallas help?" Harlow asked. "Because she's in town." Harlow wanted to get to the bottom of this, needed to know the truth. Because right now Aodh smelled of pure, unadulterated truth. Unless he was the best damn actor in the world. And maybe he was.

"Dallas can help," Everleigh murmured, moving to talk quietly with Ace.

Harlow frowned at Aodh. "Why are you here in New Orleans?" she suddenly demanded. "Did you come to kill us? To get revenge?"

"I came to find out why you'd left me! We were like family—" He snapped his mouth shut, as if he'd said too much, but she heard the pain in his voice, as vivid as it was etched into his expression before he stood and turned away from all of them.

"Wait...have you been following me? Was that you in the woods?"

"I was following you for a bit to see what you've been up to. But I left those animals for the humans, not you."

But she could hear the lie crystal clear in his voice—he'd left those kills, the dinner, for her. Not the humans.

Harlow stalked over to Aodh, stood in front of him, heart pounding. "If this is true..." The words stuck in her throat. If all this was true, then they *had* left him to rot. And he'd been imprisoned, thinking they'd just abandoned him. "I never would have left you behind."

"And I never would have tried to kill you. Or hurt you." And he was clearly horrified she'd thought he could.

But those memories were imprinted in her brain. If this was all an illusion—and it was starting to feel like it might have been—she wasn't sure where the hell they went from here. "How'd you get out of the prison?" She'd heard the story from her friend Stella, who'd told them how her grandmother had destroyed the castle in the Domincary realm with her dragon fire. And when she had, it had unleashed a dragon from a prison below it. She'd just never imagined it had been Aodh.

Why would she? Because he'd been dead. Clearly not though.

And if his story lined up with what she already knew... Oh goddess, he was telling the truth.

"An ancient female dragon destroyed everything. Her fire must have cracked the magic holding me. It had been waning anyway. I'd felt it in the last couple years, but couldn't manage to break through it. I was too weak." He growled in disgust. "But as soon as I was able, I busted out and returned to a very different world."

Oooh. Oh sweet goddess. Her heart twisted painfully. He'd been all alone, thinking they'd just left him. "Where are you staying?"

He lifted a shoulder, glanced away from her as if he couldn't stand to look at her.

It cut deep, but she swallowed her stupid feelings down. She couldn't offer to let him stay with her, not when they had cubs at the house. But maybe—

"Tomorrow morning bright and early we're going to reconvene here and figure out if you're telling the truth," Ace said as he approached them. "Dallas and the Magic Man are going to help us clarify everything. If you didn't try to kill Harlow, then I have no beef with you. But you are in this territory illegally. You didn't once try to contact King or—"

"I want to call in my favor with King," Harlow blurted. The thought of Aodh getting into hot water because he'd come here looking for answers after thinking his family had just abandoned him was too much.

Because blood didn't always make you family. They'd all chosen each other.

Ace lifted an eyebrow at Harlow.

"When King was poisoned and I stayed behind in the fae realm and hunted down that antidote, he told me he owed me. I'm cashing that in now—if Aodh is telling the truth, then he gets a free pass for being here." But her gut told her he was telling the truth. Why lie? Why show up here after all these years? They'd thought he was dead. And she felt sick about that.

Ace blinked once, then nodded. "Okay." Then he turned a sharp gaze on Aodh. "You're going to stay here tonight."

When Aodh went to open his big mouth, no doubt to snap something at Ace, Christian stepped onto the patio, having been out of sight until now.

"I've already made up a room for him," he said smoothly.

Aodh looked as if he wanted to argue, then shrugged. "Fine, whatever. I'll do whatever you need tomorrow, then I'm gone."

Harlow's heart jumped in her chest, panic punching through her. "You'll leave, just like that?"

"I can't stand to look at you. You actually thought I'd try to kill you? Much less hurt you?" Pain echoed in his words.

"It was so real," she whispered, feeling like she was being torn apart inside.

"If you leave, you'll never find that witch on your own," Axel said calmly, striding up to them. "And I assume you plan to hunt her down."

"If she's even out there," Aodh muttered. "I don't even know where to start."

Oh hell, Axel was right. Of course that was what he would be planning to do. And if Harlow had been thinking more clearly, she'd have had the same thought.

Someone had messed with their minds, had tricked her into believing the male she loved had turned on her. "It's been fifteen years," she whispered.

"Where the hell are we even going to start?" her twin murmured.

Harlow had no clue. She also had no clue how Aodh could ever forgive her.

CHAPTER FOURTEEN

"Oh, you're cooking?" Marley strolled into the kitchen, bright-eyed, clearly buzzing from her night out. It was two in the morning and Harlow hadn't been able to sleep since getting back to the house an hour ago so she'd started cooking.

For Aodh. As guilt shredded up her insides.

She shouldn't even be bothering, knew she was acting unhinged, because as soon as she was done she was taking this over to Christian's house for Aodh. No matter what happened tomorrow when Everleigh and the Magic Man did that test on them to see if they'd been spelled, she already knew in her gut that they must have been.

It was the only thing that made sense. In her bones, she'd never been able to process that Aodh had tried to kill her or the others. And he'd made a heartbreaking point—he'd have just burned them all to a crisp if he had. Not tried to stab her.

Goddess.

"Not for you," she finally said as Marley tried to snag one of her corn tortillas.

"Ooh, cranky pants." Marley sat at the island across from her, grabbed an apple from the bowl as she leaned back. "Why aren't you sharing?"

"Because she's cooking for a male," Brielle said, stalking into the room. Her twin had changed into jogging pants and a sports bra and her hair was pulled back in a long braid.

"Wait, what?" Marley sat up straight, apple forgotten. "Who? Have I met him? When did this happen?"

"Really?" she growled at Brielle, annoyed her sister had decided to spill the beans.

Her twin just shrugged and sat on the seat next to Marley. "We're telling everyone now. Because after tomorrow I have a feeling we're going to be..." She sighed, not finishing.

Not that she needed to. After tomorrow—or technically today, since it was two in the morning already—they'd be hunting down that witch who'd screwed up their lives and killed over a hundred people they knew of. And this time they'd make sure they stopped her forever. She wouldn't be locked up either. *Nope.* This was going to be a fight to the death.

Harlow couldn't just sit back and do nothing now that Aodh was back, knowing that witch had stolen all those years from them, kept him imprisoned. Hurt the male she loved.

"You're going to be what?" Marley looked between the two of them. "Stop doing that twin thing," she growled when they didn't respond.

"I just want to wait until everyone is here. Axel's grabbing the others now so you can wait three minutes," Brielle said, leaning back in her chair, her expression as tense as Harlow felt.

Lola and Bella came in a few minutes later with Axel. The kids were all sleeping, as they should be.

Bella had stayed at the house to watch them instead of going out with everyone, so she was the only one who actually looked sleepy, stumbling into the kitchen in her silky pink PJs. "It's too early to be up," she mumbled, sliding onto the seat next to Brielle.

Brielle wrapped an arm around her shoulders. "I know, but we've got something to tell everyone and didn't want you to find out last."

"Oh...thanks." She perked up slightly, even as she eyed Harlow. "You're cooking?"

"For a man, apparently," Marley murmured.

Harlow cleared her throat. "All right, ya'll are going to listen as I give you a quick rundown of what's going on. Aurora already knows, for the record. I called her," she added. She'd have been told the basics anyway because Ace had immediately contacted King, but Harlow had told Aurora regardless. "As you know, years ago the three of us did supernatural operations while in the Marine Corps. We worked with another male, a dragon. And..." She cleared her throat, tried to force the words out, but it was too hard.

Thankfully Axel finished explaining the situation for her, outlining everything that had happened years ago and then tonight.

"Holy shit," Marley breathed. "That's a lot of info to process at once. So you're cooking for this Aodh because...you feel bad?" she said to Harlow.

Brielle elbowed Marley. "She's cooking because she loved him, dummy. She feels awful. We all do."

Harlow didn't say anything, couldn't find the words, couldn't talk at all as she finished. Bad didn't even begin to describe what she was feeling.

Migas were ridiculously easy to make and they'd been one of Aodh's favorite foods. She left the zesty egg mixture in the cast iron skillet and put a cover over it before she started gathering the different toppings.

"Is there anything we can do?" Bella asked, more awake now.

"No," Harlow said, finding her voice.

"We just wanted you all to know," Brielle said. "In case we leave soon."

"We can come with you. We want to," Marley added, getting nods of agreement from Lola and Bella.

Harlow glanced at Axel and Brielle, shook her head once. "Look," she said as she started loading everything into a cloth bag. "I love you guys more than anything, but we have no idea what we're up against. The kids need you here anyway. We can't all leave them." The kids needed structure and security. And more than that, to feel safe. No way could all of them leave at once.

They started to argue, but Harlow ignored them as she packed up, then nodded at Axel to help her.

Brielle was wonderfully patient as she fielded questions and arguments from everyone while Harlow hurried out of the room with Axel. She simply didn't have the energy to deal with anything else right now.

"I feel like the biggest asshole on the planet," she said as she and Axel stepped out into the chilly night air. "We just left him in a prison."

Axel grabbed one of the bags. "We didn't know, something he'll soon realize."

"It doesn't matter! I should have known. I should have…"

How had she not realized? Of course he wouldn't have tried to kill her.

"You're not omniscient, Harlow. There was no way for you to know. We didn't realize it either, or of course we'd have scoured the damn planet for him. Other realms. We'd have never stopped looking for him."

Axel's words did little to ease the tightness in her chest, the knowledge that she'd failed the male she loved. That he'd endured imprisonment while believing she'd betrayed him. "He probably won't even eat this but I needed to do something. Goddess, this is probably stupid," she grumbled to herself. "He's not going to forgive me because I made him migas. And he didn't even want to talk to me, so…" She sighed. Hopefully he just needed time and would listen to her.

Axel didn't respond, remained quiet as they walked the rest of the way to Christian's.

Thankfully Christian stepped out the front door almost as soon as Axel texted him.

"Hey, everything okay?" The handsome vampire was in casual lounge pants and a cashmere pullover sweater.

"I just wanted to bring Aodh food," Harlow murmured, feeling stupid as she handed her bag to Christian.

"I'm sure he'll appreciate it." Christian was so damn sweet and sincere as he took her bag, then Axel's. "Would you like me to get him? He's not asleep."

"No," Harlow said quickly before Axel could respond. She knew Aodh would say no and she didn't need to have the rejection shoved in her face. "We'll be back in a few hours though for the meeting."

"Okay." Christian looked as if he wanted to say more, but nodded at the two of them before heading back inside.

Harlow quickly retraced her steps back to the street with Axel. "I didn't want him to get Aodh—he doesn't want to see us. Definitely not me."

Axel simply sighed, but didn't refute her words.

Which somehow made her feel even worse, something that shouldn't be possible. She had a feeling she wasn't going to sleep at all. Nope, she'd just count down until they returned here in a few hours.

Where she'd have it confirmed that Aodh hadn't actually tried to kill her; that she'd stabbed...well, whatever the hell that witch had conjured. Not him.

As CHRISTIAN STEPPED into his large kitchen—that was now being used far more often since he'd had a revolving door of guests the last couple years, including two dragons who were due to return fairly soon—Aodh hesitantly stepped inside as well.

The large male had put on the T-shirt he'd been carrying around earlier—the one that smelled like Harlow. "Is everything all right? I thought I heard Harlow."

"Everything is fine. Harlow dropped off food for you." He set the bags on the pristine island countertop and began unloading everything.

"Probably poisoned it," Aodh murmured, with no heat in his voice.

"Then I guess I should just toss it?"

"What? No," he snapped, frowning at Christian as he approached, sniffed slightly. His expression shifted as Christian took the top off the cast iron skillet. Surprise flashed across his hard face but it was fleeting, quickly replaced by a neutral expression.

But he wasn't fooling anyone. "Are you hungry?"

Aodh lifted a shoulder. "I could eat, I guess."

Oh, so this one was surly. Christian could deal with that much more easily than someone who moped. "Sit," he ordered, pointing to one of the stools on the other side of the island.

"I can get my own food."

"I'm well aware. But I don't want you banging around in my kitchen, so you will sit." He got out a plate, utensils, and started plating everything for him, mainly because something told Christian that this big dragon needed someone to take care of him at the moment. "So how long did you work with Harlow and the others?"

"Couple years," he murmured, his big body tense, looking like a caged animal as he sat there. "How long have you known them?"

"Few years. They're good shifters, care about the territory."

Aodh just grumbled as he accepted the food Christian set in front of him.

Instead of leaving the male in peace, as he probably should, he poured himself a glass of blood wine and leaned against the countertop as he faced the dragon. "Harlow told me about you once. Didn't say your name."

The male didn't look at Christian, just kept eating, but he was listening.

"And while I don't know her as well as Axel or her twin do, it broke her heart to think she killed you. That much I know. She wouldn't have just left you in a prison if she'd known you were still alive. None of them would have. Axel drives me insane on a good day, but I'm pretty sure he'd even come for me if I was imprisoned."

As Christian said the words, he realized they were true. And the truth of *that* shook him to his core.

So he ignored it completely and continued talking even as the fabric of his universe had just been altered. Because knowing, *accepting* that Axel would come for him if he was in danger... Oh. *No.* He wasn't ready to deal with that. "I understand being angry, being so filled with rage that you let it consume you to the point that you're not living, and it's as miserable as it sounds."

"Why are you telling me this?" the male snarled even as he tucked some of the migas in another tortilla and rolled it up.

"Because the female who just dropped off food for you didn't abandon you. So if you punish her based on something she didn't know, you're an asshole. And she's my friend." Christian shoved off the countertop, stalked out of the room, but called over his shoulder as he left. "Clean up my kitchen when you're done."

Over the years he'd allowed a few people into his life, to become his friends, and he found himself being overly protective of every single one of them. Especially the shifters who'd simply barreled their way into his life. Shifters felt with everything they had. Life was too precious to take for granted, and the thought of anyone hurting those he cared about pissed him off.

Even Axel.

Especially Axel.

CHAPTER FIFTEEN

After eating everything Harlow had dropped off, Aodh cleaned the dishes and left Christian's kitchen perfectly clean.

Because something told him the fancy vampire would come for his head if he didn't. He would have cleaned anyway—he was a soldier and he didn't like messes.

He didn't like *anything* right now, least of all being alone with his thoughts. He hadn't meant to reveal himself yesterday; had been content to follow Harlow and stew in his own anger.

Then she'd grabbed some random male at that party, had looked as if she would kiss him. His most primal side had simply reacted before he'd fully processed what he was doing. Just taken over and gone after that male—who was lucky he was still alive.

She was the only one who'd ever brought out that raw side to him.

He wanted to hate her, had planned to stew all night into tomorrow. Then she'd dropped off his favorite meal. The first thing she'd ever made for him after their first fight. That was what had made it his favorite. He wondered if he'd ever told her that?

"Hell," he growled, rubbing a hand over his face. What if she had been spelled? What if she and the others hadn't simply abandoned him to his fate?

He stilled when he scented someone—two someones. Not Christian. Strangers. He hadn't heard anything but he could smell them.

He turned off the lights to the kitchen, not needing them anyway as he used the shadows to his benefit. As he prepared for an attack, the light suddenly snapped back on and a big male stepped into the kitchen.

Definitely a dragon.

He stared at Aodh. "Who are you?"

"Aodh."

The male's dark eyes narrowed slightly, the action pulling at the deep scar on his right cheek. "Why are you here?"

"I'm a guest of Christian's."

The male started to respond but Christian strode in carrying an empty wineglass. "Rhodes, you're back early," he said, his voice light, but it was clear he liked this male. "And I see you've met Aodh already. Where's Stella?"

"I told her to wait outside while I inspected your house."

"It's warded," Christian said. "No one would get in here that I didn't allow."

The male just shrugged, then eyed Aodh.

Christian cleared his throat. "Aodh will be staying with us for...I don't know how long. I'm also having some others over in the morning —it's a bit of a story, but I'm sure you and Stella are tired after your journey."

"We are, and we brought you gifts." The male almost smiled as he spoke. "But we'll give them to you in the morning, if you don't mind. We're both exhausted."

"Of course. Go, rest, please. There's plenty in the fridge if you decide you're hungry later."

"Thank you." Rhodes looked at Aodh again, his expression dark. "Keep your distance from my mate and we'll be fine."

"Of course." Aodh nodded once, and that put the male at ease before he stalked away.

"Thank you for cleaning the kitchen," Christian said as he set his glass in the sink. "Did you need anything else?"

"No. But...look, the room you set up is nice, but would you mind if I slept in your backyard in dragon form?"

The vampire didn't even blink, simply nodded. "Of course, that's fine."

"I'll be in my camo mode, just a heads-up, but I'm not leaving."

Christian simply nodded, his expression unreadable as Aodh headed for the back door.

He found he liked the vampire, even if he seemed a bit stuffy. It had been kind of him to open his home to him, a virtual stranger.

It didn't take long for him to find a spot in the large backyard to rest. Once he'd shifted to his dragon form, a sense of peace came over him, however temporarily.

His life was one giant shitshow right now. He'd been so damn sure of himself, so sure that the female he was obsessed with, loved more than anything, had betrayed him. Now he was fairly certain she hadn't, even if some irrational part of his brain wanted to hold on to his anger.

But his anger wasn't at her, not if she'd truly not known he'd been trapped. And after seeing her devastated expression earlier, how she'd watched him in that haunted way... He knew she hadn't intentionally abandoned him.

Which meant they had a witch to hunt down.

But he wasn't sure what the hell that meant for him and Harlow. Years had passed. She'd clearly moved on, even if she felt guilty about what had happened. He'd seen her about to kiss that male last night. He was simply a part of her past now.

A footnote.

Not her future.

When he saw her in a few hours, after the witches ran their tests or whatever the hell they were doing, he'd make it clear that he held no ill will.

Then he would be hunting down that witch who'd destroyed his life. If Harlow and the others joined him, fine. But afterward, he couldn't expect things to be the same between them. Too much time had passed. *Right?*

As he closed his eyes, settled in listening to the sounds of the quiet neighborhood, the trees rustling, he allowed himself to indulge in the memory of the first time Harlow had cooked for him.

"What is this?" Aodh stared at the kitchenette in horror. Was that onion bits on the ceiling?

He shared the little space with Harlow, Axel and Brielle in between missions when they weren't able to go home. Not that he really had one anyway.

On a military base, their two rooms were connected by another room that had a shower, kitchenette and bathroom. He'd been bunking with Axel until recently—now Axel and Brielle bunked together.

Harlow glared at him. "I cooked!"

"And you're...angry about that?"

"No, I'm angry because this was supposed to be my apology. And..." She looked up, glared at the ceiling. "Something's wrong with the blender," she muttered.

"It smells good."

She gave him a dry look. She'd left her hair down today, a rarity that she usually reserved only for him. Once she'd talked about cutting it, but he hoped she never did. He loved running his fingers through the long auburn tresses while she rode him. Or when he claimed her mouth. Or any day that ended in Y.

"Don't humor me."

Snickering, he shut the heavy steel door behind him. "I'm not. It really does smell good. But you smell better," he murmured as he stalked toward her, his intentions clear. Brielle and Axel were off for a couple hours on a run.

She looked at him in surprise. "Seriously? I thought you were mad at me."

He lifted a shoulder. "I am—was. I don't like arguing with you." It ripped him up inside.

"I don't like arguing with you either." Her expression was almost mulish as she crossed her arms over her chest.

"So, let's not argue anymore." He settled his hands on her hips, tugged her close. He'd much prefer to get naked and not talk at all.

All the tension eased from her body as she melted against him. It still stunned him that only a month ago he'd been fantasizing about this—on an industrial scale. She consumed all his waking thoughts as well as his sleep. Had been doing that for almost a year and he hadn't seen an end in sight to his torture.

"Should we talk about...anything?" she hedged.

Talk about the fact that he'd mentioned mating and she'd freaked out on him? Um, how about hell no. He claimed her mouth instead, wanting her with a desperation that bordered on insanity.

And not caring.

She jumped him, wrapping her long, lean legs around him as she kissed him back hard. She fucked exactly as she lived her life, with passion and heart.

It was why he loved her, even if he hadn't said the words to her. He'd thought slowly bringing up the idea of mating to her would be the way to go, but maybe he had to be more sneaky. Just not bring it up at all.

Get her so damn hooked on him that she didn't realize it until she was just as hooked as he was. Then he'd toss mating out there. Yeah, that was what a sneaky cat would do, and he needed to start thinking like a feline.

He reached out, turned off the oven with one hand before carrying her into what had recently become their room. She was wearing workout pants and a half T-shirt so stripping her was easy.

She stretched out on the bed, eyeing him like the predator she was as she arched her back.

He growled low in his throat and pinned her to the bed, taking her mouth once again as he reached between her legs, cupped her mound.

He didn't penetrate her yet, just started teasing her clit with his thumb as he kissed her, claimed her. Because all of his kisses were claiming ones, even if she didn't realize it.

He realized he was growling aloud as the past consumed him and he forced the memory away, locked it up tight where it belonged.

Whatever happened in the next few hours, he couldn't keep thinking about the past. It would destroy him.

The only thing he wanted to do was destroy the witch who'd imprisoned him.

CHAPTER SIXTEEN

A xel shoved his hands in his pockets after knocking on the steel
reinforced door of Prima's house. He'd called her but she hadn't
answered. She hated phones, however, so that wasn't out of the ordi-
nary. But maybe it had been stupid to stop by in the middle of the night.
He took a step back and—

The door swung open and a scantily clad Prima stood there, her jet-
black hair a tangled mess around her face, her eyes bleary. "What's up?
Is everything okay?" she demanded, wiping at her gray eyes, clearly
trying to wake up. "Do we need to kill something?" She blinked again,
coming awake more quickly.

"I'm sorry for waking you up." Goddess, he was a dumbass. "I just
didn't know where else to go and I needed a friend to talk to. But it's
late and—"

She grabbed his hand, tugged him inside, then shoved the door shut.
"Come on. I'll put some tea on. What's going on?"

Prima was ancient, the power radiating off her a live thing, something she couldn't control. He wasn't sure how old the female dragon
was, and he wasn't even sure how they'd become friends, but he was
glad they had. She actually reminded him of his moms.

She was a savage fighter, terrified most people she came in contact with, had probably killed more beings than he could imagine. But had the biggest heart of anyone he'd ever met. A walking contradiction of power and generosity. She lived by her own rules, and for some reason she'd decided that she would be his friend and that was that. She also helped countless abused human females, giving them back a sense of control over their lives in a world gone mad. It was no wonder he'd taken her up on her offer of friendship. She was a rare being.

"It's been a long night," he murmured as he sat at her kitchen table.

Wearing skimpy shorts, a sports bra and nothing else, she started making chamomile tea. He was just surprised she had clothes on at all. She was more in touch with her animal than anyone he'd ever met and usually eschewed clothing altogether. "Ah, this is about you and the pretty vampire. Give it time, sweet boy. You're both young. You have time to figure things out."

A ghost of a smile touched his mouth. He was in his forties and Christian was over five hundred years old, but to her they were boys. "It's not the vampire." And something told him he would never work things out with Christian, regardless.

His vampire, who was not really his at all, had put up a barbed wire fence rigged with explosives around his heart. He didn't want to open his heart.

Axel didn't want to think about the male anyway. He cleared his throat. "Years ago..." He told her everything, poured out the whole story of what had happened, leaving nothing out. And when he finished, Prima was pouring him a second cup of hot tea.

Then she poured herself another, once again sitting across from him at the table. A beautiful bouquet of pink peonies sat in the middle, the scent pleasing.

"Aodh sounds like he was a good friend."

"He was. *Is* still, I hope." Tomorrow would confirm everything one way or another. But his instinct was telling him what he felt was real. "I just...everything is messed up and Harlow is in so much pain. I wish I could do more for her, but I feel like I'm floundering." And he was still in love with a dumb vampire who would never love him back. Which was another source of his melancholy tonight. He needed to get away from here, sometimes thought about just running away.

Then kicked his own ass mentally because he'd never leave his family, especially not Legend and Enzo. Those kids had quickly become his world, all of their world. They'd lost their parents, and even if Axel wanted to run away from his own heartbreak, he never actually would. He couldn't.

"If it turns out that spellwork was involved, that he didn't…betray us, I'll introduce you. You'll like him," he murmured, half smiling.

"He's a dragon. There's a good chance I will. Though I will challenge him to a fight. See if he's worthy of Harlow."

Axel smiled into his tea. Prima was a twin as well and had always had a special affinity for Harlow and Brielle. "Thank you for listening to me, and I really am sorry for showing up like a jackass."

Prima lifted a shoulder, clearly unconcerned. "I can sleep when I'm dead. Which will be never as I am a powerful dragon."

"And so very humble."

She grinned again, her gray eyes darkening slightly as her dragon lurked beneath the surface. He wondered if she was even aware of her beast coming to the forefront since it happened so often, the two sides so intertwined.

Axel glanced back into his mug, not because he was afraid her dragon would ever harm him, but more often than not he found that he couldn't hold her gaze for too long. There weren't many people who could. Looking into her eyes was like looking into the sun.

"I'm glad you stopped by tonight. Arthur is out of town and I found myself lonely."

"Liar," he said on a laugh. "I woke you from a dead sleep." He motioned to her wild hair. Which was standard for her. He'd only ever seen it combed neatly a couple times in the years since he'd known her.

"I'm not lying about being happy you stopped by. If you need anything, you only ever have to ask."

"I do know that, and thank you." He set the mug down, knew he needed to get home and try to snag some sleep. An hour or two at least.

She stood with him, leaving the mugs behind as they headed for the front door. "It goes without saying, but keep me updated."

"Of course."

She stepped outside with him, pulled him into a tight hug, her embrace making him gasp for air for a moment. But then she stepped back and patted his face. As she did, he was very aware of the energy changing nearby, of magic—

In the yard, a huge dragon suddenly appeared in a burst of magic, then the dragon shifted to a very large, annoyed-looking male. Arthur.

Not Prima's mate, but her lover. And Axel didn't actually understand why they weren't mated. The one time he'd brought it up, she'd shut him down by tossing him across the sparring mat they'd been practicing on and informing him that she'd never had a lion pelt before.

Soooo, he'd never brought it up again. He liked his hide in one piece, thank you very much.

Right about now the red-haired, bearded warrior looked very, *very* annoyed to see Axel. Probably didn't help that he'd just been hugging Prima and she was wearing not much clothing. But come on, Arthur should know better about the two of them.

"You're back early," Prima murmured as she leaned against one of the columns on the porch, her gaze narrowed on Arthur.

Axel couldn't read that look and was honestly a little afraid of the energy sparking between the two of them, so he simply nodded politely at Arthur.

The dragon shifter bared his teeth at Axel, and yep, that was Axel's cue to get the hell out of here.

CHAPTER SEVENTEEN

Aodh stalked into the living room, freshly showered and wearing the same T-shirt he'd taken back from Harlow yesterday.

It smelled like her now so he wouldn't be washing it anytime soon. Or ever.

As he entered the room his gaze was immediately drawn to her. Sitting on one of the chairs, she was looking at her cell phone with a look of...love. Adoration. The way she used to look at him.

From his position he could see she was looking at a picture of her and someone, but with the glare and angle he couldn't make out the whole thing.

What. The. Hell.

The thought of her with someone else, even if he'd convinced himself that they had no future and he would move on, cut out his heart.

Because that *look*. Oh, he recognized that look so well. She was looking at a picture of her and a lover. Had to be.

When she realized he'd stepped into the room, she flipped her phone over so it was facedown and gave him a weird, strained look. Guilt, maybe.

Oh goddess, he felt sick. That had definitely been her with another male.

He looked away, taking in everyone else in the room—Brielle and Axel of course, Everleigh, Ace, and three people he did not recognize. Christian wasn't there, but perhaps he'd decided to remain scarce while they did whatever the hell was about to happen.

"Aodh, this is Dallas and Rhys," Ace said, motioning to a male and female who were clearly a mated couple. "She is a powerful witch and will be working with Everleigh and Thurman," he added, motioning toward an older Black human male who was dressed as elegantly as Christian seemed to.

"I'm just here to make sure you don't mess with my mate," Rhys said in the brief lull.

The female Dallas nudged him gently in the ribs, but still gave him a look of exasperated adoration.

"Let's do this," Brielle said suddenly, standing. "Whatever we need to do, let's get it done."

Aodh nodded along with Axel and Harlow, even as he tried not to stare at her, to drink in her sharp profile. She was a long, lean, honed fighting machine. He loved her in both forms. When she was a tiger, stalking her prey, it was absolutely magnificent to watch her from the air.

And of course he loved her naked in human form too. Probably best. Definitely best. He wished she was naked right now.

Stop thinking about that, idiot, he ordered himself. *Goddess.* The others were looking at him. Had he said that aloud?

"Is that okay?" Axel asked, eyeing him questioningly.

"Yes?" What the hell had he just said yes to?

Dallas clapped her hands together once, her expression serene. The witch had dark hair, gray eyes and was as tall as Harlow. But she wasn't as sharp, lean. No, she was softer, had a gentleness about her, even as power rolled off her in subtle waves. Everleigh was powerful too; he could sense it. But Dallas was the powerhouse witch in this room and probably the whole damn territory, if he had to guess. The power was spilling out of her, likely without her conscious effort.

His own power was like that. It was the same with many older dragons. Their power simply couldn't be contained.

"If the four of you will simply stand here," Dallas said, motioning for them to move into the middle of the huge living room filled with probably a thousand books lining the walls.

Right about now Aodh wished he'd been paying attention to what they'd asked him to agree to. But he fell in line with them, standing on the other side of Harlow—and ignoring the surprised look she gave him.

"Do you have a lover?" he asked quietly, though everyone in the room could clearly hear him. Because who was he kidding, he wasn't moving on from her. Not without a fight. He wanted to know who he was up against. Then he'd decide how to kill her lover. Slowly. Painfully.

"Wait...what?" She stared at him now in pure shock.

"Never mind." He didn't want the answer, and shouldn't have asked her in front of everyone. But sue him, he'd lost his social skills while trapped.

"Okay," Dallas said quickly, taking over as she shooed Rhys and Ace back. "Everleigh and I are going to cast a memory spell. We could do separate ones but it'll be stronger if we cast it over all of you together, especially since you have different versions of that day. Once we do, I need all of you to remain still."

Aodh wasn't sure what the human male was doing there, but didn't ask. He didn't dare open his mouth again because he was afraid he'd demand to see Harlow's phone—then demand the name of her lover so he could hunt him down and kill him. Just rip out his intestines. Or maybe slice his head off. Both solid options.

Real healthy. Yep.

He watched as Dallas brought out her athame and just barely nicked her thumb, holding it over a clean white bowl. Everleigh did the same, with her own blade. Then the two females chanted quietly, and as they did, he could actually feel the air shift.

There was a sort of buzz in the air as everything around him seemed to shimmer.

Suddenly Dallas grabbed Thurman's hand and the human's eyes glowed before going all white—and there was only one way to describe what happened next.

The human basically acted as a projector, a 3-D image pouring out of him showing them a replay of when Aodh had lost everything.

The sun had recently risen, and they'd followed the scent trail of the witch to an abandoned cabin in Canada. She'd had an underlying smell of rot, one he'd never forget as long as he lived.

They were in the basement.

He'd gone down first, had wanted to take lead. Now he was at the bottom of the stairs. But then he watched in horror as "he" turned to attack Harlow on those stairs, his face angry, malicious as he spewed lies and raised a blade at her. But it wasn't him at all. It was nothing but an aberration, an *illusion*. Not him at all. Then she stabbed "him" first, sending the fake him tumbling down the stairs.

But off to the side—literally happening at the same time—deeper in that basement, he was also being stabbed by a shadowy figure. A blade punctured his chest, poison spreading through him, paralyzing him.

From this projection he could see the faintest overlay over the scene, as if reality and the spell were competing to be seen, which had to be the spell at work. They hadn't been lying—Harlow had thought he'd tried to kill her, all of them. That he'd been a traitor.

His heart was an erratic drumbeat in his chest, blood pounding in his ears. They'd spent all these years thinking he'd betrayed them. His family, the best friends he'd ever had.

And he thought they'd abandoned him.

Suddenly the vision stopped and it was as if all the air had been sucked out of the room as Thurman stumbled, collapsed into one of the nearby chairs.

And Aodh found himself tackled by Axel. "Punch me if you want, I'm hugging you!"

Emotion clogged his throat as Axel wrapped him in a tight grip and he found himself hugging the male back. They'd been like brothers, and goddess, he'd missed all of them so much.

Had never thought he even needed family until the three of them had barreled into his life. They'd made him love them. And he'd thought...oh goddess. Emotions roiled inside him and he couldn't get a grip on them.

"Later we're going to talk about what the hell you guys just did," Brielle said to the witches and Thurman as she jumped on both Aodh and Axel, wrapping her arms around them.

Harlow stood there, looking shaken and devastated as the other two stepped back. "I'm sorry, Aodh. I..." Her voice cracked, and in that moment, he didn't care if she did have a lover.

Well, he cared, but he pulled her into his arms anyway, was glad when she hugged him back tight, burying her face against his chest.

He buried his own face against the top of her head and inhaled, knowing everyone could see him doing it and not caring. He'd missed holding her. Hell, missed her friendship as much as he'd missed her in his bed. Because she'd been his everything, and this was the first time he was getting to hold her in years. Even in that prison, he'd remembered what this felt like, had wanted to hug her, hold her again.

She hadn't abandoned him. And she'd been just as devastated as he had been, thinking she'd killed him when she'd killed nothing at all.

They'd all been tricked, and that witch was going to pay if it was the last thing he did.

Aodh noticed Axel wiping away a surprising amount of wetness on his cheeks and was struck by how soft the male's heart was. Always had been, no matter how tough of a fighter he was.

"So, it appears everything is as you both said," Ace said quietly, breaking the silence.

Harlow stepped back, nodded, wiped at her own face. And he resisted the urge to cup her cheeks, wipe her tears away. "Does he have safe passage in our territory?" she asked Ace.

Ace paused. "Have you not talked to Aurora?"

"I didn't want to put her in a weird spot by asking her directly. I mean, she knows about him, about our history. I definitely told her about that." She sounded offended that Ace even asked. "But I didn't specifically ask about how long he could stay here if..." She cleared her throat as she trailed off.

Ace simply shook his head. "King wants to meet him—so does Aurora, for that matter. Call your girl. The dragon is fine as long as he doesn't cause trouble, but neither King or Aurora will say no to you.

They're not going to kick him out unless he screws up." Ace shot Aodh a hard look. "You hear that? You can stay in the territory as long as you don't cause trouble. But my Alpha will want to meet you personally in the next couple days."

Aodh would meet the Alpha. He'd do anything if it meant he got to stay near Harlow and the others. But mainly Harlow.

As Ace spoke, Harlow's phone buzzed. She winced and looked at both of them. "Tonight, actually. Aurora says we'll be hosting dinner and inviting them over."

Aodh simply nodded. He'd be wherever Harlow was. But if she invited another male, he wasn't sure he wouldn't do something stupid.

Like remove his head from his body. Now that he knew for certain the female he loved hadn't betrayed him, hadn't left him to rot, he was going to fight for her. Whoever her lover was, he wouldn't be a problem for long.

CHAPTER EIGHTEEN

Harlow stood awkwardly as Aodh stepped out into their backyard area hours later. They'd set up a few rectangular tables that basically lived out here since they all preferred to eat outdoors.

Axel and Brielle did the same, and for the first time that she could remember, her palms were damp.

After the spell Dallas and Everleigh had worked that morning, the four of them had talked a bit. But Aodh had left, wanting to go flying. It'd been clear he'd needed space, to process everything.

Not that anyone blamed him, considering he hadn't been able to take to the skies for over a decade while imprisoned. But she could still acknowledge her hurt, that he hadn't wanted to stay and talk to her.

Especially after that hug when she wanted to crawl all over him, consume him.

But...that clearly wasn't happening.

Too much time had passed. Too much had happened. They'd both been broken, in different ways. But she'd still gotten to live her life while he'd been a prisoner. He'd said he forgave her, but he hadn't given any indication he still wanted her, wanted to pick up where they'd left off. And she couldn't expect that of him.

Aodh shoved his hands in his pockets as he approached them, looking almost nervous.

"Hey." She stepped forward, feeling nervous too. "We've got food." She internally winced. Could she sound any dumber? She wanted to cover her face.

"Ah, good. I could eat." He looked at the table, the trees in the yard, the chicken coop, anywhere but her.

Ugh.

"So..." Brielle cleared her throat and Harlow wanted to hug her twin. *Yes, someone else please talk.* "I say we all just get it out in the open and talk about hunting down that sociopathic serial killer who imprisoned you."

Harlow nodded, watching Aodh's reaction.

Aodh looked between all of them. "You guys really want to team up and hunt her down?"

Axel slapped him on the shoulder. "Hell yeah."

Harlow just nodded again like a damn mime when Aodh looked at her. Because apparently she could only either say stupid things or not talk at all. Harlow was going to make sure that witch paid for what she'd taken from all of them, so many years lost. For imprisoning the male she still loved. Oh, Harlow was going to rip her apart with no mercy.

"Let's eat and talk, then," Brielle said. "I'm starving!"

Aodh looked behind him at the three-story mansion, then back at the table with the pretty string lights over it. Maybe he was second-guessing himself, but he nodded and sat down.

"I say we go back to that cabin in Canada and see if there's something we missed," Brielle said as she sat next to Harlow.

They'd all sat at the end of the table with Axel and Aodh on one side, and her and her twin on the other.

"It's been a long time," Aodh said. "Not sure that it'd do any good."

Brielle shrugged. "So? I doubt anyone lives there."

Harlow nodded her agreement.

"Why does no one live there?" Aodh asked.

"Because Donovan had someone buy it through a shell corporation. I don't know what he did with it. Bulldozed it, maybe." Captain John

Donovan had been their commander at the time, though he'd gone on to work in black ops later, then eventually he'd gone private. Harlow had tried to look for him after The Fall but hadn't been able to locate him. She hoped he'd made it.

"Why?"

"Because something about the place was off. The witch's magic there was...strong." Harlow shivered as she remembered the darkness of that place, the way it had felt as if something was scraping over her skin. Now, knowing what they did—that Aodh had been transported directly from it—made sense. If there was a sort of portal there, or if the witch had created one with dark magic, that would have created the bad energy. "Before heading back there, we should try researching any potential killings," Harlow murmured, not wanting to go down this path again. After everything had happened the killings had stopped, according to Donovan. And Harlow could admit that she hadn't dug any deeper into it once they'd left the Corps.

She'd wanted to completely erase that part of her life. To bury her sorrow.

"There weren't any more killings," Brielle said.

Axel just lifted a shoulder. "Or she got better at hiding them, or maybe she changed her killing grounds."

"We always thought there was a political bent to it," Aodh said.

She drank in his delicious voice, tried not to think about all the dirty things he'd whispered in her ears once upon a time. Tried not to want him so much, but it was useless. So she latched onto the rage inside her, determined to hunt that witch down no matter what.

"That she was a killer for hire," he continued.

"A sick killer," Harlow murmured. Because it took a specific kind of monster to kill kids. Especially in the supernatural world; it simply wasn't done. And that witch had killed entire families. Harlow glanced at the others. "It stands to reason that if she was for hire once, she's still for hire—oh shit." Harlow looked at Aodh as a thought slammed into her, kicking herself for not thinking of it before. But come on, she'd barely been thinking straight at all. "Why didn't she kill you? Why did she just imprison you?"

"I don't know, but I have a theory." He rolled his shoulders once in agitation. "She fed off my energy, kept me weak. When I was in that prison it was..."

He paused for a moment and she wanted to pull him into a hug, touch him, comfort him.

"Almost like I was in Hibernation. I didn't have to worry about food or anything else. I was in a semi-hibernated state but sometimes I was aware of more than I wanted to be. It took a bit of time, but I eventually realized I was under a castle, and that I was in a fae realm. And they had no clue I was there. Or at least the king at the time didn't."

"I scented you," Harlow murmured before she could rein in her mouth.

He blinked. "What?"

"When we rescued Rhodes...the dragon staying at Christian's. When we were hauling him out of the dungeon, I swore I could scent you, but I thought I was losing my mind," she whispered. And the guilt of that just kept chipping away at her insides. She'd scented him and then left him there. Hadn't even put two and two together when she'd heard the story about the dragon escaping—and she wanted to wallow in her stupidity. Goddess, why hadn't she realized?

"It's not your fault," he said as if he read her mind, but she wasn't sure she believed him. "There would be times where I was mostly lucid, then I'd fall into almost fuguelike states where time would pass but I wouldn't remember it. I became so exhausted that I would sleep deeply, but it wasn't a natural sleep. It was as if someone or something was siphoning my energy. Her, obviously."

"Could this witch have been part fae?" Axel asked. "Or maybe living in the Domincary realm? Because she'd have to be at least somewhat near you to take your energy."

"It could explain why the killings stopped." Brielle lifted a shoulder. "But so could a lot of other things."

There was simply too much they didn't know, and the thought of hunting her down seemed almost impossible.

"Look, I don't expect you three to help me find her," Aodh said. "You all have lives now. Good ones. So—"

"I'm gonna stop you right there," Axel cut in before Harlow could. "We're doing this. I can't even imagine what you went through or the kind of pain you experienced thinking we'd all abandoned you. But it didn't happen, as you now know."

"Yeah, shut up with that," Brielle added, glaring at Aodh.

Harlow just watched him because her throat was clogged with more emotion. She hadn't cried in years, and now it was like her eyes just wanted to rain all the time. How could he think they wouldn't help him?

Before she could respond, their back door opened and...everyone poured out at the same time, including King and Aurora and their dragonling Hunter.

Even Dallas and Rhys—with Willow—rounded the side of the house. Luna, a human friend of theirs, was with them, talking to Dallas excitedly.

Harlow was glad for the distraction even as she hated anyone pulling her focus from Aodh.

But as he turned, breaking eye contact, she could breathe again.

As everyone approached, all of them talking at the same time, she quietly scooted her chair back and stood, hoping to go hide. Or something. She wanted to hide away from the world right now.

But that hope was dashed when Willow flew at her, tackling her to the ground with happy little chirps.

"Oof." Laughing, Harlow wrapped her arms around Willow's neck and kissed her face. "Baby girl, I've missed you, but I think you've chonked out a bit."

Willow chirped indignantly, just further proof that the baby dragon could understand everything.

"I'm just playing. You're a perfect dragonling in every way."

As Willow preened, stretching her gray wings out to their full length, Hunter, another dragonling and very likely her brother—they weren't totally sure—body checked Willow before chirping maniacally and rolling onto his back, clearly amused. Of the two, he was the more mischievous one.

That was all it took for the two of them to start rolling around like loons on the lawn. Everyone ignored them because they were used to it.

Harlow snickered and hurried to their shed, grabbed a long metal pipe with bite marks in it and then whistled loudly. Out of the corner of her eye, she saw Aodh talking to Axel and just couldn't make herself go over there.

She couldn't make small talk with the male she'd wanted to mate. The male she still loved. Sure, he might now understand that she hadn't actually abandoned him, but she couldn't expect him to just be okay, to want to start over with her.

The two dragonlings came to attention, flying directly for her until she threw the pipe high into the air. Then they changed course and shot straight up, their flying substantially improved in the year and a half since they'd been rescued. They'd be badass warriors one day, she was sure of it.

The get-together was turning into a party, everyone getting louder and laughing more as food was brought out, and she was glad to have the dragonlings as a distraction.

But she knew her relative solitude wouldn't last long.

Aurora made her way over to her, casual in jeans, a thick navy sweater and boots. Her chestnut-colored hair was down tonight in soft waves and a soft blue glow emanated from her. Since "coming out" as a rare phoenix, she didn't hide what she was as much anymore. And Harlow liked it, even though she would always have a low-grade worry for her. Phoenixes were coveted for their blood, and Harlow would always view Aurora as a younger sister, no matter how much time passed.

"So...how are you?" Aurora's voice was gentle as she reached her.

Hunter immediately swooped down, kissed Aurora, then Harlow, then shot back into the sky. Willow did the same, and then the two of them took to the skies, chirping and executing impressive tricks as they headed off into the neighborhood. They were now more secure in their abilities and went off on little flying excursions but she knew they'd be back soon.

"Things are interesting." She figured that was a neutral enough answer as she turned to look at everyone—mainly Aodh.

And saw that he was talking to the pretty Luna. The human scientist who Harlow really liked. But she was also noticing how adorable the female was for the first time. Her tiger swiped at her insides, not liking the burst of jealousy. Luna was over all the time since she and Marley had become close friends—and often played guitar together.

"That's not really an answer." Aurora linked her arm with Harlow's. "Walk with me."

Falling in step with her, she allowed herself to be guided around the side of the house, away from everyone and toward the front yard. Their property was walled in, the original owner liking their privacy, and Harlow was grateful for that now.

"I've heard a recap of everything from Ace, and I'm not asking as your Alpha," Aurora said as they reached a wrought iron bench under a two-hundred-year-old oak tree. "But as your friend."

"I'm...sort of a mess." Leaning forward on the bench, she covered her face with her hands for a moment. "I don't like feeling like this." Being out of control wasn't something she was used to. And there was no way she could get her emotions in check right now.

Aurora gently rubbed her back. "I'm sorry you're dealing with this. And it feels so hollow to say this, but if there's anything you need, I'm here."

"I know." Sighing, she sat up, stretched her long legs out. "And thank you. We might be leaving the territory soon, just to give you a head's up. I need to talk to Ace about the rotations he's got me on."

"It'll be fine," Aurora assured her.

She'd known it would be. They had enough security for the territory now and were always training pups coming up in the pack.

"If you need anything for your travels, just ask."

"Would you mind reaching out to Nyx in Biloxi, ask if she could transport us to a couple places? Or at least one?" Because Harlow knew that once they formulated a plan of attack, they'd want to move fast. And if they found the witch, they'd definitely want to move on her quickly. But she wanted to talk to the Magic Man first, as well as Dallas. Talk about ways to overcome spells meant to fool your eyes. Because that witch had tricked them once and she could easily do it again.

"Of course. Do you know where you'll be going?"

"No...not quite." There was too much in the air, but after tonight they'd figure things out.

If it was the last thing she did, she was going to slay that witch. She might not have a future with Aodh anymore, but she would give that to him. Give him retribution.

CHAPTER NINETEEN

"You planning on ignoring me all night?" Aodh's deep, dark voice wrapped around Harlow as he pulled up a seat next to her.

Lights twinkled above them, strung up in the trees, creating the perfect party atmosphere.

The get-together was thankfully winding down, with Rhys, Dallas, Willow and Luna gone. And Harlow was really trying not to be so happy the pretty human with hair a color similar to her own was gone and away from Aodh. "I'm not ignoring you." *Liar, liar, pants on fire.*

He snorted softly and took a sip of his beer. "All right, pumpkin eater," he murmured, calling out her lies. But then he shifted direction, apparently letting it go. "I don't even like beer, but for some reason I missed the taste of it. I missed the taste of a lot of things while imprisoned."

It almost sounded like his voice had dropped an octave, as if he'd been talking about her, but when she looked at him, his expression was impassive. So, maybe he hadn't meant anything by that. Goddess, she was screwed up. She wanted him desperately, but what was she supposed to do? Jump him? Ask if he wanted to go get naked and make up for lost time?

He hadn't made any indication he wanted more from her. And while it slashed her up, she could at least help him get retribution for all his suffering. Not go all pervert on him.

Her muscles tightened as she thought of him locked away and she wanted to rush out into the night and savage that witch. But that obviously wasn't happening with no freaking idea where the female was. Harlow would have to practice patience. Unfortunately. "Are you staying at Christian's or...did you want to stay here?" She hated feeling like they were strangers.

"Christian is a perfectly nice male, but I'd rather stay here if you have the room."

"We've got a couple rooms free." Or you know, *her* room. But she wasn't going to offer that when she had no clue if he'd take her up on it. And oh goddess, how embarrassing would that be for her to offer and him to say no? Then they'd be stuck working together as they hunted down the witch. No. Better to keep things professional.

Professional, she ordered herself.

"I'll grab my stuff from his place, then." He snorted again. "It's not much."

She sat up straighter as his words hit home. Of course he wouldn't have much of anything. "What do you need?" Her brain had basically been mush. "I, ah, we, saved some of your stuff. Not a lot, but it's still yours. And we can get you any sort of basics you need."

He stared at her, his eyes flashing to his dragon. "You saved my stuff even though you thought I betrayed you all? Thought I tried to kill you?"

She turned away, unable to look at him for long. It hurt too much. "Yeah. What you did, or what we thought you did...couldn't erase the friendship we'd had."

"Friendship," he murmured.

Yeah, *friendship*. One she'd cherished as much as the relationship with her twin, Axel and the others. "I've been thinking about our next move," she said, wanting to change the subject as she watched Aurora hug the others goodbye. She'd already gotten her hug. And she couldn't think about her battered heart.

She could, however, focus on revenge.

"Because the more I think about your energy being drained... She had to have stayed close by you. Or at least moved in and out of the fae territory in between taking your energy. I've been there so I saw how lax their security was. So maybe she didn't live there, but I don't think it would hurt to return and check things out. Maybe find some fae to talk to. She could be pretending to be one of them, or maybe she is one of them. We need to at least see if we can pick up a trail, clues, something."

"The fae were driven from their home because of dragons." His tone was dry. "Pretty sure we won't be welcome in their territory."

She snorted because yeah, it would be tough to get information from anyone in that realm. But it was worth a shot. "I've got some other ideas too, but thought it wouldn't hurt to return." A thought struck her and she looked at him. "Unless it'll be too hard for you?"

He shook his head, watching her closely. Too closely, damn him.

"I'm about to crash," Axel said, approaching them, yawning. "But I just spoke to Christian and he's going to drop off your bag. I made the executive decision and you're staying here. Harlow can show you to your room because this lion is tired." He stalked off without waiting for a response.

Aodh laughed, the sound curling through her, warming her.

"I'm glad some things haven't changed. So...Axel and Christian? I got sort of a vibe between them," Aodh murmured.

Harlow felt the band of tension in her chest ease a fraction at the natural shift in conversation. This felt more like old times. "Not sure what's going on with them. Christian's mate died centuries ago and I don't know if he'll ever move past it." It was depressing as hell because Harlow could see how much the male wanted Axel when he looked at him.

And vice versa. But Christian had put up a wall, one she wasn't sure anyone would ever knock down or climb over.

"So what were you and Luna talking about?" *Oh, real smooth, Harlow.* She wanted to kick her own ass. Why not just let her claws out? *Ugh.*

"The little human?" He seemed surprised by the question, but shrugged. "Robotics mainly. She said a lot of stuff I didn't understand," he said on a laugh. "Did you get enough food tonight? I didn't see you eat."

"Oh, yeah, I'm good." She stood, stretched, thinking about going for a run soon. It was either that or climb out of her skin. "You want me to show you where your room is? Or did you want more food?"

Lola and Bella were moving like whirlwinds, currently cleaning up the table of food, and she felt bad for not offering to help. But she was at max capacity for things she could do today and was basically done with everything. Even herself. She just wanted to shift to her tiger and run free.

"This is a nice home," he said quietly as they made their way to the second floor.

The small talk felt wrong, maddening, when the two of them had used to joke about everything under the sun. But she supposed she couldn't expect anything more. "Yeah, we bought it right before The Fall. It was supposed to be our landing place after...well, after we rescued Aurora from some dragons."

"Where's Star?" he said suddenly, though he'd never actually met her.

But Harlow and the others had talked about their family enough. Of course he would remember. "In Scotland. Mated to a dragon. They're the Alpha couple of a territory over there."

He looked faintly surprised, but nodded. "Interesting."

"Is there anyone you want to reach out to? Or is there anywhere you need to be, I guess? So much has changed." And she couldn't imagine coming out of an imprisonment or Hibernation with everything so different and no family. But he'd never had a clan, not that she knew of.

He'd been a lone dragon, or so he'd told them.

"I'm where I want to be," he said quietly as they reached the door to the guest bedroom.

There was so much she wanted to say, but her brain refused to cooperate. "Okay. Ah...bathroom's there." She pointed. "You'll be sharing it with me." She'd intentionally given him the room that shared the same bathroom as hers. Because of course she had. "You can use any of my stuff in the shower," she added, reaching out and running her hand over his head out of habit. "Can't believe you cut your hair."

Then she froze, realized what she'd done. How casually she'd touched him, as if she had a right to.

"Ah, sorry." She didn't have the right to touch him, not anymore.

But he just watched her carefully, heat simmering in his gaze. "I'll let it grow out again." Then he stepped back and disappeared into his bedroom without another word.

She shoved out a breath and nearly collapsed against the wall, barely caught herself. She wanted all or nothing with him. She could jump him, and after that look he'd just given her, she was pretty sure he'd take her up on her offer. But just sex alone would never be enough for her. Not when it came to Aodh.

She wanted forever.

~

AODH RAN a hand over his face as he leaned against the shut door, pushed out a slow breath. When Harlow had touched him so casually, the way she'd done a thousand times before, it had taken him off guard.

Because it had felt so right.

He'd wanted to lean into her touch—to pull her to him and claim her mouth. Take her right on the floor in the hallway.

His dragon was riding him hard now, his hunger for her growing with each second that passed. Being so close to her today, yet feeling that chasm between them as if an entire planet stood in their way.

He didn't know how to fix anything, to make things right again. He couldn't just ask her to jump into bed with him—even if he thought getting naked with her was the smartest thing to do right now.

But she'd been keeping him at arm's length. Maybe...she wanted to let him down easy, tell him she'd met someone else.

No, he hadn't scented anyone on her and there had been no male here tonight with her. But...

He sighed. She wouldn't have been so cruel to invite a lover anyway, wouldn't have flaunted it in front of him. There were too many things to think about, obsess over, and he wanted none of that now.

He finally took in the generous-sized bedroom. The dark wood furniture looked French to him, but wasn't overly small. Two large windows faced the backyard, sheer curtains pulled over Roman-style shades.

The bed itself was king-sized and would have to do. He glanced at the door to the bathroom, thought about showering, but a buzzing energy hummed through him, his dragon desperate to fly first. After being kept from the skies for so long, without his consent, the need to fly was always right under the surface. Competing with the need to claim Harlow. At least he could take care of one of those needs tonight.

Leaving the lights off, he opened the curtains, then the shades and finally the windows, letting in a blast of chilly air.

Breathing deeply, he savored the fresh air, the freedom as he looked up at the moonlit sky. Down below he saw the females Lola and Marley talking and laughing in front of a small fire pit, glasses of something in their hands.

They weren't paying any attention to him so he quickly climbed down the side of the house, stripped and shifted, taking to the skies in a whoosh of magic.

As he flew higher, he glanced down and saw a large tiger trotting down the street.

Harlow.

She and her twin looked similar, but he'd know Harlow's haughty strut anywhere. Brielle stalked like a predator, and while Harlow did too, she had attitude.

Something he loved about her. She was a beautiful apex predator, secure in her place in the world.

He'd seen her take on various predators when they'd worked together, and it had always been with efficient savagery. She and Brielle had often gotten naked in human form to distract prey—and then gone in for the kill.

And while he didn't like the idea of anyone, anywhere, ever seeing her naked, he still loved to watch her work.

Curious, and okay, obsessed, he followed her from above, wondering if...she was going to meet a male, perhaps.

Then he debated how he would kill any male she slept with. Fire seemed too easy, though that was how he would dispose of the body.

But she only went to what he realized was a track for running, and started doing laps, faster, faster, as if she was trying to break a record. Then she headed back home, and by the time he'd changed into his human form and scaled the side of the house, the shower was running in their adjoining bathroom and his bag was now on his bed.

He listened to the flowing water on the other side of the door. She was in there all alone, naked.

And it took every ounce of self-control he had not to simply incinerate the door and join her. To worship her body as he brought her to climax over and over.

But it had only been a mere day since she'd discovered he was alive and hadn't actually tried to kill her. She'd lived with the thought that she'd killed the male she loved; that had to have broken her trust in a sharp way, no matter that she knew the truth now.

He couldn't expect her to just jump right back into things the way they'd been before. Right?

CHAPTER TWENTY

Harlow accepted the mug of coffee Ace slid her across the huge countertop in King's pack's mansion—the one Aurora mostly lived at now with her mate. "Thanks."

"No problem," he said around a yawn.

"Late night?"

"Yeah, dealing with some vampire shit."

She frowned before taking a sip of her coffee. "What kind of issue are we talking?"

"Don't worry about it—because I know why you're here. You're taking time off for a bit?"

"Yeah. So are Axel and Brielle."

He filled up his own mug as he nodded. "Yeah, I figured. I already started reworking the schedule around the three of you, so we're good."

"Thank you." She'd woken up early this morning after only a few hours of sleep, but mostly tossing and turning, unable to rest when all she could think about was Aodh. So she'd decided to get in yet another run, then come talk to Ace. "And I don't know if I need to talk to King about this but…I'm putting a pin in his offer."

"Also figured that, and I'll let him know. The offer isn't going anywhere, so no rush anyway. The humans we rescued have been relocated to that territory and they all adore you, so…I really hope you think about the offer."

She nodded, glad to just be able to tell Ace and not have to worry about hunting down King for that conversation. The hierarchy of the pack was smoother like that, and she knew that it freed up King to worry about bigger-picture issues. Years ago he hadn't delegated as well as he did now, but since mating with Aurora he was much better at it. He had good people at the top and they handled a lot of the day-to-day smaller issues. "You're the best."

"True," he said around a half yawn, half grin. "So, you and Aodh. He's the reason you don't date or hook up or anything." Not a question.

"Good job, Sherlock."

Ace simply grinned. "Why aren't you currently in bed with him, then? After years apart I'm surprised—"

"It's complicated. And not something I want to talk about." Last night he was the reason she'd tossed and turned. His scent so close, toying with her, making her crazy. But it couldn't be so simple as just jumping into his bed as if no time had passed. That was what she kept telling herself anyway. Though if he gave a hint that he'd open his bed to her, she was there. Goddess, she was pathetic. *Ugh.* Even though deep down it'd destroy her if he only wanted sex and not more, but she knew that she'd still give in to all her desires if he said the word.

"You sure? Because I'm great with advice."

"Not looking for advice, and I'm certainly not talking about it here in the pack's kitchen. Nosy wolves," she muttered, knowing that just because there wasn't anyone else in the kitchen with them didn't mean anything. This house was full and there would be plenty of ears eavesdropping, intentionally or not.

She didn't like the idea of her personal business spreading out to all the nosy people of New Orleans. *No, thank you.*

"Probably wise. So yeah, you're good to take off. But what else do you need? It sounds like this is a nasty threat, and while I can't take off long term, I can take off a bit of time and help you guys out. And I know a handful of others who'd love to step in as well."

She blinked in surprise.

"Why the shock?" He took another sip of his coffee.

She did the same, mainly to give herself a moment to think. "I, ah... thank you. That's a generous offer."

"You're part of the pack. All of you. And so is that arrogant dragon by extension. Maybe not for good, but once you two figure things out he'll be pack too. And news flash, you're very popular here."

Not sure what to say, she drank her coffee again.

"Cat got your tongue?"

"Ugh, I don't even know what to say to that. Stop being so nice!"

"Hey, I'm always nice."

Yeah, but he usually gave her a hard time about anything and everything. It was their thing, a brother/sister relationship she'd come to adore. "Right now I don't think we need anything," she finally said. "Not that I can think of anyway. But once we track down the witch, we might need backup. And fast. So whoever helps us will need transporting abilities."

Ace nodded. "I'll start working on setting something up. And you know King and Aurora are going to be involved, right? She's not just gonna let you head off into this without any help and neither is he."

"I..." She hadn't really thought about it.

Ace gave her a dry look then. "I don't know if it's just felines in general or you tigers. But you make me crazy. You're not a freaking island, Harlow."

"Hey, I know that!" She had a crew she loved, had worked with since she was a cub.

"Do you? Because Aurora, Lola, Bella and Marley didn't even know about Aodh."

She rolled her shoulders before draining the rest of the coffee. She had stuff to do and still had another stop to make—she wasn't going to deal with all this. "I don't have time for this, Ace."

He just sighed and pulled her into a quick hug. "You make me crazy."

"All wolves make me crazy," she murmured, hugging him tight. Sometime in the last year he'd become one of her closest friends. Which was why he was often so bold in just saying what was on his mind. And damn him, he really did give great advice. She just didn't want to hear anything right now.

Why did the people in her life insist on being all logical?

He snickered as he stepped back. "Keep me updated when you leave, and with where you're headed. And yeah, that's an order as well as a request from your friend. I want to be kept up to date on everything—I need to know you're safe."

She mock saluted him before hurrying out the back door into the expansive backyard, and wasn't surprised to find Hunter lounging by the huge pool the pack used almost all the time.

Five house cats were draped over the dragonling's snoozing back, but he opened his eyes, saw her and chirped softly, probably so he wouldn't wake the tiny felines.

They all stirred anyway, one of them jumping off his back and trotting over to her. The little Abyssinian cat had a long, lean body with a burnt sienna coat Harlow loved. And she was fearless in her curiosity, something else Harlow respected.

Harlow sat on the grass, wincing at the wetness on her butt even as Angel, as she'd dubbed the cat, jumped into her lap, already begging for cuddles. "I can't stay long today but you're the most beautiful baby ever," she murmured, scratching behind her ear.

Hunter made an annoyed chirping sound, making her chuckle.

"And you're the most adorable dragonling, Hunter," she said, looking up at him. "I wish I could stay," she murmured into the cat's furry head, nuzzling her gently. Next time she'd shift to her tiger form—the cats were always wary at first, but then had a good time tumbling with her. And often Brielle came too.

"I see you're one of them now," King said into the quiet as he stretched out next to her, seemingly not caring about the damp grass.

She hadn't even heard him, which said a lot for how stealthy he was. "One of who?"

"Hunter's cat posse."

She laughed, the sound startling a couple cats nearby into popping their heads up and skittering off. "He really is a wonderful weirdo. And hell yeah, I'll be part of his posse."

Hunter stretched in response, slowly easing his wings out, giving the rest of the cats time to jump off him. As they scattered, he turned and shook his little tail at them before jumping into the air and flying off.

"You'll get no argument from me. So." King shot her a sideways look. She blinked. "What?"

"What kind of firepower do you need for your hunt?"

"Oh...I honestly don't know. I'd planned to meet up with Thurman after coming here."

King nodded, looking out at the huge yard and the cats now lounging everywhere. It was a bit odd to see cats on a wolf pack's property but...she was a cat too and didn't feel in danger. That was the thing with animals—they all had that innate ability to sense danger.

"Good," he finally said. "And I know you talked to Ace, but anything you need, just contact me or Aurora. You don't need a go-between, and I'm going to dare overstepping and speak for my mate—she might be hurt if you don't reach out to her first."

"Of course." Harlow nodded, understanding that this wasn't an Alpha's order. "I'll let you both know before we leave. We'll probably stop by and give her too many hugs and kisses."

He grinned before jumping to his feet. "We're good, then," he said as she stood next to him, still cuddling Angel.

But the cat jumped down from her arms and ran off to join one of her playmates.

King walked her to the big open gate of their property, and then she headed to meet Thurman. As she walked, she received a text from her sister—and froze.

Mom and Dad are here early. Just arrived.

Then she snorted when she realized her twin was messing with her. They weren't supposed to get here for almost a month. *Ha freaking ha. I'll be back soon.*

Not kidding. They're here! Then she added an attachment, a clearly covertly taken picture of her parents talking to Aodh. Her mother was patting his arm.

What. The. Hell. She sent a bunch of random emojis, then pocketed her phone and started jogging to Thurman's.

Hmm, maybe the Magic Man had a spell for this? She sighed, doubting it.

～

HARLOW WAS glad Thurman had wanted to meet at a little breakfast diner run by avian shifters, as opposed to the compound where he and his family lived—and now her friend Hyacinth since they were shacking up. It was closer to home and she was antsy to get back to Aodh. Oh yeah, and her parents and the others.

But mostly Aodh.

Thurman rose as she approached the outdoor seating area, the only person outside on this chilly morning.

"Hey," she said, giving him a quick hug. "You sure you don't want to sit inside?"

"I like the chill in the air," he murmured, his smile soft as he sat back down.

"Me too." She was a Siberian tiger, so the cold made her want to run around and play. As she sat across from him, a human male with blond hair pulled back in a bun brought out a steaming cup of coffee with a side of milk.

"I told him what you'd want when you got here."

"Is that, like, part of your seer abilities?" she asked, not bothering to keep her words quiet when it was now common knowledge about Thurman.

He grinned. "I just remembered from your visits. And if I had to guess, you'll be ordering sausage, with a side of bacon."

She snickered before pouring the milk into her coffee. "You would not be wrong."

"So, you want answers," he said into the quiet once their server had taken their orders and disappeared back inside.

The diner was small, with four tables outside and only six inside. Normally it was packed but clearly it was too cold for most people this morning. Or maybe she'd just gotten lucky with some privacy.

"You'll be hunting the witch," he continued, before she could respond. "And I know *that* because of my seer abilities, but I'd have guessed after what we saw at Christian's house."

"How are you, by the way? You don't seem affected at all by what you did." But it had to have drained him.

"I was a bit tired afterward, but..." He lifted a shoulder, all elegance even in that simple action. He wore a cashmere sweater today the color of wheat, and dark slacks. "I'm fine now. More than, actually."

"Good. And yes, we'll be hunting the witch. We're not quite sure where to start. We'd thought about returning to the cabin in Canada or starting in the Domincary realm, see if we can find anything there." Aodh had been kept prisoner there, after all.

"The cabin will give you nothing," he murmured, his eyes going hazy. Not fully white in that creepy way, just a faint haze over them. He was definitely seeing more than she was. "The fae realm has many possibilities. You'll have to follow your instinct, and you'll have to stick together. I can sense the darkness, and she's strong. She serves no one but herself, and that makes her the most dangerous of all. Once, she took payment for her crimes, but would have been committing them regardless."

His voice was slightly deeper as he continued, almost in a trance.

"She likes her life and will not give it up. She'll never stop her destruction, never stop tearing lives apart. And she knows the dragon is awake, was there when he was freed. One day she plans to come for him. For you." His gaze snapped to Harlow's, his normally dark eyes still filmed over. "She knows he will never let her crimes lie, and she'll come for you because of your link to him. Not for a very long time. If you leave her be, you'll have a family, a long life, and then she'll come, the tendrils of her magic stealing into your life as she rips everything you love apart. But if you go now..." He coughed slightly, the haze slipping away, and he gave her a clear-eyed look.

Harlow held her breath, waiting.

"I cannot see what happens after you track her down."

Dread settled in her gut, hard. "Because I die?"

"No. The future isn't written in stone, but often I can see which way it might go. Now, I cannot. Nothing is written in stone because the choices have not yet been made. The one thing I do know with certainty is that you and your pack must trust each other. Trust your family."

Well this was...sort of helpful at least. Even if the heavy ball in her gut was crystalizing. "The Domincary realm is the right place?"

"It's a good start. Once you get there, if you listen to your gut, it will not fail you." He paused, his eyes going hazy for another moment. "A... keeper of books will help you. Or...lead you in the right direction." Then his gaze snapped back, his eyes dark once again. He slightly shook his head, as if coming out of a dream.

She was silent as the server stepped outside with their food. Thurman's was a loaded omelet with a side of red beans and rice, and she'd basically gotten a plate of meat. Plus another plate of beignets because, come on, they were delicious and she needed the fuel.

"So, if we do nothing, we'll be attacked later. But if we hunt her down now, we might die," she said to clarify.

"You could die either way."

She already knew her decision, was fairly sure the others would agree. They were going after the witch now. Not just because of what she'd done, but because of what she *would* do.

She was a menace, killing anything and anyone that got in her way. Harlow intended to stop her. Kill her for taking Aodh. "Thank you. This is very helpful."

Thurman nodded as he passed a small cloth bag over to her. "I already know your decision—these amulets will protect the four of you when you go into battle, but they won't last forever. I've never sensed something like her before. She sucks everything around her dry. Or that's not right—everything she finds useful. She doesn't kill without purpose. She likes the power."

Even though her stomach tightened more, Harlow nodded as she cut into one of the sausage links. "When we hunted her years ago, we gathered what little information we could. We never got her name, but I do know that she takes energy from those around her and uses it as her own. I don't know that she's inherently powerful, but once she's hopped up on enough power, she can wield it for her own use."

The witch had managed to stab Aodh, incapacitate him, and that was no easy feat. Though she'd been on her home turf, had surprised them in that small basement.

"We got so close before," she murmured, more to herself than him.

"And you will again. I have faith in your abilities," Thurman said quietly.

That might not be enough. He'd told her what he saw, gave her two paths, but both had the same result.

They faced off with evil no matter what.

CHAPTER TWENTY-ONE

As Harlow hurried back home, she couldn't get the Magic Man's words out of her mind. He'd given her spelled amulets for the four of them, but like everything, they had a shelf life.

He'd also said, *I can sense the darkness, and she's strong. She serves no one but herself, and that makes her the most dangerous of all.*

So that was awesome. An enemy with no perceivable weakness.

But as she reached her house she shelved everything about their mission, including literally tucking her amulets away so her parents wouldn't see them, before bracing herself to see her parents.

Who she absolutely loved—but their arrival timing was just plain inconvenient.

She didn't bother heading inside, but rounded the house and found almost everyone enjoying breakfast. The boys, Phoebe and Marley weren't there, but everyone else was.

Her parents jumped up as she approached, both rushing at her with arms open, making her laugh.

"My sweet baby." Her mom was faster, wrapping her up in a tight grip, lifting her off the ground before her dad took over and lifted them both.

Which just made her laugh again. "You guys!"

"We've missed you," he growled, kissing her cheek, even as her mom peppered her other cheek with more kisses.

"Goddess, you two." She ducked away, or tried to, but her mom hugged her again.

"You'll understand when you have kids. I've missed your smell," her mom murmured. "My two troublemakers."

"Two?" Axel called out from the table.

"Fine, three," her mom tossed over her shoulder, but she didn't let go of Harlow even as she stepped back, cupped her cheeks in her hands. "You look good. Healthy."

"Thanks. You look great too, both of you," she added, looking at her dad.

Her mom was two inches taller than her, and her dad another five. They were both stunning and always stood out wherever they went because of their striking looks. Her mother had passed down her beautiful hair to both her and Brielle, as well as her sharp cheekbones. They'd gotten their father's darker eyes and slightly darker skin tone. Where her mother's people originally hailed from Siberia, their father wasn't sure where his family came from, not completely. Somewhere north, is where his parents had always said.

Which could mean any number of things, but their dad was pretty sure it was what was now known as Alaska. Her mother's people had crossed the Bering Sea and started making their way farther south. And by people, it had been five of them. Because again, tigers were rare so their history was fairly murky too. Her father said his grandparents did the same, and by a twist of fate their parents had met in Florida—and that had been it for the two hippie vegetarian tigers.

There was never going to be another one for either of them. Their bond was too deep. Because once a tiger committed, that was it.

Something Harlow understood, though she was studiously ignoring looking in Aodh's direction. It just hurt too bad.

"So, you guys are early," she said when her mom kept hugging her.

"Yes," her mom said, guiding her to sit at the table with the others. Her hair was in two loose braids and she had on an intricately woven tunic with gold tigers sewn in, and plain black leggings.

Brielle's single braid was slightly ruffled, her hair frizzing a little, so that told Harlow all she needed to know—she'd taken all the original hugs and kisses like a boss. Even Axel's hair was down and mussed.

"We decided we couldn't wait any longer, and oh—" Her mother looked at Axel. "Axel, your moms are coming next month anyway. They decided to visit and we thought it would be better to split the time so we didn't take up too much space."

"You guys could have come at the same time," Harlow protested.

"I said the same thing," Brielle murmured, with Axel nodding.

"Well I'm glad you split it up," Bella chimed in. "We get spoiled even longer."

"Shameless," Axel muttered, but laughed as he did.

"That's right," Bella agreed. "My parents are coming in the spring." And she looked positively thrilled about it.

"Speaking of spoiling, when are Phoebe and the boys getting back? We brought presents," her mom said.

Because of course they had. They'd met Phoebe, Enzo and Legend at the beginning of the year and had immediately adopted them as grandchildren. Their love seemed to be endless. The three kids were orphans, but had been officially adopted by their crew and that meant they had a big extended family now.

"They're gone for a few more hours. Marley took them to meet up with Aurora."

Likely for practicing flying. No one other than their tight-knit group knew that the kids were rare phoenixes—which was why Aurora was their teacher.

"What about my presents?" Harlow asked as she took the glass of water Aodh set in front of her.

Her mother gave her a dry look. "Your father and I are your presents."

She giggled and paused at the look Aodh gave her, raised a questioning eyebrow at him.

But he just shook his head, looked away when her mother spoke again.

"We've also met your friend, Aodh. He tells me that you two used to work together."

Oh, thank the goddess they didn't know any more. She wasn't sure she had the energy to unload anything else. And definitely not right in front of him. "Yep."

"Well that's great. We also hear that the four of you might be leaving soon?" There was more than a hint of disappointment in her mom's voice.

But her father gently took her hand in his as he sat next to her, across from Harlow at the table. "If you do, we understand."

Harlow looked at Brielle, who simply lifted her shoulder a fraction—meaning she got to be the spokesperson. *Ugh.*

"Well, we actually do have something to take care of. It's important or we wouldn't—"

"Oh, you don't have to explain," her father said, an easy smile on his face, his dark eyes crinkling at the corners.

"We understand how important your work is. Lola told us you'd be saving lives," her mom added.

Well, taking a life was more like it, but probably saving them as well. Because once that witch was dead she couldn't hurt anyone else. Harlow glanced at Lola, gave her a grateful look.

"We just worry about you," her mom continued.

"Nothing will happen to your girls on my watch." Aodh's deep voice wrapped around her, piercing right through to her heart as he oh so subtly slid an arm around the back of her chair as he stretched out.

The action could be nothing, but Aodh was intentional. What...was he doing? Because he wasn't removing his arm either.

"My girls are fierce, but I'm glad they have you and Axel as team-mates," her mom said, beaming at him.

Her father's expression was a bit more reserved, but she was going to ignore the weird energy that had just popped up and enjoy the fact that her parents were here.

Because very soon, probably tonight or in the morning, they needed to leave. If they were going to hunt this nameless witch down, they had to start soon. The Magic Man had indicated that heading to the Domin-cary realm was the right move so she wanted to jump on that now.

CHAPTER TWENTY-TWO

Aodh sat on the end of Axel's bed as Brielle shut the door behind him, Harlow and Axel. He was surprised by how clean the bedroom was because back in the day Axel had been an absolute mess.

Even the Marine Corps hadn't been able to beat it out of him.

But...people changed, he knew that.

His obsession for Harlow hadn't, however.

Never would.

Harlow handed him a small amulet tied on a leather strip and very purposely avoided touching his fingers.

Yeah, that wasn't going to last for long—he wouldn't let it. The longer he was around her, he knew he wasn't letting her go. Wasn't walking away. She was his, and he was going to make his move tonight —but not until they were alone.

He turned the amulet over in his palm, inspected it carefully. It was a slightly glowing shade of violet and was warm in his hand—the magic buzzing off it palpable. As she handed the others to Brielle and Axel, she said, "These are from the Magic Man. I didn't want to say anything in front of everyone else, but apparently what we're up against is dark shit, to paraphrase. We already know that though. And these won't protect us from everything or forever. They're good for about a month."

Aodh slid the leather over his head, felt his dragon push curiously at the warm magic against his chest, then immediately settle back down.

"What else did Thurman say?" Axel asked as he slipped his over his head.

"To trust each other. And that if we head to the Domincary realm, we're on the right path."

"That's it?" Brielle asked.

"I mean, no, we talked for a while. He sees the darkness we're running to and says if we don't find it, she will find us eventually. And he was pretty specific in his word choice of 'she.' Also..." She sighed as she looked between the three of them. "He said that if we waited, we would likely have long, happy lives, but that one day she would come for us."

"I'd rather hunt her down now than have her come here," Aodh murmured. Harlow and the others had a family, people they loved, and he didn't want any of that messed up. Knew they'd never forgive themselves if their family got hurt.

"Same," Harlow agreed, with the others nodding. "He also said we need to stick together," she added. "Oh, and that a keeper of books will lead us in the right direction."

"No other words of wisdom?" Axel pushed.

Harlow lifted a shoulder. "He's not a god."

"I know, just wondering."

Aodh had met seers in his long life—not many, because they were rare. Usually a trait in human families, as it seemed to be with Thurman the Magic Man. And while they could see what might happen, nothing was ever set in stone. Which was why he would heed the advice, but he trusted himself and he trusted his team.

At that thought, something shifted inside him. For all the years he'd been stuck in that prison, he'd thought they'd abandoned him. Now that he was with them again...he couldn't believe he'd ever thought they could be capable. Especially after what he and Harlow had shared together. Doubt and loneliness had suffocated him as much as those magically spelled walls.

Never again.

"So…" Brielle set her hands on her hips. "We head to the Domincary realm, see if we can find anything or anyone who might know something about you being captive? A keeper of books, apparently. And see if we can track her down?"

Nodding, Aodh stood from the bed and resisted the urge to pace, though his dragon wanted out. He didn't want to go back to that damn place but there was no choice. If the human seer said going back there was the right choice, then it was what they had to do.

"And if we come up short, or the Magic Man is wrong, I say we head to Montana, talk to Prima's niece," Axel said. "Prima's already smoothed the way for us."

Aodh knew from their previous conversation that the female named Victoria had a huge research library and was connected with other healers and supernatural librarians all across the globe. They'd created a sort of network since The Fall, apparently.

Smart.

He just wished they'd had something like that before. Human law enforcement agencies had been notorious for not sharing information, and unfortunately supernaturals had been much the same. Were likely still the same to an extent. "We could split up, two of us going to the Domincary realm and two going to—" He didn't get to finish because Harlow swiveled on him.

Her expression was hard. "No. We stick together."

He agreed, but he wanted to needle her a little, get his Red riled up. "Just because the Magic Man said—"

"Not because of what he said. Because *I* say." She stalked toward him, all fierce warrior in that moment. And okay, all moments. She was a fighter to her bones.

"Is that right?" His voice dropped an octave as, inevitably, his gaze fell to her mouth. He wanted to take her right there on Axel's bedroom floor. And for the way he felt, he didn't give a shit if the other two stuck around and watched. That was how far gone he was for her. She made him lose all sense of everything, even himself.

"Yep. We're not going to give her a chance to come between us again." There was a wealth of emotions in those words, her eyes sparking fire.

He'd started to respond when the door burst open and one of the young twin boys raced in, held a finger to his lips and dove under the bed. Aodh glanced at Axel, who just shrugged.

A moment later the other twin, this one more disheveled, raced through the door, looked at all of them suspiciously. "Where is he?"

"Who?" Axel asked, playing dumb—as Harlow snuck out of the room.

Damn it. Sneaky, sexy tiger.

"You know exactly who!" The little boy threw himself at Axel with the freedom of a child who knew he'd be caught. That Axel would never let him down.

Aodh had never experienced that, not as a child. Times had been different back then, or maybe his clan had been different, small as it had been. He'd been raised as a warrior. Taught to fight, to kill, to gather intel. The way of his people. Then he'd been sent out into the world on his own.

Dragons had been out to the world, then gone into hiding over the course of his first lifetime. He'd seen nations rise and fall and then the same happen again. Over all his lifetimes, he'd never had remotely what he'd had with Harlow and the others.

A kinship. *Friendship.* A sense of belonging.

And...he wasn't letting all of that go without a fight. Wasn't letting her go at all. As the room erupted into chaos he followed after Harlow, but was too late.

She'd somehow covered her scent and he couldn't figure out which direction she'd headed once he reached downstairs. Instead of tracking her, he headed back to his room, and left the adjoining bathroom doors open.

She'd come back eventually and he was going to talk to her once they were alone.

Hopefully more than talk some sense into his fiery tiger. He wanted her naked underneath him. Or on top of him. Didn't matter.

When they'd been naked in the past, nothing else had mattered. They could have that again, he just knew it.

CHAPTER TWENTY-THREE

Brielle zipped up her small duffel, figured that she was covered with enough clean clothes for however long this thing was going to take. And if she stank, then whatever. She'd just shift to tiger and clean off in a lake or something.

A soft knock on her door made her pause. "Come in."

Her mom peeked her head in, a smile on her face. "Hey, sweet girl."

Brielle snickered as she set the bag on the floor. "You're the only one who calls me sweet."

"Well of the two of my girls, you're the sweet one." She shut the door behind her and Brielle saw that she was carrying a mug of steaming hot chocolate, given the scent.

"That's not a high bar." Neither she nor her twin would ever be considered sweet.

Her mother just shook her head as she handed her the mug, then sat cross-legged on the end of the bed. "Sit with me. I'd like to talk before you leave."

They'd decided not to leave until the morning, wanting one more solid night of sleep. And Brielle had planned to search out her parents anyway, to spend some more time with them. She'd just wanted to be packed first so they could leave when it was time with no fuss. "Of course. Where's Dad?"

"Talking with Harlow in the kitchen." Her mom wrapped an arm around her shoulders as she sat, laid her head against Brielle's. "I've missed you two so much."

"We've missed you too."

"We raised you two to be independent, strong tigers and...I still can't help but worry."

"What are you worried about?"

Her mom gave her a soft smile. "All the things." She cleared her throat. "How would you feel about your father and I moving here?"

Brielle blinked. "I'd love it. Are you serious?"

Her mom shoved out a long sigh, as if relieved, as if she'd actually been worried about her response.

"How can this surprise you? We'd both love you to be here. I just never thought you'd leave the compound."

Her mother again gave one of those soft, serene smiles. "We lived there because all of us could exist in peace. We all love creating art for the world. But times have changed, and with supernaturals out to the world, and you and your sister more or less settled...we've been discussing moving here. And for the record, so are everyone else's parents. It seems clear that you guys won't be moving anytime soon, and we want to be here when you all start raising your own families. This territory is more stable than ours as well. There are only pros to moving —you and your sister being the only two that matter."

Raw joy burst inside her. She loved and missed her parents, but had never thought they'd want to move. What her mom said made sense, however. "I don't know that we'll be starting families or anything soon, but you're right, we're not leaving. This is our territory now." They'd put down roots, and with Aurora now mated they weren't going anywhere. She was their new Alpha.

"Good, then. I believe that Kartini, Athena and Taya's parents will move to Scotland once we move here. I'm not saying it will be next month, but by the end of next year it's our goal to be settled here."

"We can help you find a home and—"

"Oh, I know, and I'm not worried about that." Her mother took the mug from her hand and set it down on the nightstand before sitting again and turning toward her. "But I also want to talk about your sister and that dragon."

Ohhhh. Brielle had a feeling that was the real reason for this private conversation. "Ah, what about them?"

"They look at each other the way, well, your father and I look at each other. But there is no mating scent. No scent at all on either of them. And Harlow seems troubled. I try not to pry, but I'd like to know what's going on."

Brielle pulled in a breath, tried to find the right words. Because her mother was right, she almost never pried. Which was probably why Brielle and Harlow told her everything anyway.

Everything except about Aodh. Her twin's heart had been shattered, and Brielle hadn't wanted to break her trust by telling anyone about him. Now things were different. "It's complicated between them. And..."

Brielle poured it all out, just telling her mom everything that had happened all those years ago. And by the time she was done, her mom pulled her into a big hug.

Brielle was surprised to find her eyes wet as she buried her face against her mom's neck. "I couldn't do anything to help her," she whispered. "She was in so much pain. And while the years made it better, she never got over him. I don't know what'll happen to her if he's hurt on this mission," she said as she leaned back, swiping at the stupid tears on her face. It would destroy Harlow, even if she was currently fighting her feelings. Or whatever the hell her dumb twin was doing right now. Because avoiding Aodh was dumb. Those two loved each other and could have each other! She wanted to shake both of them.

"If something happens, you'll be there for her. We all will. But he seems pretty tough."

"He is." They all were.

And Brielle knew they were going to need every ounce of training they'd ever had to take down this threat. Because there was no way she wanted the witch hunting them down later.

Sure, they'd have home field advantage, but they would also have a hell of a lot more to lose.

No, they were going to take the fight to that bitch and make her regret every life choice she'd made.

CHAPTER TWENTY-FOUR

Harlow paused in her bedroom doorway to see Aodh stretched out on her bed as if he had every right to be there. Gritting her teeth, even as raw lust slammed through her, she shut the door behind her. "What are you doing here?"

She'd planned to grab a few hours of sleep before they left, and while she could function on much less sleep than humans, they needed to be in full fighting order for this. She knew that down to her bones.

Being around him now was just going to screw with her emotions. Well, make them worse than they already were.

He slid his hands behind his head, his elbows out, his body language so damn casual she wanted to throttle him. Or screw him until they couldn't walk.

Maybe both.

"We need to talk."

She growled at him, but instead of responding, she stalked to the bathroom and shut the door. Maybe if she ignored him, he'd go away. She simply couldn't deal with an argument or anything else right now.

And he'd wanted to push her before when she'd told him that the group wasn't splitting up. Because they absolutely were not. She wouldn't lose him again.

Nope.

No way.

Not happening.

And she sure as hell wasn't going to get into an argument about it right before bed. Right before their mission.

After stripping, she got into the shower and turned it on full blast, glad for the hot water.

When she heard the door open, she froze. Wait, no, he wasn't— She swiveled as the shower curtain was ripped back and Aodh got inside as if he had every right.

Oh, and he was completely, gloriously naked.

"Are you crazy?"

"Yep." He glared down at her, his expression dark and hungry.

The air charged between them, an electricity buzzing as she felt his thick cock brush up against her abdomen.

At the feel of his reaction to her, heat slid through her, making her inner walls clench with an unfulfilled need. One that only he'd ever been able to quench.

She stared at him in shock, her gaze traveling over his scarred, muscular chest, over his ripped abs, down, down... *Oh sweet goddess.* She couldn't have bit back that moan if she'd tried. She'd missed every single inch of him. Especially the many, many inches between his legs.

"I guess we'll be talking later," he growled before he pinned her against the tiled wall and claimed her mouth.

Just took over like he had every right to.

She should really stop this. *Right?* For reasons she couldn't even think of. Probably because they didn't exist. She didn't want to talk or argue, but this? Oh, she wanted this more than her next breath.

She wasn't going to stop this wild ride unless the earth opened up and swallowed them. Maybe not even then.

His tongue invaded her mouth as he cupped her mound—and slid two fingers into her slick folds.

Goddess, he was just taking over completely.

She nipped his bottom lip as she reached between their bodies and wrapped her fingers around his thick cock. He was so damn hard, his erection thick and heavy in her hands.

They hadn't been with each other in so long, but it was like no time had passed as she fell into this with him.

He growled into her mouth, the sound rough as he slid another finger inside her.

The feel of him stretching her, pinning her in place like this, had heat curling to every part of her. She'd never let herself fantasize about him after what had happened. Sometimes she'd almost been able to convince herself that he'd never been a part of her life.

But the memory of him had been imprinted on her so deep, she'd never been able to fully pretend. He was part of her, always would be.

Now that he was here, his hands and mouth on hers, her own on him, water rushing over them—she was going into sensory overload as need built inside her.

Long dormant, there was a volcano building and she wasn't going to last.

Not when her inner walls were already tightening around his fingers, wanting all of him. "Hard at first," she rasped out against his mouth. "In me now." She needed all of him.

He didn't balk at her demand, didn't say anything as he pulled his fingers from her.

She clutched onto his shoulders and lifted herself up as he moved his hips, positioning his erection right at her entrance.

As he slid inside her, she pulled her mouth from his, sucked in a sharp breath at the invasion. She hadn't been with anyone since him.

The thought was unimaginable. She'd committed to him and that had been that. There would never be another for her.

As emotions swelled inside her, she buried her face against his neck as he clutched onto her ass, gripped tight.

His breathing was rough, unsteady as he remained buried deep inside her, the water pounding around them a background she was barely aware of. "So damn tight."

She clenched her inner walls around him as she savored the bite of pain as he dug his fingers possessively into her.

He sucked in another breath.

She nipped his shoulder, barely breaking the skin. And he bucked against her, the thick head of his cock hitting that sweet spot as she raked her teeth over him.

She closed her eyes as he began thrusting inside her, filling her, hitting her nerve endings in that perfect, perfect way.

She rolled her hips against his as they found an erratic rhythm that matched the beat of her heart. Nothing about this was smooth as he slammed into her, over and over.

Each time his cock hit that spot, her inner walls tightened even more. And as if he'd just been inside her yesterday and remembered exactly what she liked, he reached between their bodies and teased her clit oh so gently.

Just barely skated his thumb over the pulsing bundle of nerves. And she lost it, the orgasm punching through her.

She bit him again, partly to mute her cries and partly because she wanted to mark him. Wanted everyone on the damn planet to know he was off-limits. Tigers were as territorial as dragons and— She jumped slightly as he gently nipped her shoulder right back.

He cried out his own release as he started coming inside her, his arms tightening around her as he continued thrusting.

Harder, harder. Until they both rode through the pleasure. As they came down from their climaxes, she didn't feel relief, but keyed up. Hungry for more.

But he surprised her as he slowly eased out of her, keeping her pinned against the tile wall.

"I missed you," he murmured, his mouth finding hers again, those three words so raw and honest.

Instead of the hard claiming she'd expected, he kissed her gently, almost sweetly as he ran his hands over her breasts, down her waist, to her hips and back up again, as if he was memorizing the feel of her.

She did the same to him, skating her fingers over his broad chest, lower, around him, everywhere she could touch. Since she'd never thought this would happen again, that she'd never see his face again, she took her time, savoring every moment.

"Step back for a sec," she murmured against his mouth.

He gripped onto her hips instead, started kissing along her jaw as he *sort of* moved back. The shower was normal-sized and he was an above-average dragon shifter so there wasn't much room anyway.

She snagged her combo shampoo and body wash—why did people need more than this?—and poured some in her hands before she ran her fingers all over his short hair. She missed his long hair, but this was hot too.

He moaned slightly and paused as she gently washed his hair, massaging his scalp as she arched her back, brushing her nipples against his chest. Because she wanted every part of her body touching his.

It was impossible, but she didn't care. She was going to sleep draped on top of him later because now that they'd crossed this line, that was it. No going back.

His erection prodded against her abdomen and she smiled at the feel of his thickness. "Ready to go again?"

"It's been years," he growled, snagging the same bottle she had and manhandling her as he turned her around. "This thing isn't going down all night."

"Promises, promises." She leaned her head back as he washed her hair, doing the same to her scalp before he started working the shampoo into the rest of her hair.

"I missed stuff like this. Just showering together. Having coffee together." His words were quiet, his tone full of too many ragged emotions. "Holding you in my arms."

"I'm so sorry, Aodh," she whispered, glad she was facing away from him. "If I'd known—"

He wrapped an arm around her, pulled her back against his chest. "No. No apologies. I know you wouldn't have left me, and I never should have doubted you. Any of you," he growled. "I want to burn her and anything she owns or cares about to ash, until the ash doesn't even exist."

His rage reverberated around them so she turned in his arms, wrapped her own around him and kissed him hard. She didn't want him to focus on revenge now, not when they had this small moment together.

Tomorrow they'd be officially on the hunt and she knew how that went.

There'd be no time for this.

Because life was a giant punch in the dick sometimes. She'd just gotten him back, and she was terrified life would steal him away from her. And she wasn't sure she'd survive losing him again. If she did...

Goddess, she couldn't go there. So she kissed him harder, forcing thoughts of the future and past out of her mind as she focused solely on the here and now.

On his wicked mouth and thick cock as he slid inside her again.

AODH HAD WANTED to talk to Harlow about the mission, and okay, about them. But when she'd turned her back on him, shut him out of the bathroom, something inside him had snapped.

Now he was glad she hadn't wanted to talk—because this was a hell of a lot better.

He fell back onto the bed as she basically shoved him down. They'd both climaxed three times in the shower and he wasn't remotely done.

And he knew she wasn't either. She'd tried to braid her damp hair but had done a half-assed job as they'd stumbled into his room.

Her tiger was in her eyes now as she climbed on top of him, for just a moment, before they flashed back.

Normally he liked to be in control—it was often a battle between the two of them who got to be on top. But right now he was savoring every single second as she climbed up him, straddled him, took his cock in her hand.

She watched him as she stroked him impossibly slowly, squeezed tight once. He swallowed hard, his balls pulling up tight as she stroked him again.

"I missed you too," she whispered, her words a response to something he'd said who knew how long ago in the shower.

"Take your hair down," he demanded, even as her words rolled over him. Goddess, he'd needed to hear them.

She paused, gave him a slow, wicked grin as she reached back and pulled the little black hair tie free.

He snagged it, slid it on his own wrist even as she finger-combed her hair, letting it fall around her shoulders and over her full breasts.

Reaching up, he cupped them as he slowly rolled his thumbs over her hard nipples, wanting to take his time now. They'd been frantic in the shower, the first two times up against the wall. And the third time, he'd taken her from behind.

As he teased her she lifted up slightly, then slowly, slowly pushed down on him, taking all of him inside her. "I haven't been with anyone since you."

He froze, all his muscles pulling taut as he stared up at her, scented the truth of her words.

The soft gray smokeless fog of his mating manifestation poured out now, engulfing the entire floor as he watched her. He wanted to say something, anything, but couldn't find his voice as she started to slowly ride him.

Probably better, because he didn't trust himself anyway. She hadn't been with anyone? He'd tried not to let his mind go there, tried not to think about the past at all.

Because she'd thought he was dead. He'd assumed that of course she'd moved on.

He should have known better. Tigers were like dragons in that way. Possessive and obsessive.

Clutching onto her hips, he couldn't help but get lost in the vision of her as she continued riding him, faster now, her breaths coming in shallower.

His own were the same, that familiar need already building in him. It was so fast, the need to come inside her, mark her, claim her forever. It was like his body was making up for the lost years.

It didn't take long for either of them to reach their peak, and when she arched her back, her climax close, he reached between their bodies and teased her clit, gently pinching it.

She jerked against him and he felt the sudden rush of her release as her orgasm punched through her.

His own wasn't far behind and he joined her, finding another release that still couldn't take the edge off, couldn't give him any sort of peace. He wasn't sure peace would ever come between them. Not tonight.

Hours later, he realized that they weren't going to get any sleep if they didn't stop so he pulled her naked, yawning, on top of him, wrapped his arms around her and inhaled her sweet scent.

She splayed over him, her gloriously naked body plastered against him.

"I haven't been with anyone either," he murmured suddenly, startling a laugh out of her.

She lifted her head, her silky hair falling over his chest. Then she smacked his stomach. "Stupid," she muttered.

He just smiled, enjoying the rightness of this moment, of the feel of Harlow wrapped up in his arms as they drifted to sleep.

Because in a few hours they were going into battle. However he wanted to look at it, at the end of the day that was what it was. They were hunting a monster. A very powerful one who'd somehow gotten the drop on him and could create visions of things that weren't there.

To stop her, they had to be at the top of their game.

CHAPTER TWENTY-FIVE

Harlow didn't want to get up—ever. Could just stay here lying across Aodh's big body all day.

But...they had to leave soon. Which meant actually getting up, getting dressed. *Ugh. Stupid.*

Aodh trailed his fingers up and down her spine gently, the feel of him touching her perfection. But this moment couldn't last. Unfortunately.

"I don't want to get up," she growled into his chest.

He sighed, slid his hand lower to her ass, cupped it. "I know. Let's just tell the others we're not going today."

She nipped his chest, then looked up at him, sighed. "We can't do that."

"I know." His gaze landed on her mouth, then he met her eyes again. "At the risk of sounding like an insecure dick, especially after last night... When we were at Christian's, you hid your phone screen from me. It looked like you and another male..."

He cleared his throat and for a brief moment she saw a look of raw vulnerability on his face. Which made sense, considering he'd thought she'd abandoned him. "You think I was hiding a picture of me and another male?"

"I believe you when you said you hadn't been with anyone. But... Forget it. I'm being stupid." He closed his eyes, leaned back slightly against the pillow.

"Hold on," she murmured, slipping from the bed before he could stop her. She never wanted him to doubt her. To doubt them.

She'd left her phone in her room hours ago so she snagged it, then unlocked it to show him what she'd been looking at as she curled up next to him again.

It was a picture of the two of them, as well as Brielle and Axel. Someone had taken it after a mission. They'd all been in cold weather gear, a little rough around the edges and filthy, but they'd been smiling. Her hair was tucked under a toque and she'd had something streaked on her cheek. Dirt or ash. Her head rested on Aodh's shoulder, and they had their arms around each other. He wasn't quite smiling, but he looked pleased with himself. Her other arm was around Brielle, with Axel on the other side of her twin, his smile more of a smug grin.

Goddess, those had been some good times.

Before everything had gone to hell. For so long she'd tried to bury that time in her life, but now she was unpacking all of it, embracing it, holding on tight.

"Jesus," he murmured, almost touching the screen with his finger. "I don't even remember who took this."

"Me neither." But she remembered Axel tossing his phone to someone and telling them to take the damn picture as proof that they'd survived. "But that's what I was looking at. I'd saved it online, then when the world went to shit I uploaded it to this phone." She'd also printed out a physical copy that she had hidden in one of her drawers.

Now she'd be pulling it out and framing it, no need to hide it anymore.

"I'd only looked at it once," she continued. "Until the other night. Hey." She sat up suddenly. "What happened to that guy you threw at the block party?"

His expression went dark as he handed her phone back to her. "The one who got close to you? The one I'm pretty sure you'd planned to kiss." There was a bite to his words.

She felt her cheeks heat up. She'd been trying to do anything to get Aodh out of her mind—and now she wondered if the dreams she'd been having the past few months had been because he'd broken out of that prison. "I hadn't decided one way or another if I would kiss him—and I thought you were dead."

"Guy's lucky he's walking," was all Aodh said as he claimed her mouth hard and fast before sliding out of bed. "And we've gotta get dressed now if we're ever going to get out of here."

Yeah, she knew that, even though she didn't want it to be true. She wanted to say goodbye to everyone as well—and they had to contact Nyx, let her know that they were ready to roll out soon.

Sighing, she headed to her own room as he started gathering his things.

Back to reality. Unfortunately. If only they could use a finding spell on this bitch. But they'd tried in the past and it had proved useless.

So old-fashioned tracking her down would have to do. Good thing they were all ace trackers and had a starting point. Sort of.

As she gathered her things, there was a soft knock on her door. "It's unlocked." When the door opened, she was surprised to find Dallas on the other side.

"Hey, I'm sorry to stop by so early."

"No, no, come in." Harlow glanced behind the witch, looking for Rhys.

Dallas smiled softly. "He's outside with Willow, who will want to see you before you go. But I wanted to talk to you alone."

Surprised, she nodded. "You can shut the door," she murmured as she tugged the bathroom door shut too, giving them the illusion of privacy.

Aodh would likely be able to hear anyway, but she didn't care. Harlow wouldn't be keeping secrets from him regardless. "What's up?"

"I know you guys are leaving soon and I…" Dallas sighed, as if struggling with something. "I created a couple spells. I know the Magic Man gave you some things, including warded amulets to keep you safe, but I played around with some of my magic. Using my blood. Not blood magic, however," she added.

145

Harlow nodded, understanding. Actual blood magic was when someone else's blood was used—usually without consent—for dark purposes. It was dangerous, and likely how the energy witch had taken Aodh. But Dallas was a rare, natural-born witch and used her own blood on occasion. At least that was Harlow's understanding. "You don't have any blowback when you use your blood, right?"

"As long as it's for the greater good and not for personal gain, no. I'm so glad you understand," she said on a smile. "I believe that helping you is for the greater good if it stops someone from killing others. So…" She opened the satchel slung across her body, pulled out a small quilted, zippered pouch. "Only one of them is a sort of finding spell. And I know what you said before, that you'd tried one on her. This isn't an exact finding spell, it's something that you can use if you think you're in the near vicinity of her to at least know if you're on the right track. But it won't pinpoint her location if she's got herself warded from being found —and it seems likely she does."

"What's the downside? Because I feel like you're leaving something out."

"You can only use it once, and you have to be in the same territory as the witch. So if you used it here and she was somewhere else, like the Latore realm or the Domincary realm, then it wouldn't help you. You'd get a null response basically."

"Ah." She nodded. "So only use it if we think we're close?"

"Exactly. I wish I could give you something more precise. That said, I've added a bundle of other spells, including one that will repel a confusion spell. But it will only work for the one who uses it, so if she confuses all of you, you'll have to fight it hard." She then opened up the pouch and pulled out the little vials. Each one was roughly two inches high, cylindrical, and each held a different colored liquid. Dallas quickly went over how everything worked, pointing at them as she went—but she'd thankfully added a short note on the outside of each.

So, spells for dummies, thank you very much. Because Harlow wasn't sure she'd remember everything otherwise.

When Dallas was done, she tucked them away in the pouch and handed them to Harlow. "If I'd had the energy and time, I'd have made more. But this took a lot of my reserves. And these vials won't break—they're spelled too," she said, half smiling. "So while I don't recommend slamming them against anything, they're tough and will withstand traveling."

Harlow could actually see the faint dark circles under Dallas's eyes. "This is amazing and unexpected. Thank you."

Dallas took her hands in her own, squeezed gently. "Your family has always been so welcoming to me. You were one of the first groups of shifters who didn't make me feel ashamed of who I am, and you opened up your home to me and Willow. I'm more than happy to help. I just hope it's enough." There was a hint of worry in the female's tone.

But Harlow pulled her into a hug. "Thank you. And we'll be okay. We've all got claws and teeth and know how to use them."

Dallas laughed lightly, but the sound was strained.

Harlow understood. They were going up against an energy witch who'd once imprisoned one of their own, had made them see something that wasn't there. That alone terrified Harlow on a level she didn't want to think about. Being able to distinguish reality from fiction was something every soldier had to be able to do in battle if they wanted to survive.

But it didn't matter—they were going after her better armed and with more knowledge now. They would win, she had to believe that.

But at the back of her mind, she knew that they might not—that what had happened before could happen again. Only this time, they might not survive to fight again.

"I don't want you guys to leave." Enzo had his arms crossed over his chest as he glared at them, his final glare landing on Harlow.

They'd all gathered in one of the downstairs living rooms this morning before the sun had even risen. This was the place where they often crashed, talked, ate, just hung out. In addition to the rest of the household, Nyx and her mate Bo were there. Because the half-demon didn't let his mate out of his sight for the most part.

Something Harlow could respect. She didn't want Aodh out of her sight either.

"I know," Harlow murmured as Enzo climbed into her arms, all wild feral animal. This kid owned her heart. She hugged him tight before he jumped off her, attacking Brielle with a hug next.

Legend wrapped his arms around Axel, buried his face in his stomach and held tight before moving on to Harlow.

"I haven't forgotten what you asked me to do, so you know I'll be back," she said. After thinking about it, she was pretty sure Legend wanted her to help him set a trap for Phoebe's boyfriend. It seemed like something a little brother would do.

He looked up at her, eyes glistening with unshed tears, but he held a finger to his lips and basically shushed her in admonishment.

She bit back a grin and nodded.

They'd already hugged everyone, already said their goodbyes, but the kids were taking this goodbye especially hard. Which surprised her, because they often went off on missions. And they'd never had a big farewell like this, not with everyone gathered.

But maybe this one felt harder because the kids understood the danger. Hopefully they didn't fully understand, but she knew they listened to everything that went on in the house and were aware of the dangers of the world.

"They'll be back soon," Aurora murmured, her arm around Phoebe's shoulders as she gave Harlow and Brielle a look that said they better make it back.

She'd wanted to come with them, but they'd ultimately decided against it. This was something the four of them had to handle. It was their job to finish. And Aurora had her hands full with running the territory with King. Not to mention Phoebe and the boys needed her, needed another phoenix to guide them as they grew older.

Nyx delicately cleared her throat as she looked pointedly at Aodh. "As soon as you guys are ready."

Unlike Nyx, who was a demigod and could transport anyone she touched along with her, Aodh could only transport himself places. Which said a lot about the witch who'd been able to incapacitate him and restrain his powers—because Aodh was ancient, and taking him down had either been a stroke of luck on that witch's part, or raw power.

Harlow really hoped it had been stupid luck.

So before Nyx could take the rest of them to the Domincary realm, Aodh was going to transport himself to the realm, take a picture of where they wanted to go, then bring it back to Nyx. It didn't matter that Nyx had been there before—a lot had changed in the last seven or so months since then and she needed a fresh image to work with.

Harlow was just grateful that Nyx was helping them, though she knew it was as a favor to the New Orleans territory. Regardless, it would save them a lot of travel time.

"Here." Harlow handed her phone to Aodh, since he didn't have one of his own. "Just take the picture then get back here." She knew it sounded like an order and didn't care. She hated the thought of him leaving her sight for even a few minutes.

He looked at her, his expression unreadable, her phone in his hand as he prepared to leave. "I'll be right back. And for the record, as soon as we're done with this mission, we're getting mated. And I'm not asking. The only reason I'm not pushing you now is because if things go side-ways, I'm not taking you down with me. So deal with it, Red. I spent too long in that prison. I'm not going to live with any regrets. And neither will you."

Then he winked out of existence, just disappearing and leaving her to deal with a bunch of people staring at her.

So that was great. She closed her eyes as she tried to process every-thing he'd just said.

Because...*wow*. They'd barely talked at all last night—or this morn-ing, whatever. They'd had a whole lot of sex—though it was more than just sex to her and she'd seen his mating manifestation. She knew it was more to him too. But they hadn't actually talked about it.

To be fair, talking had never been their specialty.

"Oh my God," Lola breathed. "That male is so hot for you."

She cut a glare at Lola—who just grinned.

"I like his style," Bo murmured, his tone approving.

Harlow glanced over at her parents, who were both...smiling. *What the hell?*

"Thank the goddess," Brielle murmured, a smile on her face too.

She closed her eyes again, breathed deep, because she didn't want an audience right now as she tried to hold on to his words tight, keep them close to her heart. Her mind was still rebelling around the fact that he was here, that they'd spent hours together in his bed. That her future was different, so much *better*, than she'd dared hope.

And now she was terrified to even hope that they had a chance. The truth was, she'd wanted to mate *before* this mission because if something happened to him...she wouldn't survive losing him again. She wouldn't want to.

But how selfish was that? Because what if something happened to her? He would die along with her. That was how it was with dragon mates. No, she couldn't risk that, couldn't risk him dying because of her. Not when he'd just escaped that prison.

Before she could fall down the rabbit hole of her mind, he was back in a puff of wind, right in the spot he'd left from. He held out his phone to Nyx, then grabbed Harlow's hand, squeezed tight.

She linked her fingers through his, squeezed back, a wave of relief flooding her. He was hers. No matter what happened—hell, even if she died—she would die knowing he belonged to her and vice versa.

"Okay," the petite demigod with long, dark hair and peaches-and-cream skin said as she looked at the screen. "Anyone not going with us, back up."

As the others did just that, Harlow grabbed her twin's hand too and they all stood in a circle, joining up—and fell into time and space.

There was really no other way to describe it as Nyx transported them other than being in the middle of a tornado. Then, they were standing on cold, barren ground looking up at a cloudy sky with two violet moons peeking through the clouds.

It was colder than Harlow remembered the last time she'd been here, but quiet—no doubt the reason Aodh had picked this spot to transport to.

"I'll be waiting for a call or direct contact from you," Nyx said into the darkness, her eyes on Aodh. "Either I or Bo will have our phones on us at all times. I wish we could help but we can't leave our daughter for long. And our territory needs us too."

Harlow wouldn't have expected them to help. This wasn't their fight. "We just appreciate your assistance. This is saving us a lot of time and we're in your debt." She held out her hand, clasped Nyx's arm in the way warriors did.

The petite female seemed surprised, but returned the gesture. "I hope you catch this monster."

Brielle clasped Nyx's arm too, but Aodh and Axel just placed their fists over their chests in a sign of respect—they weren't touching the female with her mate so close. And Harlow was glad Aodh wasn't touching her at all.

Because she didn't want him touching another female but her. Ever.

Reasonable? No.

Also, she didn't care.

After Nyx and Bo left, they all turned in a circle, placing their backs to each other in a subconscious sign of trust as they took in the quiet surroundings.

"I can't sense any life nearby," Brielle murmured.

"We're maybe a mile from the castle," Aodh said. "It's why I picked this spot."

They knew from intel—because Starlena had sent people back here to keep tabs on the fae and she'd given that information to Aurora and King, who'd given it to the four of them—that when the royal fae had been run out of the castle, they'd scattered a solid eight hours on foot toward the mountains and were starting to build a stronghold there.

As of now they were living in tents as they rebuilt, but it sounded as if someone decent had taken the weak king's place. So that was something.

But now the four of them were considered enemies in this territory, no doubt about it. And the fae hated dragons, so they'd have to be stealthy no matter what.

"You're team lead on this." Harlow turned to Aodh. "So what do you want to do?"

"Now that I'm here again…" He sighed, looking around. "We need to find a keeper of books for the fae. Make them talk to us."

"Force isn't going to get us anywhere," Axel murmured.

Unfortunately, Harlow agreed. "We won't force anyone, but we will use persuasion and some form of payment." She patted her backpack.

They'd all brought various valuable items from their realm in case they needed them.

"The important thing is, we get a keeper of books—or I'm just going to say librarian—to talk to us. Get them alone and convince them to share their knowledge," Aodh said.

Brielle and Harlow both nodded. It wasn't much as far as plans went, but it was where they had to start. And record keepers, or keepers of books, would have recorded all sorts of information on the history of the fae over the years. Their histories were never kept in one place and usually not in the main castle—because of the threat of attacks. Not to mention the fae had a system similar to what humans had once used—the cloud. The fae's was built with magic, but whatever worked, as far as she was concerned.

They simply needed to know if there had been strange deaths in the last fifteen years. Unexplainable ones. Missing people. Anything that might help them find the witch.

"I say we shift and head to the building site of the new territory," Aodh said. "Normally I'd say you could all ride me but I think there's merit in me taking to the air and the three of you staying on the ground. This territory is too foreign to us and I don't want to miss something."

As she nodded, the others did the same. She quickly stripped, packed up her clothing, then shifted.

The others followed suit and she had to force herself not to stare at Aodh like some giant perv. They were here for a job. And the sooner they completed it, the sooner they could move on with their lives. Together.

CHAPTER TWENTY-SIX

"What's that look?" Aurora slid her arm through Bella's as everyone dispersed, heading for the kitchen to grab breakfast.

But Bella wasn't hungry. Just frustrated that three of her best friends were off on a dangerous mission and had decided they didn't want her or any of the others going.

Nyx and Bo had returned just to let them know that the others were in the Domincary realm and that they'd be available to transport if any of them called with an emergency. But they hadn't stuck around long.

"What are you talking about?" Bella smiled serenely.

"Really? You're gonna lie to me?" Aurora lifted an eyebrow.

"Omitting something isn't a lie. But I have nothing to hide... I'm just thinking of ways to help the four of those stubborn jackasses." She wanted to be with them, helping them. But they'd decided that "it would be best" if they went off and handled things alone.

Aurora snorted and tugged her in the direction of the front door. "I'm not letting them go off alone."

Bella blinked in surprise as Aurora opened the door and didn't even mind when she basically propelled her outside into the cool morning air. "You're not?"

"Heck no. I didn't tell the others, but once Nyx and Bo returned, they actually headed out to pick up Ace and drop him off in the same spot as the four of them. He's going to be tracking them and keeping an eye on them. They have an arsenal with them and so does he. I know they're capable, but I couldn't just let them go off without backup."

"They'll realize he's following eventually."

Aurora snickered. "I know, but they won't be mad at him. Harlow loves him and they can just be pissed at me if they want. I don't really care." She lifted a shoulder. "Those felines think they can just run off into danger and we'll all just be okay with it."

"You say felines like I'm not one."

"Oh, I know you are. Felines are the bane of my existence and the loves of my life," she said, throwing her arms around Bella and hugging her tight. "I just can't stand the thought of anything happening to them," she whispered. "To any of you."

"Pretty sure that big dragon won't let anything happen to any of them either."

Aurora sniffed once as she pulled back, wiped away a few errant tears. "No joke."

"So he's definitely moving in here when he gets back. I was thinking we should get him some clothes and other things and move him and Harlow into a bigger room. We could get it all done while they're gone." Because they would be coming home or Bella would be hunting down that witch herself.

"That's a great idea."

"I just wish I could do more." She looked up at the brightening sky, watching the leaves of the oak trees shift with the wind as she inhaled the scent of her city. Sometime in the last couple years she'd put down deep roots here in a way she'd never done anywhere else.

"Well, I suggest that you and Lola go into research mode, then."

She looked back at her Alpha. "What?"

"Brielle has a bunch of notes from when they were originally hunting that witch, and they'd planned to go see the healer Victoria in Montana if this trip is fruitless. Why not get a head start and reach out to her yourself? I might have already paved the way for you and so has Prima. She's expecting your call."

"So you're just taking over and handling shit like a boss," Bella said, nodding in approval. "I love it, and yes, I'll get together with Lola and we'll see what we can come up with." Before The Fall she'd been obsessed with crime podcasts and "murder shows," so helping to hunt down a serial killer—or whatever that witch was—was something Bella could get on board with.

Anything to help her family.

CHAPTER TWENTY-SEVEN

Aodh kept his camouflage in place as he flew a lazy loop over another village. It was the fourth one they'd passed, along with a couple inns on the side of the road in between villages. And of course, various farms.

The villages were bustling with activity, non-royals living their everyday lives. These were the people who actually contributed to keeping the kingdom and territory running. They provided so much of the necessities, and now the royal guard and others who'd inhabited the castle were no doubt discovering just how much.

The rest of his team were in the nearby forest, waiting for him to finish scouring this area since he was the only one who could get close while it was still daylight out. The sun had risen not long after they'd arrived so he'd ended up flying in camo mode while carrying them. The others couldn't camouflage themselves enough to blend into any of the villages well. Not in the daytime anyway. At night it would be a bit easier.

He hadn't seen any other types of shifters in any of the villages he'd flown over. So they would stand out. Even with his ability to naturally camouflage, he still had to be careful since someone might overhear his wings flapping, even if they couldn't see him.

When he spotted a large building next to one of their holy sites, he silently landed and shifted to his human form, keeping his camo in place.

Cold rolled through him as his feet connected with the cobblestones, but he ran so hot it didn't affect him too much.

Two huge doors to the worship building were open, but he couldn't hear anything inside. Time worked differently here so he wasn't even sure what day it was. Clearly not one of their worship days.

He moved up the stone steps silently, saw two marble statues of different fae goddesses in the interior. Moon goddess and...something to do with harvests. He wasn't certain about fae religion. But he did know that the record keepers were often holy people or librarians—the two were sort of interchangeable in this realm. There wasn't quite a mirror in the human one to equal what the record keepers did here.

He heard a murmuring of female voices speaking an ancient fae language, and when he stepped into the main worship building he spotted a couple females in long robes speaking quietly in front of a dais.

Luckily the fae didn't have the same type of scenting abilities that shifters had so he wasn't worried about anyone discovering him that way.

Ignoring them, he hurried through the rest of the building, searching for anything that might be useful for their purpose—which at this point was like trying to pin down a tiger: almost impossible. He was hoping to catch the scent of the witch more than anything. *Or hey, how about a bright neon sign pointing in her direction.*

But really, if he couldn't catch her scent, he was hoping to find some sort of legal "wanted" type of document. The fae had the equivalent of "wanted" posters in their realm that humans had used at one point when trying to bring a fugitive to justice.

When he found nothing, he moved on to the building next to it because it had the same official look—almost like a library. Now that was where he might find something useful.

The front doors were similar to the house of worship, except they were closed. As he contemplated opening them—and hoping no one saw a door open by itself and figure out something was off—one of them opened and a female reading a book strode out. Her purple robes flowed behind her, and even if he hadn't been in camo mode, he didn't think she'd have seen him anyway. She was so caught up in the heavy tome in her hands. She had a similar build as the other females he'd seen in the holy building—tall, slender with gently pointed ears. Though she had paler skin while the other females had been brown-skinned.

He moved like a ghost, slipping through the door before it could shut behind her, and allowed it to naturally close behind him.

As he stepped into the huge antechamber, he looked around at all the books.

They were everywhere, on all the walls, reaching high above him up to the third floor. There were also at least fifty shelves on the first floor visible to him. A library.

This was it. They should be able to find the record keeper here.

HARLOW WATCHED movement in the town as it slowed to a trickle through her binoculars. Aodh had returned to them hours ago, then left again to do aerial recon while they waited for the right moment to infiltrate the library. The timing was more of a guess at this point. But after dark was a must.

She, her sister and Axel were all in different trees, keeping watch from the edge of town.

Breaking into a library was one of the more benign things they'd ever done, but hopefully they'd be able to find something to help. Or someone—a keeper of books.

They were armed with a couple bags of tricks from the Magic Man and Dallas at least so that should cut down on a lot of time in finding the witch.

Harlow stilled when the trees rustled unnaturally at a sudden gust of wind. She readied herself for a fight, but then Aodh was there in a burst of quiet magic, standing naked and tall at the bottom of the willowy purple tree that had no match in the human realm.

"No one's gone in or out in the last hour. I say we move in now." His words were quiet as he started dressing in dark clothes. "We can lie in wait and try to catch whoever comes in for the morning shift. See if we can get them to help us."

She jumped down from the tree in a silent move, already dressed in dark gear. Moments later both Brielle and Axel were there. They all pulled on balaclavas to hide the majority of their faces, then quietly made their way to the edge of town, following Aodh's lead.

The Magic Man had told her to follow the direction that felt right. And this felt right. Which was of course making her question everything. Harlow didn't like vague. She liked cold, hard facts.

Things she could sink her claws into.

It was easy to avoid detection since no one was around. And as they reached what she was just going to call a library, they used a side entrance, Aodh picking the lock with ease.

So clearly his imprisonment hadn't dulled those skills.

As he eased the door open, they waited for an alarm, but nothing came. Even so, it could be silent, a magic alarm linked to someone or something.

They stepped into a small room with a few benches and couches as well as some small round tables. A sort of reading or resting room? Research room? Soft glowing balls of light hovered over each of the tables, no doubt powered by fae magic, illuminating the quiet, cozy space.

Didn't matter what the room was—it was empty, thankfully.

Aodh motioned for them to continue so they hurried through to another door. He paused as he peered past it, then she saw the moment his big body relaxed.

He turned back to them. "Looks clear. We do a quick sweep of the aisles, then use one of Dallas's spells to see if we can find anything useful."

In the past they'd been following the trail of the witch based on her killing pattern. They'd come so damn close a few times before that fated day in that little cabin. Looking back, Harlow realized the female had led them into a trap.

Harlow shelved that thought as they all moved into the dimly lit library as a unit. They peeled off in different directions, no weapons out because they didn't plan to hurt any fae. Not unless necessary.

Harlow moved down one aisle, then another, breathing in the slightly musty scent of the pages, but also a sort of citrusy scent, maybe whatever they used to clean.

And this place was clean and tidy, no dusty tomes sitting on the shelves. Unfortunately, she didn't read the language of this fae realm, but hopefully one of Dallas's spells would help with that. If they'd had Bella with them, she might have been able to help, considering how many languages she spoke. At least Aodh could communicate some-what, he'd said, so she was hoping that when the time came they wouldn't struggle with a language barrier.

Once they were done searching the aisles for any signs of life, they reconvened at one of the four tables in the center of the huge room. All the windows were two stories above them, letting in moonlight, but there was no way someone would see them unless they passed by a window on the second or third floor. The room was octagonal, with shelves lining all the walls.

And there were so many books.

Harlow set her backpack on the table in front of them and pulled out her bag of tricks. "The only one that I can think might help is a finding spell. Maybe we can 'find' something that might help us?" It was so vague, she found herself frustrated even saying it out loud. But all they needed was a point in the right direction. And if they could find one of the fae's records of various deaths, including murders, then maybe they'd be able to figure out a pattern. It was what they'd done before, though they'd had better technology.

Hopefully tomorrow they'd be able to talk to an actual fae record keeper, but they had access to this building now and she wanted to take advantage.

Everyone nodded so she pulled the clearly marked vial out and poured the contents onto the middle of the table. It was a liquid, but more viscous than water. Almost like gelatin. The shimmery aquamarine blob trembled for a moment before it rose in the air, then it started floating down an aisle—then another and another, then up the stairs.

They were careful to avoid any windows as they followed the blob until it reached a heavy-looking wooden door on the second floor.

It trembled and shook, vibrating in front of the door until they arrived.

Aodh tried the handle, smiled when it opened.

He'd barely opened it an inch when the blob flew right past him into the dimly lit room.

They all froze to see a female in heavy-looking purple robes dozing in a plush lounger, her feet propped up. A thick book was in her lap, but her head was lolled to the side, her breathing soft and steady.

The blob hovered right over her lap before dissipating in a whoosh over the book.

The noise had the female with long, silvery white hair opening her eyes.

She stared at all of them, her eyes widening in horror as she opened her mouth to call out for help.

But Brielle moved fast, covering the short distance to the female in the chair, clamped her hand over her mouth.

The female shot out a blast of light from her fingers, but it bounced off Brielle with a fizzle—*thank you, Magic Man, for the amulets.*

"We're not here to hurt you," Harlow said quickly as she tugged her balaclava off. She was going on instinct now, and threatening this female wasn't going to get them anywhere. The Magic Man had said a keeper of books would help them, and *hello, keeper of books.* "We need help, that's all. We're looking for a murderer. Or murderess, I guess." Then she winced, realizing this female might not understand them. *Damn it.*

Brielle removed her hand from the female's mouth and stood back, removed her own balaclava and held up her palms.

The fae looked between the two of them in surprise as she closed the book in her lap. "Twins are rare among the fae. But they're a sign of good fortune," she murmured in heavily accented English.

"You speak English," Axel said as he took his own mask off.

The female gave him a withering look as if to say *duh*, but didn't respond otherwise. She looked at Aodh next. "If you truly don't wish to harm me, I want to see all your faces. I will not have a conversation with you intruders while you're masked up, hiding like cowards."

For some reason Harlow felt ashamed, but she shook off the chastisement from the older female. "We used a spell and it led us to you. Or maybe your book," Harlow said, glad that Aodh was taking off his mask without comment. "We're searching for a serial killer. Do you know what that is?" Sometimes not all things translated.

"I do. And I'm not sure how I may be of help."

Harlow looked at Aodh. "I say we tell her everything." The spell had led them here after all.

Aodh's expression was hard for a moment, then he said, "What do you know of the dragon that was kept prisoner under your territory's castle?"

The female's eyes widened in clear surprise. "Ah...nothing, really. It was a big topic of gossip for a few weeks after the dragon invasion but we have no real knowledge of how it got there." Her expression shifted slightly, anger in her regal face. "Our former king was greedy and stupid so we only had our speculation. Why?"

Aodh cleared his throat, looked at Harlow, raised his eyebrows.

She nodded. Her gut was just saying to lay it all out there.

He lifted a shoulder and turned back to the fae female. "I was that male. I was locked away under the dungeon by a witch. A very powerful energy witch. She fed off my energy for years, and as far as I know she didn't leave this territory for long, if at all. When those dragons invaded, the magic holding me in place cracked and I escaped."

The female looked at all of them, then motioned to the other comfortable seating. "I say we all sit," she said even as she sat back in her chair, tucking her long legs underneath her. "Are you members of the clan that destroyed part of my kingdom?"

"No," Aodh said. "But I'm not sorry about what they did. Your king deserved it."

The female gave him a soft smile, as if amused. "Are all of you dragons?"

"No," Harlow said, but didn't give the female any more.

"So, you're hunting an energy witch that imprisoned you? You escaped many turns of the moons past. Do you think she is still here?"

There was something in the female's tone... Fear, maybe? But Harlow couldn't pin it down. Hell, she was probably just afraid to be confronted by four shifters dressed like burglars in the middle of the night.

"We don't know," Harlow said. "We hunted her once before. Many, many years ago. Then...she tricked us and imprisoned my friend." She nodded at Aodh, who growled low in his throat. She frowned at him.

"We are more than friends."

Oh, sweet goddess. Really, *now?* Harlow looked back at the fae female. "She killed hundreds of shifters in our realm, and afterward she disappeared. My...dragon was imprisoned, and we made some bad assumptions and bad decisions. It's possible she'd been hiding out in this realm, using a sort of glamour to blend in. And we don't know what we're looking for. We came here originally to see if there were some sort of records of deaths. Unusual ones or—"

"Unusual deaths? How?" The female sat up straighter.

"Ah...entire families being murdered or going missing. It's what she did in our realm. It was why we were hunting her. But it's highly possible she changed her M.O. She could have been operating differently here, especially since we believe she was hired for political purposes back in our realm."

"We're just looking for a lead," Aodh added. "She needs to be stopped. She has no respect for life, not even those of children or babies."

Oh, damn, his words hit their mark, Harlow realized as the fae female's face hardened ever so slightly. Because that was something most supernaturals had in common—kids or pups were to be protected. Always. And if anyone went against that code, they lost the right to life.

The female opened her book as she said, "My name is Minerva. And

I don't know how much help I can be, but..." She flipped through the book in front of her and finally stopped about halfway through. She turned it around and held it out for them to look at.

"Is this a children's book?" Brielle said as they all stepped a little closer, her expression wary at first.

There was a picture of a beautiful female with long, blonde hair in the middle of a forest, but all around her the vegetation was dying. Leaves in the trees were blackened at the edges, curling into themselves. And, oh, there were dead birds all around the edge of the dress the female was wearing. The page itself was stunningly illustrated and the frame around the image was some kind of gold embossing.

"This is more for youth, not children exactly. Teens, or young adults, I believe you would call them. But it's fiction."

"Why are you showing us this?" Aodh demanded.

Harlow shot him a sharp look, raised an eyebrow to warn him to watch his tone. Because something told her this female wasn't going to respond well to rudeness.

He simply gave her a dry look because apparently that was him being polite.

Minerva flipped the page over and on the next two pages were more illustrations. In this one, the female in the beautiful dress was dragging what looked like a bag of bones with her. Actual human bones. Harlow could tell, given the very accurate shapes. Or fae bones—humans and fae had the same body structure.

Wow.

"Um, this is kinda dark," Axel murmured, clearly offended for any youth reading it.

The female lifted a shoulder. "Perhaps."

"Again, why are you showing us this?" Aodh stepped back to the door then, slung it open and stepped outside, clearly looking for others.

Oh shit, was she stalling them? Harlow wanted to kick her own ass for getting so taken in with the wonderfully illustrated pictures.

Sighing, the female set the book down on the table and stood with them. "Because this is a recent fictional tale about fae going missing. Not necessarily *entire* families, but we've had some strange disappearances in the last decade or so throughout the entire realm—and recently those disappearances picked up. I'd say roughly seven turns of our moons. And the author of this book lost her younger sister and father. They disappeared, and no one knows what happened to them for certain—it was assumed they were killed by a sea monster."

Harlow sucked in a slight breath as she digested what this fae was saying.

"Recently she published this book to much acclaim. I was reading over it earlier and fell asleep. She claims this book is fictional, but given her background, now...I wonder. The author of this book...well, she claimed that her family was stolen by a beautiful monster and sucked dry until they were nothing but bones."

"What aren't you telling us?" Harlow asked, watching the female's face closely.

Minerva adjusted her robes, her expression tightening. "The author of this is named Vita. She's my niece. When her father and sister disappeared, she had a wild tale about someone coming in the night and stealing them away but there was no proof. And she's always been a bit of a wild child, telling unbelievable stories. No one took her seriously—she wasn't there when it happened either. Her father had gotten a contract job in another part of the realm. Vita didn't want to go because she doesn't do well with too many people, so she stayed behind."

When the female paused slightly, Harlow raised her eyebrows because it was obvious there was more.

Minerva cleared her throat before continuing. "Later, her father's and sister's horses were found wandering near a river, their belongings along the river's edge. Scraps of clothing were found as well. Their deaths were ruled as likely death by a sea monster. The river they were near was known to be avoided because of it."

Harlow's gut tightened as she looked at the open book again. "What about her mother?"

"She died giving birth to Vita's sister," Minerva whispered. "She was my sister. And I admit I was so frustrated with Vita at the time, I thought she was lying. I thought her fanciful tale was a way to deal with her grief instead of reality. But..." She looked over at the book, frowned. "Perhaps not."

Again, there was a strange scent coming from Minerva, almost like guilt, but not quite. She wasn't telling them everything, Harlow was certain. "Do you have a list of all the disappearances?"

"No, but I know Vita does. She tried to show it to me once, but I thought she was looking for things that weren't there, trying to make sense of senseless deaths when sometimes the world is simply cruel. Oh goddess," she murmured, picking up the book again, flipping through the pages. "What if she was telling the truth and this book is about real deaths in our realm?" She stared down at the tome in horror.

"We need to speak to her," Aodh said, his tone hard. "How far does she live from here?"

Minerva blinked, looked up at them. "In the village, but you will be noticed. And I do not know if she would welcome you anyway."

"We're hunting the female who might have killed her family," Harlow said quietly. "She'll talk to us."

Minerva paused, then nodded. "I cannot simply show up with the four of you. It will be too overwhelming. I need to speak with her first, give her a warning."

"You mean give you time to go alert someone to our presence." Aodh crossed his arms over his chest.

The female gave him a dry look and pulled out a small orb from her pocket. "I could have done that at any time. But I chose not to because I sense you're telling the truth. And I believe you were brought to me for a reason, because of my connection to Vita. So, what's it going to be, dragon?"

He shot a glance at Harlow. "You go with her, then we'll follow later if her niece welcomes us."

Minerva nodded and looked Harlow up and down. "I have robes that will fit you. We're the same height and the robes will help you to blend because you cannot be walking around dressed the way you are. We'll need to cover up your hair again as well, and your ears."

Harlow resisted the urge to tell the female that she could easily sneak around in the dark and simply track after Minerva unseen. Instead she nodded. "Okay." Robes it was for now.

Then she'd return to the rest of her crew—or more likely, her crew was simply going to follow them. No way was Aodh letting her out of his sight. Same with her twin and Axel.

Because they were on the tip of discovering something big. She felt it in her bones.

CHAPTER TWENTY-EIGHT

"What kind of shifter are you?" Minerva asked as they strode down the quiet cobblestone street. The village was quaint, with homes that reminded Harlow of chalets. She didn't know much about architecture but she thought the style might be called Bavarian. Snow covered most of the roofs and there were soft, magical lights on each porch, simple glowing orbs not suspended by anything. But no one was outside in this chilly weather.

"You know asking that is frowned upon."

"So is breaking into a library and threatening a record keeper."

Despite everything, Harlow snorted. "I think I might end up liking you."

The female sniffed slightly, as if that was a given.

And damn, Harlow did kind of like this fae. She'd held her own with the four of them when she could have panicked. "I'm a tiger."

Minerva stumbled slightly, but Harlow reached out with her supernatural speed, steadied her. "I'm not going to attack you."

"Oh, no, I just...I assumed wolf, to be honest. Tigers are quite rare, are they not?"

"We are."

"It is fascinating, is all. So you're a twin and a tiger, that's double good luck." But there was an odd note in her tone.

Harlow didn't feel threatened, however, so she left it alone.

"How has your territory fared since the dragon attack?" Harlow murmured as they turned down a side street. Another cobblestone road, but this one had more lights, and what looked like shops instead of homes, including a pub that was lit up. A few fae stumbled out, but no one paid the two of them any attention as they kept to the other side of the road.

"Our village, and many others around the realm, are fairly insulated. We never depended on the king or any of his guard to function. Though they came through here and took what they wanted on occasion." There was a bite of rage to her words, barely suppressed.

"Took things? Like...people?"

The female nodded, her expression stiff. "Among other things. They called it taxes, but it was always unjustly taken."

Harlow felt a punch of aggression roll through her. It wasn't her business what went on in this realm, but... "You can leave, you know. Our territory is diverse. Run by an Alpha wolf but he's got all sorts of different shifters in charge."

"Ah, you're from New Orleans, then."

She looked at Minerva in surprise. "Good guess."

She tilted her head slightly, the action ridiculously regal. "You're one of the closest territories to us from the main portal. And after the dragon attack, we made it our business to find out more about your territory and the Nova realm." There was a hint of anger at the words "Nova realm."

"Those dragons were justified in what they did," Harlow said mildly. Really, it was only one dragon who'd destroyed everything while the others had watched.

"I know." She sighed. "Doesn't mean I condone violence."

Harlow snorted softly. "Sometimes that's the only way shit gets done. And for the record, Starlena allowed everyone but the king to leave alive. That was ridiculously generous." Especially for a dragon as ancient and powerful as her—she'd been out for blood.

Minerva was silent for a long moment. "Perhaps. And as to what you

169

said about leaving, this is my home and I've been working with others to make changes. I won't leave my territory unless it's the last option. I...have hope we might have a new leader emerging. A fair one."

"Yeah?" Harlow didn't know much about the fae in general. And what she did know, she didn't like. There were exceptions of course, but they tended to be insular and snobbish, to put it lightly. Bigots, some would say.

"A female warrior is currently leading the rebuilding of the new castle stronghold. The things being reported to my superiors are promising."

Interesting. Harlow filed it away to tell Aurora and King later. They were always gathering intel on neighboring territories and realms. Knowledge was definitely power.

A few blocks later, they were nearing what Harlow knew was the edge of the village. The homes had started to grow farther apart, and from her recon earlier, she was familiar with the layout to an extent.

"This house," Minerva murmured as she opened a little gate and strode up a short walkway.

Little animal figurines were on the railing around the patio, some mythical and others from the human realm, including two Siberian tigers. *Huh.* A faint sprinkling of snow dotted all the figurines, as if a wind had blown some of the snow from the roof down onto them.

There weren't any lights on outside, but Harlow could see a soft glow coming from inside, the light outlining the curtains covering the windows. And she'd noticed smoke coming from the chimney as they'd approached.

"Vita, it's me," Minerva said as she knocked, three sharp raps of her knuckles.

There was a bit of rustling inside, then the door creaked open slowly. "Aunt?" The female was petite, not like Harlow had imagined. She had the typical pointed ears of the fae, but unlike Minerva, her wings were visible, a gossamer, pale pink and shimmering behind her. They disappeared when she saw Harlow. "Who are you?" She didn't look directly at Harlow, but at a spot over her shoulder.

"My name is Harlow."

"We have much to discuss," Minerva cut in. "May we please come in?" She glanced behind her, but Harlow knew no one was on the street. Well, other than her crew, because they'd definitely followed.

It didn't appear Minerva had realized that, however.

Vita finally nodded and stepped back, letting them in.

Inside was much warmer, the fire crackling in front of two worn-looking chairs. A steaming mug of something was on a table in between the chairs, as well as a sketch pad.

"Why are you here? Is something wrong?" Vita looked between the two of them, her expression tight. But the female was stunning, her shimmery white hair and once again visible wings making her seem almost ethereal.

Minerva took off her robes, so Harlow did the same, though unlike Minerva's fancy dress underneath, Harlow still had on her burglar gear.

Vita's eyes widened as she took in Harlow again, looking at her ears for a long moment. "What are you?"

"A shifter. And I'm not alone. I'm in this realm hunting down an energy witch," she said before Minerva could beat around the bush. Harlow was just going to get right to it. "And it sounds like it might be the same one who killed your family."

Minerva sucked in a breath, but Vita looked at her. Well, in her direction, because she still didn't look her in the eye, but at a point on her shoulder.

However, Harlow understood that Vita's focus was on her.

The petite female nodded, then motioned to the chairs. "No one else believed me." Her words were blunt, her voice soft as she sat in one of the chairs.

Minerva murmured something about getting refreshments and headed toward the small attached kitchen.

"Can you tell me what happened?" Harlow asked.

Vita tapped the armrest of her chair as she stared into the fire, the action rapid, clearly a tic. "My father and sister left for a job. The night it happened, I saw it, even though I was back here. But no one believed me," she repeated. "They thought I was crazy or lying. But she took them and she drained them dry. Then she dumped their bones with all the others. All the others," she said again, her tapping a continuous pattern.

"When you say you saw it…how exactly?"

"I saw it in my mind. I was here, they were there. But I saw it in my mind."

There was a clank of noise from the kitchen, as if Minerva had dropped something.

"She does not believe me. Doesn't believe me."

Okay, so Vita had more than one tic. "Are you a seer, then?" Harlow asked.

Vita shook her head slightly. "Fae can't be seers. Just humans. Or maybe witches."

"Says who?" Harlow asked.

"It's common knowledge," Minerva said as she returned with a tray of cheeses and what Harlow assumed was a fruit local to this realm.

"Sometimes common knowledge is just stupid assumptions. The humans in my realm once assumed dragons didn't exist, or shifters in general. But here we are. So." Harlow shook her head at the tray Minerva offered, not caring about food. "Do you mind explaining everything you saw?" Her gaze strayed for a moment to the sketch pad. It was mostly lines, but she could see that soon it would be a person.

"She followed them at night. And she stabbed them with an athame, right through the chest, but not quite in their hearts. She took my father first. Then…" The tapping increased and Vita looked back at the fire. "Then she took all their energy, all their magic. It wasn't much, but she drained them until they were husks. And she'll keep draining fae until she's done here."

Oooh, no. "Do you know why she came here?"

"She brought the dragon here, then the dragon left."

Yep, this female was a seer. Likely neurodivergent as well, if Harlow wasn't wrong. Which might explain why people hadn't listened to her. Goddess, people sucked in all realms apparently.

"Now she takes magic where she can find it. Our land is in an upheaval so it's been easy for her. So easy." She whispered the last part, her tapping continuing.

"Stop tapping," Minerva murmured.

Vita stopped, but Harlow could see it agitated her to do so.

Harlow glared at Minerva, then looked back at Vita, softened her expression. "You're not bothering me. Tap away. I'm sorry about your sister," she continued, hoping to put her at ease, but she still meant the words. "I have a twin and it would destroy me if anything happened to her."

Vita started tapping again, then looked at Harlow, right in her eyes for just a moment, before she looked at a spot on her shoulder once again. "Twins bring luck."

"That's what I'm told."

"How will you kill the witch?"

"I'm not sure yet, but I got close once. I'm friends with the dragon you saw in your mind."

Vita stopped tapping, blinked once. "Are you a tiger?"

Well, that was interesting. "I am indeed. I saw the tiger figurines on your patio. They look like my twin and I when we're in our other forms."

Vita looked in the direction of her aunt, who was hovering by the hearth, looking as if she might split apart from nerves at any moment. "Will you please retrieve my book?"

Minerva sighed, but nodded and disappeared into a back room.

"I saw your book back at the library. It's beautiful. You're very talented."

"Thank you." There wasn't much emotion in her voice, just the slightest hint of inflection. "No one believed me so I told the story of my visions the only way I could. It is surprisingly popular."

"How popular?" Harlow asked.

Minerva strode back in carrying a thick tome that was a copy of the one she'd had back at the library. "It's in all the territories, and every library I'm in contact with has asked me to reach out to Vita." Her voice softened now as she looked at her niece. "I think it's more popular than you realize. People of all ages love it. Your illustrations...they're breathtaking."

Harlow wondered how they made copies. She doubted printing

presses existed here, but she guessed magic was the simple enough answer.

Minerva set the book in Harlow's lap as she continued. "This is why she wants you to see the rest of the book. And why I was surprised when you told me you were a tiger."

Frowning, Harlow looked down at the pages, saw a Siberian tiger that looked just like her or Brielle stalking through a dark forest. Eyes were watching from the shadows, almost blending with the leaves. She couldn't read the words, but the image told a tale itself. The tiger was on the hunt and danger was all around her.

She quickly flipped through the pages, watching as tigers, a lion, a dragon and a wolf hunted a witch. The wolf looked a whole lot like Ace too. *Hmm.* As she got to the end, there was a tiger lying in a patch of grass, crimson spreading around her.

Icy fingers slicked down her spine as a sense of foreboding overtook her. "One of the tigers dies at the end?"

"This isn't the end," Vita said. "I'm working on the second book. It's a duet."

"What happens?"

"I don't know yet. I haven't seen that part... Your friends are at the back door. You may let them in."

Harlow looked up and blinked.

Minerva's lips pulled into a thin line, but she stalked off, muttering under her breath about rule breakers.

"So you haven't seen the end? But do you know how we can find the witch?"

Vita shook her head as she looked back at the fire. "No. No. I cannot see her in my mind. Not now. Only when I sleep. She is hungry. Very hungry. The dragon fed her so well and now she craves the same power once again." Her voice had taken on an almost rhythmic quality as she spoke.

Harlow was aware of the others coming in with Minerva, but kept her focus on Vita.

"When you see her in your dreams, what do your surroundings look like? Could you maybe draw them for me?"

Vita nodded, then stood without a word and headed to the back of her house.

"She'll be in there a while," Minerva murmured, rubbing a hand over her face before she collapsed in the now free seat. "She gets lost in her drawings."

"Did you know she is a seer?" Harlow asked, annoyance popping inside her. "Because something tells me these aren't the first visions she's ever had." They were so damn specific—she'd written an entire book about them with incredible details.

Minerva was silent and the others remained in the kitchen, happy to let Harlow do the talking. They were so quiet, so still, it was likely Minerva could almost forget they were there. The four of them might be tall, the males huge overall, but they were really, really good at blending in.

"Fae aren't seers," Minerva finally said.

"Well, I think we can both agree that's bullshit."

Minerva frowned at her. Then she spoke again, her voice lower. "If the former king had ever found out about her abilities, he'd have had her executed or used her for his own gain. He'd have taken her from her home. So the family just denied her abilities to the point where I believed they didn't exist." She covered her face for a long moment, clearly in shame. "Or I tried to."

Harlow glanced back at the others and stood, having nothing left to say to this record keeper. She moved in next to Aodh, slid her arm around him as they waited for Vita. "There's food if you're hungry," she murmured.

But they all shook their heads.

Harlow leaned into Aodh, simply holding him, taking this small break of time to enjoy the sensation of having her arm wrapped around him. Touching him. She'd gone so long without him. This time together was a gift.

Luckily it didn't take as long as she'd feared for Vita to return with a few pages of sketches. Not overly detailed but filled in with color enough that the places were easily identifiable.

"It is too late for you to go anywhere else tonight. You will stay here.

I have an extra room and enough food." They came out almost like orders, but Harlow had a feeling that was simply the way Vita communicated.

"They can't stay here." Minerva stood at her niece's words, faced all of them. "It is illegal for them to even be in this realm. If you're caught housing shifters—"

"Then I will face the consequences. What will they do to me anyway? The royal guard does not come here anymore and the new queen is not a bigot. She will change the laws soon. Change the laws." The repetitiveness seemed to come and go, but was definitely a part of her speech pattern.

Harlow's heart ached for this female. It seemed that her entire life her family had denied and tried to suppress her seer abilities. Had they even acknowledged her other differences? Harlow pushed back her anger because it wasn't the issue right now, but she still hated it for this kind fae female who was helping them. She'd gone through life not truly being seen.

"We don't want to put you in any danger," Harlow said quietly. Because even if Vita was willing to open her home to them, Harlow wouldn't allow her to be hurt because of their presence.

"You will not. There is more danger in the forest than in my home. You will sleep well here, and in the morning leave on the rest of your journey."

Harlow looked at the others. Aodh lifted a shoulder, clearly not caring one way or the other. "We'll stay if it's not an imposition. But I think after we leave, you should find somewhere else to stay for a while. If this witch learns of your book, she could come after you if she realizes that you're literally telling the truth about her crimes."

"This is my home. I will not leave," was her only response.

Something Harlow understood. She wanted to tell the others that she suspected Ace was following them. Or was at least in the territory, if Vita's book held the truth. But she decided to hold off until they were alone.

She liked Vita, but her crew were the only people she truly trusted right now.

CHAPTER TWENTY-NINE

Flavia kept the heavy book gripped tight under her arm as she made her way down the salt-covered sidewalk next to the cobblestone street, trying desperately to keep her gait steady.

There weren't many people out this late, likely because it was so cold. Little snow flurries had started falling, and though it wasn't much, school had been let out early in preparation and people were staying inside with their families.

Which put a dent in her plans. The family she'd targeted would be locked up tight tonight, and she'd planned to take their son when he walked home from school. She'd had everything arranged perfectly, but this snowfall had wrecked everything.

Though that might be a moot point regardless because of the book she'd just stumbled across in a local shop. Other than a tavern, it was the only place still open after sunset.

Some young brats had been raving about the book, and she'd glanced over, fully prepared to tell them to quiet down. And then she'd seen the display.

There were nearly two dozen copies of a beautifully illustrated book in the style of human fairy tales on a revolving rack in the middle of the aisle. Around it had been a forest scene created with little figurines, including a tiger, a dragon and a witch.

Curious, she had glanced inside the tome because the dragon figurine had looked so similar to her former prisoner. The male she still dreamed about—the desire to suck out all his power was a living thing inside her. She felt hollow now without all that power, and the hunger only grew worse every day that passed.

When she'd started skimming the pages, ice had formed inside her, crystallizing down her spine. Instead of finishing what she'd read in the shop, she'd bought it and hurried out.

She needed to be alone, to see if this was as bad as she thought it was. It couldn't be what she thought it was.

It simply…had to be a coincidence.

The walk to the cottage she was renting for a couple weeks only took fifteen minutes but as the need to flip open the book and devour it took hold, time seemed to stretch on and on.

"Finally." She slammed the heavy wood door behind herself, letting her glamour fall away as she hurried to the table in the kitchen.

With trembling hands, she flipped open the book and started reading quickly, her heart racing.

Despite the little figurines from the shop that had depicted a hideous monster, in the actual book a beautiful blonde witch was hunting fae in a far-off, fictional realm. And "heroes" from another realm were hunting her for crimes she'd committed years ago.

As more cold snaked through her, she looked around the quiet cottage, realized the drapes were still open. She'd never been careless before, but she was shaken to her core. She hadn't paid attention to anything as she'd rushed inside to read.

Taking a deep breath, she shut the drapes, then started the fireplace with a burst of magic. The little action made her feel more at ease immediately. Grounded her.

As she returned to where she'd left the book, she forced herself to think calmly, rationally.

Someone was clearly writing about her. But how? She'd been very careful when killing, always had been.

She flipped a few more pages, looked at the detailed illustrations of her favorite kill of the last few months, then flipped to another image of where she'd dumped the bones.

The drawings were beautiful, but far too detailed. As if someone had been following her, watching her. But that wasn't possible.

As anger surged through her, she turned back to the other page and traced her fingers over the fluid lines, remembering the delightful kill a couple months back. Flavia had broken her pattern and murdered a highborn lady who'd been rude to her in the market.

But not before she'd made the female pay. She'd trussed her up like a turkey, rendered her mute with a simple spell, then tossed on a glamour spell so she looked like the woman. Glamour spells like that were difficult, but it had been at night so if there had been any fractures in the illusion, the female's husband hadn't seen them.

Besides, once she'd gotten naked, the stupid male hadn't cared about anything but mauling her breasts and getting himself off. As he'd started climaxing, she'd let the spell drop, slit his throat, and stolen all his energy.

The moment had been *absolute* perfection. The kind she lived for.

Because of his recent climax, his energy had been stronger, wilder, and she'd very much enjoyed forcing that female to watch Flavia screw her husband. She'd killed her afterward, of course, and then she'd done something else she'd also never done.

She'd left that bitch naked to be found by her servants instead of draining her dry.

This book didn't reveal any of those details. No, it told a much simpler story of a rampaging witch stealing people's souls. Which wasn't quite the truth.

She didn't have a thing to do with souls. But their power, their strength and gifts...those were hers for the taking.

And the illustration of the highborn lady's bedchambers, the dress she'd been wearing that night—it was all a mirror copy.

So someone knew what she was doing. Shutting the book, Flavia looked at the front of the book, saw the name on the cover.

It likely meant nothing, would be a pen name of course. And there weren't things like social media in this realm so she would have to hunt down this author a much different way than if she'd been in the human realm. Well, *before* The Fall. Now things were just as difficult there.

Not like that mattered now. *Focus, focus,* she ordered herself.

"My lady, I've just finished your laundry." A sweet female voice called out, the sound of the back door opening and closing. "I meant to get this to you hours ago but the snow has been awful..." The female who owned the cottage stepped into the kitchen, a basket in her hand filled with clean linens. Her eyes widened when she spotted Flavia at the kitchen table. "Who are you?"

Flavia cursed herself for her stupid mistake. She should have checked the locks before allowing her glamour to fall. Unfortunately now the female who had been excellent at keeping this place clean was going to have to die.

Flavia gave her a sincere smile as she stepped around the table. "I'm visiting my dear friend," she said as she approached. "And you must be Rhona. Here, let me help you with that." She plucked the basket from the female's hands, but then she dropped it intentionally.

As she did, she withdrew her athame from her skirts and plunged it into the female's chest, striking her heart.

"This isn't personal," she murmured as the woman stared at her open-mouthed, the pain catching up to the receptors in her brain. "I hadn't planned to kill you at all. Blast it," she muttered as the female slumped forward, getting blood all over the newly laundered sheets.

Hefting the female up, she took her to the bedroom, laid her on the unmade mattress and straddled her. As she did, she twisted the knife and breathed in deeply, the faint power from the fae female lingering in the air.

And as Flavia sucked in the energy, more and more of it released from the fae, wanting out, wanting to find a new home inside Flavia.

By the time she finished, the female was nothing but bones inside her utilitarian clothing.

And Flavia barely felt any stronger.

"What a waste," she muttered. Staring at the bones for a moment, she then flopped on the bed next to the female.

This wasn't supposed to happen. She'd liked staying here, had picked out families in neighboring towns to target in the coming days. Families with more powerful fae, the kind that would feed the hunger inside her.

She glanced over at the bones, frowned. Then she sat up. "I'm not dumping these," she said to the empty room. She wasn't going to waste her time.

Not after that book had been released. It was too dangerous to return to her dumping grounds. She needed to leave this realm—it was the only thing that made sense if she wanted to survive.

But she would need more strength before she ran. And supplies.

Going to the window of the bedroom, she pulled the drapes back, looked at the flickering lights from the nearby houses.

This town was small, provided textiles for the realm. And they were fairly cut off, with the nearest town an hour or so by horse.

If she wanted power, she could wipe out this entire town tonight. All she had to do was move quickly. Unfortunately she couldn't tease her prey, draw it out how she preferred.

Tonight was simply about gaining raw strength. Then she would leave, never to return.

She would start over somewhere else, taking what she wanted, where she wanted. And the new world in the human realm would do just fine.

Things were different since The Fall—wilder, less civilized.

Perfect for her needs.

CHAPTER THIRTY

"Do we trust them?" Harlow kept her voice low, even though they'd retreated to the nearby forest, using the night and trees as cover. Her gut was telling her that they could trust Vita. She didn't seem capable of lying, and the scents rolling off her had been so pure. So real.

"I trust the hot one," Brielle said as she took a bite out of an actual block of cheese she'd snagged from the plate of food. "Vita," she added, as if they'd thought she was talking about the older fae.

Harlow shot her twin a surprised look. Not because of the cheese thing, but the hot comment. Normally her twin was professional to a fault. "You can't cut off some cheese like a civilized tiger?"

Brielle ripped another bite right out of the block with a feral grin.

Axel snorted and said, "Yeah, I think Vita is telling the truth. And Jesus, can you imagine going through life having your whole family deny who you are?"

Aodh had his arm firmly around Harlow's shoulders. "I trust them both, even if I don't like Minerva."

"Then we're agreed because I trust them too," Harlow said.

"Then we stay the night, and in the morning, see if we can find our target from the drawings," Aodh said. "They were quite detailed and I think I might ask Vita if she's able to draw some of those images from an aerial view."

"Good idea." She pinched his butt.

He raised his eyebrow, but didn't respond otherwise.

"Oh my goddess," Axel grumbled. "You two are taking the guest room tonight and Brielle and I will sleep by the fire. I can smell your damn pheromones."

Her twin stretched and nodded as she polished off the cheese. "Sounds good to me. I wonder if she's got more of this cheese. It's delicious," she murmured.

Once they returned to the warm house, they found Vita and Minerva talking quietly in the kitchen. Minerva almost looked resigned to having them there, and okay, Harlow didn't blame her. They could get Vita in trouble by staying at her house, and Harlow never wanted any danger to befall anyone because of her. But especially not a fragile fae who was sharing all her knowledge at great risk to herself and asking for nothing in return.

"I'm sorry for my attitude earlier," Minerva said to them, her tone sincere. "I just worry about my niece. And perhaps I'm not showing it in the right way."

Brielle shrugged. "No worries. We look out for our family too." Now there was the faintest hint of a bite in her twin's tone. "So I know you won't say a word to anyone about us staying here." Oh...yeah, more than a bite. Yep, Brielle was definitely threatening Minerva. "And I also know that once we leave in the morning, you're going to take your niece back to the library with you or to your home, and keep her safe."

"Oh, I do not need to leave," Vita said quietly.

"We'll see." Brielle kept her hard gaze on Minerva as she spoke.

Minerva just nodded, her face slightly pale. "I will keep my niece safe."

Harlow shot Brielle a *calm the hell down* look, but her sister just lifted a shoulder, her tiger in her gaze.

Ignoring Brielle, Harlow looked at Vita. "I wanted to ask if you would mind drawing us some aerial views of the places you've seen in your dreams? Or visions," Harlow corrected as she changed the subject and silently told her sister to chill. She wasn't sure what was up with this sudden aggression.

Vita nodded once, her pale wings visible again, but they were pulled up tight against her back. "I will start on them now and give them to you in the morning. I do not mean to be a rude host but I need time to decompress and sleep. The guest room and bathroom are open for you to use. And any food is yours to take. Please help yourselves."

Minerva sighed as her niece left, then started for the door, but paused as she grabbed her robes hooked by the front door. "Please try to be out of here before the sun rises. She has lovely neighbors but...I still worry about her. And," she added, shooting a look at Brielle, "I will be back in the morning and do my best to convince her to come stay with me. If she won't, I will stay here with her."

"You'll convince her. I have faith." Brielle unstrapped her blades then, a practically feral expression on her face as she held them loosely in her hands.

"What the hell was that?" Harlow murmured once Minerva had left, the door thudding shut behind her. Minerva wasn't as understanding or supportive as she should have been, but she didn't seem bad at heart. And she'd been helping them freely. They certainly didn't need to piss off anyone right now when they were covertly hunting in this realm.

Brielle gave a tight shrug. "She denied what Vita was her whole life. It pisses me off. Someone needs to take care of that little fae."

Harlow wanted to ask her twin if she planned on volunteering for that role, but the energy rolling off Brielle right now was too chaotic and aggressive as she started stripping.

"Come on," Harlow said, grabbing Aodh's hand as her sister shifted to her tiger and flopped down in front of the still crackling fireplace.

Axel had started stripping too, was no doubt about to shift, and Harlow simply needed to be alone with Aodh. Tonight had been far more fruitful than she'd imagined. That spell Dallas had given them had really come through.

As Aodh shut the door to the little bedroom behind them, she turned, and found herself quickly pinned to the nearby mattress.

"What are you doing?" she murmured against his mouth, or tried to, even though she had a pretty good idea what he was doing. And approved.

Oh, how she approved.

"I think that's obvious," he growled.

"We can't do anything, we're on a mission." But she was already pulling her shirt off. Because self-control? She had none when it came to him.

He snickered as he tugged his own shirt off. "Really didn't even have to convince you, did I?"

"I'm just saying for the record," she whispered, "that this is totally unprofessional."

"Good thing we're not getting paid, then. And I'll be unprofessional all day long if I get to eat your pussy," he continued as he practically ripped her shoes and pants off.

Heat engulfed her at his words and she had to remind herself to try to be quiet as he buried his face between her legs like a male starving.

She hissed in a breath but managed to keep her mouth shut as she arched off the bed. He teased her with abandon, and every time he let out a low growl, it reverberated through her, adding to her pleasure.

She clutched onto his head tightly as he pleasured her, focusing on her clit with the most perfect amount of pressure. It didn't matter that years had passed, he'd remembered everything she liked. And she knew it wasn't going to take her long to come, but she wanted him inside her first.

Hell, she was desperate for it.

For all of him. "I want to mate you," she rasped out as he sucked on her clit. The words just popped out fully formed before she could think about them.

He froze, looked up her body as she stared down at him. "Now?"

"No. *Yes.* I mean...obviously I want to now, but I know we can't. When we get home though...you're mine forever, dragon." Once they mated each other, it would send them into a frenzy and all they would want to do was hole up and screw for weeks. So that had to wait.

In response, he sat up, then shoved his pants all the way off, inch by slow inch, revealing the hard planes of his hips...his gorgeous cock.

Her gaze traveled lower, over his thick, muscular thighs, then riiii-ight back up to what was directly between his legs. Call her shallow—she'd missed all of him, especially this part. Probably more than was healthy. But whatever.

His dick was beautiful, and if she'd been a poet, she would write an ode—or a sonnet?—to it.

Her inner walls tightened as he climbed up the bed, over her, caging her in against the little mattress they very well might break. The dark smoke of his mating manifestation filled the room, surrounding them, wrapping around them like a living creature.

And his scent was delicious, making her light-headed as he brushed his mouth over hers. "I don't want to wait. We mate tonight."

"Aodh—"

"No." He grabbed her wrists, held them above her head, pinning her in place.

If she'd wanted to fight him, she could have, but she savored this sensation of him holding her down. Something about it grounded her, made her feel secure. "If we mate now—"

"Then whatever the future brings, we're together. Forever."

"If something happens to me, then—"

"We go together. I'm not living in a world without you, Harlow. I already lived in a cold prison where I thought you left me behind. That was bad enough. I won't live in a world where I know you're gone. I can't."

"But you've barely been out of that prison." And she was terrified that if something happened to her, it would kill him too. Because that was how dragons mated—literally for life. When a mated dragon died, so did his mate. And vice versa. As far as she knew, they were the only shifter that mated that way. "This wouldn't be fair to you." And she loved him too much to shackle him like that.

"You could never shackle me," he growled.

Oh, had she said that aloud?

He loosened his grip on one of her wrists, cupped one cheek gently. "If you die tomorrow, or a hundred years from now, I don't want to be left behind. But if you're having doubts—"

"No!" she shouted, then winced. "Never," she whispered. "I just hate the thought of something happening to you because of me. I want every damn person, human and supernatural alike, to know you belong to me. I want my scent and bite mark on you." Heat flooded her, her canines already straining at the thought of getting to claim him. She was a very, very possessive tiger.

"If it happens, it happens. You and me, this thing has been burning bright from the moment we met. I don't want to wait until after this mission."

"I don't either." Though she knew it'd be a hell of a lot harder to leave tomorrow when all she wanted to do was mate until they couldn't walk, she would.

"Good. We're stronger together anyway."

Hell yeah, they were. She grabbed the back of his neck, started to yank him to her, but he was faster, crushing his mouth over hers in a sure claiming.

His mating manifestation was all around them now. It was the only thing she saw other than him, as if it was cocooning them, protecting them from the rest of the world.

She arched her back, her breasts brushing against his chest, her already hard nipples pebbling even tighter at the friction. All her muscles were pulled taut as she wrapped her legs around him, squeezed tight.

She used to fantasize about what he would feel like naked against her, skin to skin. Before they'd gotten together, and then even after, she'd dream about him, count down until she got him inside her again. It had been her greatest, and only, obsession.

"I need you in me," she whispered, trying to be quiet as she arched her hips up to meet his. But energy was building inside her, a desperate hunger only he could quench. She felt as if her entire body was engulfed in heat as a low buzz of raw energy hummed through her.

He reached between their bodies, sliding a finger inside her, then two, curling them against her as he withdrew, then pushed back in.

She sucked in a breath, her heart a wild beat in her chest as he continued slowly teasing her.

She clutched onto his ass, gripped hard. "I don't want your fingers."

"Shh," he murmured, brushing his mouth over hers as he withdrew his fingers.

She bit his bottom lip. "I'll shout the house down if you don't get inside me right now." She was also a very impatient tiger.

He smiled against her mouth, nipped her back. "I've missed every single thing about you," he growled as he thrust fully inside her. "Especially your impatience."

She gasped at the way he stretched her, even though it hadn't been that long ago that they'd done this. But the sensation of his thick erection pushing inside her, knowing where this was leading other than orgasm, was everything.

She dug her fingers into his back, unable to stop the tight, possessive grip as he pulled back, slammed into her again.

As he flicked his tongue against hers, the gentle teasing at odds with the hard pattern of their hips, she felt her canines start to lengthen and tore her mouth from his, buried her face against his neck.

A sense of rightness punched through her as she scraped her teeth against his neck.

And his answering groan sent streams of pleasure ribboning through her as he stretched her, claimed her.

When he reached between their bodies again, this time teasing her clit, she bucked against him, ignoring the way the bed creaked. They definitely weren't being as quiet as she'd hoped, but there was no way around that now.

Blood rushed in her ears as her orgasm started to build, shoving up to the surface as her inner walls started clenching around his erection, tighter and tighter.

"Come for me," he growled as he tweaked her clit, the pressure against the sensitive bundle of nerves enough to send her over the edge.

As her climax surged through her, she scored the side of his neck, breaking his skin and sinking deep.

"Harlow!" he cried, and she felt him give in to his own pleasure and start coming inside her.

As he did he pulled back suddenly, and while she wanted to grab him, bite him again, he did the same to her, burying his own face against her neck.

When she felt his teeth pierce her skin, her entire body jerked with the pleasure and another orgasm slid through her, this one smaller, chasing that first one until she collapsed against the sheets. A sense of peace rolled through her, like nothing she'd ever experienced.

"I love you so much," she whispered, cupping his face with her hands. It was as if she'd broken apart, only to be put back together, newly whole. "And I'm glad we didn't wait to mate."

"I love you too—and I'm not done."

She snorted out a laugh, then froze when he stared at her. "What?"

He reached up, ran his thumb gently over the sensitive area he'd just bitten on her neck. She could already feel her skin healing, but something else was happening, as a tingle of awareness spread through her. "It's me," he whispered. "It's like a tattoo of me on your body, in dragon form. I mean, it's *exactly* like me, right down to the way my tail curves when I'm flying." There was a note of awe in his voice.

She sat up, shoving at the tangle of sheets, and paused, her eyes widening as she saw the little tiger symbol on his neck where she'd bitten him.

The bite marks were already healing as well, but there was a tattoo-like symbol of a Siberian tiger that looked just like her, the little tail swishing midair. "You have one too." She reverently touched the mark, her heart expanding as the mating bond slid so fully into place she wanted to burst from joy at the pleasure of it.

"What is it?"

"It happens with tigers." She was still whispering as she rubbed her thumb back and forth over the symbol on his neck. "When a tiger mates with their fated mate, a tattoo-like symbol appears on their bodies. It can be anything, from a symbol of their mate, or in our case, a very clear representation of the other. My parents have them too." Though theirs were on their inner wrists.

"I've never heard of that before."

She kissed the mark, the warmth of pleasure inside her expanding. "I know it can happen with wolves too, but I don't know about other shifters. Aurora and King have the same thing, though theirs didn't appear until weeks after their mating. She freaked out the first time and, oh my goddess, I don't know why I'm talking about them."

He laughed lightly, sliding off the bed and pulling a small mirror off the wall and bringing it to her.

Because he clearly understood her. As he held it up, she tilted her head, looked at the small symbol of Aodh, a fierce, detailed midnight-dark dragon against her neck right where he'd bitten her. She swore his amber-orange eyes practically glowed at her.

Eyes wide, she gently touched her neck, traced her finger over the mark and saw he was doing the same to his.

"I like that I've got you on me." Pleasure filled Aodh's voice as he put the mirror back, joined her on the bed again. "And now..." He grabbed her hips, flipped her onto her knees. "I'm going to show you exactly how much I like it."

A shiver rolled through her at the hunger in his voice and she spread her legs, ready for him to take her again, to keep claiming her until they had to face reality in the morning.

Until that time, she was going to enjoy every single moment of this night with her mate.

Her fated mate, the male she'd been destined to find. No matter what happened, no one could ever take this from them.

CHAPTER THIRTY-ONE

Harlow blinked in surprise as her twin quietly stepped out of Vita's bedroom, looking pleased with herself—and only wearing a silky pink robe far too small for her tall, lean frame. It was clearly owned by the petite fae. Her sister would never buy something so frilly, and besides, she'd have never packed something like that for a mission anyway.

Harlow blinked again as she moved into the hallway from the guest room. "Really? You're hooking up with someone now?" she whispered, beyond shocked.

Brielle shrugged. "Didn't expect to meet my mate on this mission, but..." She lifted a shoulder and stepped past Harlow as if she hadn't just dropped a grenade. Then she paused, turned to her sister and pulled her into a hard grip. "Congrats," she murmured, hugging Harlow tight.

Tears sprung to Harlow's eyes, but she brushed them away. "Oh yeah." She hadn't forgotten about her own mating, but her sister's declaration of meeting her mate had thrown her. Brielle had to be kidding, right? Her and Vita?

"Oh yeah?" Brielle snorted. "I can smell the mating bond and...you're fated mates." Brielle's eyes teared up too as she touched Harlow's neck gently. Then she turned, headed back down the hallway. "Come on, I'm about to make my future mate breakfast and you can help me."

"Wait, *you're serious?*" she shouted, far too loudly, as she hurried after her sister into the kitchen. Brielle had just met Vita.

"Pretty sure you don't need me to repeat myself," Brielle murmured as she started filling a pot with water.

"What are you doing?" Harlow stared at her sister.

"Are you having issues comprehending this morning?" Brielle lifted an eyebrow. "Has the mating bond made you loopy?" she said on a laugh. "I'm clearly making tea. Vita said she likes it for breakfast."

Harlow covered her face for a long moment. "I just... She's your mate? She's so small!" And fae. Far too delicate and fragile. The thought of having a fragile mate made her want to break out in hives.

Brielle stilled, setting the pot down as she turned to Harlow. Her tiger was in her eyes. "And?"

"Oh sweet goddess, I'm not insulting her," she hissed out as quietly as possible. "She's stunning, obviously, I just...she's delicate, that's all. And you guys just met!" And Vita was very feminine, the opposite of her sister.

Brielle stalked forward, not looking any less deadly in the ridiculous robe. "Good thing I was born with teeth and claws. I'll destroy anyone who messes with her."

Holy. Sheeeet. "She's really your mate?"

"Yep. She came out last night to get something and we started talking. It took like five minutes but my tiger recognized what she was to me. And I'm not going to let anything happen to her."

"I'm so happy for you," Harlow whispered again, not wanting to wake anyone—where the hell was Axel anyway? Aodh was in the shower, but she didn't want Vita to hear them talking about her. She ignored that voice of worry in her head that wanted to ask a bunch of questions—like, how would this work since Vita lived in a different realm and was fae? Her sister had always supported her, and she was going to bite back any questions because she was certain her twin had already thought of them.

The tension in her twin's shoulders loosened slightly and her expression shifted. She looked almost stunned. "I…still can't believe it. I feel like I've been hit with a dragon's tail right across the face."

"Kinda like how I felt when I met Aodh." So yeah, she got it. But still. This was…unexpected.

"Mom and Dad are going to be so happy that the two of us are mated —well, I will be soon." And Brielle seemed annoyed by the wait. "I'm going to need to court her properly after this."

Despite the shit of everything going on, Harlow let out a laugh and pulled her twin into a tight hug. Now they had even more of a reason to see this through. As she stepped back, the rear door opened and Axel strode in, shirtless, his pants hanging low.

"Snowed like crazy last night. Few inches at least. Pretty sure I flashed some of Vita's neighbors so we should probably roll out soon." He winced slightly. Then he stared at Harlow, inhaled deeply. "Congrats," he murmured, rushing forward, pulling her into a hug. He gripped her even harder as he continued. "Two of my favorite people in the world. I'm so glad you took that leap of faith." When he stepped back his eyes were slightly wet, but he quickly turned away, wiped at them before he cleared his throat.

"Thanks," Harlow murmured, then paused. Wait until he heard about Brielle. "You hear that?"

They all paused, and Harlow's heart rate kicked up even as Brielle said, "Hoofbeats. A lot of them."

Then a bell sounded from somewhere fairly close, the gong heavy, ringing over and over. She'd seen a big bell in the center of town when they arrived so that had to be it.

Vita and Aodh came out at simultaneously, no doubt having heard the same thing. Aodh only had on pants, but Vita was dressed in a tunic and leggings, and was carrying fur-covered boots.

Her cheeks flushed pink when she glanced at Brielle, but then she looked between the rest of them. Or at their shoulders; she didn't make eye contact. "Everyone stay inside. I need to see what's happening."

Brielle stepped forward. "We're not letting you—"

"I'm not asking." Vita shook her head impatiently as she slipped on one of her boots. "That bell means something is happening, that we have riders coming in from another town. I need to go out with the rest of my neighbors or they'll wonder what's wrong."

"I think one of your neighbors might have seen me naked," Axel said. "Not in lion form, but when I was coming out of the forest. I hadn't fully put on my pants yet."

"It's fine, regardless. I know my aunt worries but I have good neighbors. And I've helped a lot of people in this town with my visions. She and my family denied what I am, but my neighbors have been more open. One of them…is a half-shifter. And I know for a fact that other half-shifters live in this town. No one would turn you in, and honestly, I don't know if there would be anyone to turn you in to anyway. The royal guard isn't what it used to be and this conversation is over. Over," she repeated. Then she lifted up on tiptoe, kissed Brielle briefly, then hurried out the front door.

Harlow blinked in surprise, but Axel didn't seem surprised at all so maybe he'd known they hooked up last night. And Harlow was glad to see that Vita had a backbone. She might be delicate physically, but she was going to hold her own with Brielle or anyone, that much was clear.

"I'll head out the back," Aodh said, already stripping his pants off. "I'll go into camo mode and follow her."

Harlow nodded, beyond anxious to get outside and see what was going on. Especially since the hoofbeats were getting louder.

She looked at her twin and Axel and nodded when they gave her a questioning look. They'd lived with each other long enough to basically read each other's minds. "We take to the trees," she said, just to make sure they were all clear.

Aodh crushed his mouth to hers. "I've got your six."

"Always."

As he hurried out the back door the rest of them did the same, but they remained dressed.

Harlow hurried to the edge of the cottage, peered around the wall and watched as fae on horseback kicked up the fresh snow, heading toward the downtown area. Near the library and the other main buildings. Looked like they wouldn't even need to shift; they could just head in the direction everyone was going. "Let's grab hooded tunics for now," Harlow murmured.

Once they had their heads covered, they started out on foot, circumventing the main road but heading in the direction Vita had gone. Brielle was tense as they hurried, clearly in protective mode, which was new for her twin.

Though Harlow couldn't see Aodh, she knew he'd taken to the air, would be circling above looking for any danger.

The mating link between them was strong, a warm pulse in the air she felt all the way to her soul. He was hers and she was his. No matter what happened, no matter what the universe threw their way, she was mated to the male she loved.

And she was glad they hadn't waited.

CHAPTER THIRTY-TWO

A odh slowly circled the downtown square where much of the town had gathered around the fae who'd ridden in on horses. There were only a dozen of them, and none of them looked to be guards or soldiers of any kind. They were dressed in simple tunics and leggings, and they all had one thing in common—they stank of raw fear.

A dark-skinned female in purple robes was standing in the middle of a gazebo, trying to get everyone to quiet down.

Harlow, Brielle and Axel were on the outside of the crowd, not standing near each other but strategically spaced out. Vita was standing with a family of four—parents and two young daughters. Her neighbors, no doubt. He was close enough that he'd overheard them talking, knew the girls' names were Mave and Keeva. And Vita's aunt was next to her as well, also in purple robes.

When the dark-skinned female called out again, everyone quieted and a male from the incoming group stood next to her, said something loudly in his language.

After being imprisoned for so long in the Domincary realm, hearing so many conversations, Aodh understood most of what the male was saying.

"I come from your neighboring town, Nairn. Our entire town has been slaughtered, save for a few of us. She came in the middle of the night, killing us household by household. We don't know what she is, but she's powerful and angry." His voice broke and he covered his face for a long moment.

One of the females who'd ridden in with him stood next to him now, her voice softer, but everyone was deathly quiet so her words were clearly heard.

"We barely managed to escape. We hid away some of our children as we raced here for help. Someone needs to ride on to the royal guard, but we fear there won't be enough time. She's a monster. A beautiful monster, stealing everything until nothing but bones are left. She's some kind of mage or witch." The fae female's voice shook slightly. "We don't know what direction she will go next, but you all need to be prepared. To run, if necessary. We tried to fight her with our magic, but it wasn't enough. It was like she simply consumed what we threw at her and it only made her stronger."

Aodh quietly landed, kept his camouflage in place as he shifted to his human form. He drew closer to the outside edge of the crowd, moving in Harlow's direction, but was careful not to get too close to anyone. Just because they couldn't see him didn't mean they wouldn't feel him if he bumped into them.

A murmur went up as people started talking among themselves.

Aodh needed to talk to the fae who'd just ridden in, get the location of their town and any details possible. If the witch had taken to massacring an entire town, she would be drowning in power. Though something had to have triggered her to cause her to kill an entire town overnight.

Or maybe she'd simply gotten tired of small kills spaced out. Didn't matter.

The only thing that did was stopping her. And they had to do it now, when they knew where she was, or at least the vague direction.

While he didn't relish the idea of revealing himself to an entire town of scared fae in this moment, he knew it would take too long to get the fae who'd just arrived alone.

So he maneuvered his way to the raised gazebo structure and

dropped his camouflage. He held his palms up, ignoring the awkwardness of being naked—until someone from the crowd screamed. Either because of his nakedness or the clear fact that he wasn't a fae. He was simply too large to be one of them, not to mention the shape of his ears gave him away.

"Oh Jesus," he muttered. Then in their language, he said, "I'm hunting this witch, and—"

The purple-robed female next to him blasted white energy out of her hands at him, her eyes widening when the light bounced off him, slamming into the platform they stood on. The wood beneath him sizzled under the impact, a dark scorch mark left behind.

"Really?" he growled, his dragon in his gaze now. He'd put his hands up in the universal sign of *I come in peace.*

One of the fae withdrew a sword, but Vita was shoving her way through the crowd. "Stop attacking him!" the small female shouted.

Aodh didn't need her help, but appreciated it even as a sense of protectiveness swelled inside him. It was clear Brielle had claimed the fae female and he'd do anything to keep her safe now too. The female had given them shelter and was helping when she didn't need to.

She was one of theirs now.

There was a low murmur as someone from below helped her up onto the raised platform, just lifting the petite fae up. "He's not here to hurt you."

Her voice wasn't overly loud, but everyone had quieted to listen to her, which told him that people respected her enough to hear what she had to say. At least enough to shut up. She was looking off to a point in the crowd, somewhere in Brielle's direction.

"He's here to help us, so please, no one else attack him. He and his friends are hunting this witch and all they wish to do is stop her. I've helped enough of you in town, warning you of impending disaster, that you know I'm telling the truth. We need to give them whatever they ask for." She paused for a moment, then said, "If you've read my book, then you already know the truth. They're here to help us and we need to help them do that."

There were more murmurs and nods before the purple-robed female shouted out a short order, telling everyone to let Vita continue—even as she gave Aodh a wary look. Still, she unhooked part of the bottom of her robing, taking off a large swath of fabric, and handed it to him with a pointed look.

He wrapped it around his waist as Vita continued to speak. He was also aware of Harlow moving closer to the stage, winding her way through the crowd so subtly it was impressive. Her hair might be covered with the hooded tunic, but he could pick his female out of any crowd, anywhere.

Vita turned to the small group of fae who'd arrived from their neighboring town. "He needs to know everything about what happened. Any detail you can give, now. There will be no time to waste."

The fae looked nervous, but nodded.

Minerva climbed onto the platform as well, spoke quietly with the female who'd blasted Aodh with energy. Then Minerva looked at him. "Can you stop her?"

"We're going to try."

She nodded once, then motioned to the newcomers. "Come this way. We will speak in private now."

There was a lot of murmuring from the crowd then, but Aodh ignored them, waiting for Harlow, Brielle and Axel to join them before stalking off with the fae.

They convened in the library they'd broken into the night before, with the two fae who'd spoken to the crowd looking even tenser.

No wonder; they'd lost friends, family, perhaps children.

"I'll speak plainly," he said brokenly in their language.

"We speak many human languages, including English," Minerva said. "They do as well."

He nodded, continued quickly. "We're not familiar with this realm so we're going to need a map as well as any details you can give us of your village."

"I'll grab the maps you'll need," Minerva murmured, hurrying off.

"What details are you looking for?" the male asked, his accent heavy but his words clear.

"When did the killings start? How was she discovered? Did she leave the town or did you escape before that happened? Anything that might be relevant. Also, are you certain the children you hid away are safe?"

"I don't know exactly when the killings started, sometime in the night. I'm the, ah, I think the human word is law enforcement, for our village. Someone came to me hours ago, told me they'd seen a stranger in the local pub and people were dying as she stole their souls. I admit I thought he was drunk and seeing things, but after I confirmed it I sent out scouts to the rest of the town..." He cleared his throat. "From what I can tell it started at a cottage on the outskirts of town and seemed to spread inward."

Oh goddess, Aodh knew exactly where this was going.

"We tried to fight her, but she just laughed and blasted us with magic. I woke up while she was killing one of my men and slipped away. We don't have any mages in our village and no way to fight that kind of evil, so I spread word and everyone who could escape did. Most of them ran into the nearby forest. I told them to keep running and not to stop until they reached a neighboring town. We went in different directions, hoping to spread the word and gain help. We need firepower and magic users. That is the only thing that will stop her."

"No." Harlow stepped forward then, having already pushed her hood back. "The more magic you use on her, the more she'll suck up and become even more powerful. We're going to take her down the old-fashioned way," she said as Minerva returned, two scrolls in her hands.

Meaning with claws and steel. And fire. Lots of dragon fire.

"Why should we trust you?" the male snapped, his voice reverberating with rage. But underneath it was fear.

"Because they have no reason to lie to us." Vita spoke for the first time since arriving in the library, and it was clear she at least knew this male from the faint familiarity of her tone. "And the witch imprisoned him," she said, pointing at Aodh. "He was the dragon underneath the castle we all heard about. The one who escaped. He wants her dead as much as we all do."

Someone sucked in a surprised breath, but that was the only response.

Minerva ignored everyone as she stretched out the maps on a nearby table, speaking quickly. "This is where we are. This is the quickest road to their town but…ah, you will fly, I take it?"

Aodh nodded, glad when Harlow moved up next to him, leaned gently into him. Having her shoulder against his grounded him.

Brielle and Axel had moved up as well, were looking at the map intently.

"Okay, then you can clearly see the quickest route." She looked at the fae male. "What forest did your people escape to?"

From there, the male pointed out where the others had run and gave a quick recap of the surrounding areas, highlighting all the information they might need.

The witch wouldn't have gotten too far, not unless she had the ability to transport. And since that ability was so very rare, and she'd long since stopped being able to take his powers, she would still be in the realm.

Aodh thought about sending one of his crew to the portal that bridged this realm with the human one, to guard in case she managed to escape them, but immediately dismissed the idea. They couldn't split up. And she would not escape them.

"We leave in two minutes," he finally said, turning to his crew. "Say your goodbye now," he added to Brielle.

Brielle simply nodded before pulling Vita into a private corner to speak. It was clear that once they returned she'd be claiming this female for good if Vita would have her.

"What happens if you fail?" the female with the purple robes asked.

"We're not planning on it. But I suggest sending a message to your royal guard, regardless. Some of your mages might be able to come up with a way to trap her at least."

The female snorted softly. "They will not be able to help. They were not even able to hold the castle when dragons invaded."

"Then you pray to your goddess and fight. That is all I can suggest." He rolled up the map, turning from her, because he didn't plan to fail. But then he paused, eyed who he assumed was a high priestess of sorts, given the differences in the way she and Minerva were dressed. And the fact that she'd packed a punch with her magic blast before. "The female,

Vita, she'd better remain unharmed. Or I'll finish what those other dragons started in this realm and not stop."

The female's eyes narrowed at him. "We would never harm Vita. She is one of our own. We did not take her as seriously as we should have before, but...she has helped many people in town with small matters. She is loved. No one will harm her."

Aodh nodded, turned to his female and Axel as Brielle stepped forward. "The fastest approach will be from the sky. How do you prefer to attack?"

"I'll stay in this form for now," Harlow said. "Might be easier to infiltrate smaller places."

"We need to take her down outdoors," Axel murmured, his arms crossed over his chest. Small spaces were how they'd gotten in trouble before.

They all nodded in agreement, ready to go.

"The wolf following you is in the woods by my house," Vita said quietly as she approached. "He wishes to go with you."

Aodh snorted and looked at Harlow. Seemed her friend had definitely followed, not that Aodh was surprised. He thought he'd caught Ace's scent more than once. And it seemed clear that Vita had seen the male in her vision, or however that worked. There'd been a wolf in the pages of her book, so yeah. "Let's go grab him," he murmured, taking Harlow's hand in his as they stalked out of the library.

This was it. They weren't letting that evil witch slip through their fingers this time.

CHAPTER THIRTY-THREE

"Congratulations, by the way," Ace said as he crouched low with Harlow and the others on Aodh's scales, the wind rolling over them as her mate flew higher. "I'm happy for you and I can't wait to get to know your mate." Her friend's expression was so sincere it warmed her from the inside out.

When she'd first settled in New Orleans, she hadn't been sure if she'd stay—had thought she might move to Scotland eventually and live with Star's clan—but she'd developed deep roots, made friends who were more family than anything. And she wasn't giving up any of it.

"Thank you. Still can't believe you followed us," she murmured.

"Like you didn't scent me?"

She just lifted a shoulder and glanced down below at the countryside flying by beneath them. Aodh was flying lower than normal as they headed in the direction of the massacred town. "Unless she's killed everyone, we're going to need to set up a triage."

"Only after we kill her." Axel's voice was hard as he looked over at her, his hair slightly ruffling in the wind. "We can't let ourselves get sidetracked even if it means leaving someone in pain. Because if we don't stop her, how many more will die?"

They were all crouched down low, Aodh's back wide and long enough to transport all of them. And with the angle he was flying at, they were blocked from most of the wind. But it was still damn cold up here, even for her tiger blood. "I know." She looked away from Axel, continuing to scan below them. She hated that he was right.

As soon as they landed, picked up the witch's scent, they had to go on the hunt. They knew what she smelled like too from the last time they'd almost caught her, and Harlow and her twin were incredible trackers. Hell, all of this crew were born trackers. If anyone was going to find and neutralize the threat, it was them.

And it had to be now.

They'd been flying for twenty minutes, and though they'd told the fae from Vita's town to stay behind, she wasn't sure they would listen. This was their home. They would want to protect it, something she respected.

When Aodh suddenly dipped lower, she knew why—she scented the witch. A scent she would never forget. A faint floral scent that might be pleasant, almost happy, but underneath it was rot. Garbage. Death.

Scanning the landscape, she spotted the quiet, calm village. Far too quiet for this time of morning. There were no fae to be seen anywhere, no animals either.

Just an eerie quiet across the territory as Aodh descended on the picturesque village. He set down right at the entrance to the village, before a sloping bridge that was more for decoration than anything, then let his camouflage drop.

They all slid off his back, and as they did he shifted in a burst of magic. Harlow handed him loose pants, but he didn't bother with anything else, not even shoes as he slid his backpack on.

Using hand signals, he motioned for them to cross the bridge. He and Harlow would take one side of the town, the others would take the opposite. They weren't splitting up per se, but they couldn't be up each other's asses for this either.

There was too much ground to cover. And no time to lose.

Harlow withdrew one of her blades from her back sheath as they crossed the small bridge, listened to the faint gurgling of the flowing water beneath, though some of the stream had frozen over.

The scent of the witch was faint, but as they moved over the bridge, deeper into the town, it got stronger.

Aodh put his hand on her hip, motioned that they would go left, start checking into the far too quiet butcher shop at the edge of town.

Inside, the scent of blood was there of course, but...not fae. There was nothing at all there, no signs of life.

In the coffee shop next door it was the same, and it was clear the place had never been opened at all this morning. Which lined up with what the fae townspeople had told them.

Ten minutes later, the five of them convened at the end of the main strip of shops.

"Fae bone remains at the pub," Brielle said, her expression grim. "Just like that male said."

"A lot of them," Axel added.

"We found some remains, bones only, outside what looks like their local jail," Harlow said.

"Come on." Aodh's voice was tight as he motioned toward the homes on the next stretch of road. "We look for signs of life and try to catch her scent trail."

Fae towns and villages all had a fairly similar layout. They were often built by a body of water on a long, usually winding road with shops and places of business on one side, and homes on the other. Then there would be outlying homes, usually those of nobles or wealthier individuals, or fae who liked privacy. She hadn't seen any far outlying homes like that on the way in. This was just a small village nestled near a thick forest and running stream.

As they neared the first house, Harlow could already smell the death trailing on the air, the iron scent of blood unmistakable.

She moved quickly, heading around the right side of the cottage, Aodh going around the other side while Brielle moved in through the front door.

Harlow eased in through a side window that was partially open, the sheer white curtain flapping slightly in the breeze.

Axel headed to the back of the house and she knew Ace would be moving in behind one of them.

Four of them had operated as a team for so long, and it didn't matter how much time had passed. And she'd worked with Ace long enough to know that he was a huge asset. They all knew what to do when infiltrating a place. They didn't bash open the front entrance. No, they infiltrated from multiple points instead.

Harlow's boots were quiet as she stepped into a bedroom. The bed itself was longer than most human beds, but narrow, the bedding a simple sunshine yellow. It was empty. The covers were rumpled.

Frowning, she glanced back at the window—maybe someone had snuck out of it just before she'd arrived?

There were many scents in the room—four, all with a similar sort of underlying smell. All members of the same family. But there was something else there—the rot. Not active, but the witch had been here at one point.

As she reached the bedroom door, there was the slightest shuffling sound. So faint, like a mouse scurrying across the wood floor. From the closet. She didn't turn to it, however, not wanting to give herself away.

She stepped out into the hallway, came face-to-face with Aodh.

His expression was grim. "Dead fae female in the kitchen. Bloody, no bones though. Just looks as if she was struck in the head and left to bleed out," he spoke subvocally so only she could hear.

Harlow held up a finger, pointed to the bedroom. *Someone in there*, she mouthed.

He nodded and they moved in together in a fluid motion. He grabbed the bed and lifted it up in the air while she ripped open the closet door and froze to find a little fae girl on the ground, her arms wrapped up around her knees, her eyes wide as she stared up at Harlow.

Oh goddess, she hoped this wasn't an illusion. Sheathing her blade, she crouched down so that she was eye to eye with the girl. "We're here to help," she whispered in broken fae. She didn't speak it well, but could say a few sentences.

The girl launched herself at Harlow, taking her by surprise as she started sobbing into her neck. She said something in her own language, the words not clear, but the intention behind them, crystal. The girl's body trembled as she continued to cry.

"We need to get her out of this house," Harlow said as she hurried from the room, taking her toward the front of the house instead of the back where she guessed the kitchen area was. Because it didn't take much to guess that the dead female was this girl's mother. And Harlow wasn't letting her see that.

"Can you ask her how long she's been hiding?" Harlow said to Aodh.

Harlow tried to keep her voice soothing as the girl continued to cry. She'd never done well with crying individuals, but kids were the worst. She just wanted to take away all this girl's pain and felt absolutely useless.

Sniffling, wiping at her face, the girl leaned back and spoke.

Aodh quickly translated the girl's words. "She came in and hurt my nanny. My daddy yelled at me to run so I opened my bedroom window and pretended to leave, but hid instead."

"Can you tell her that I need to set her down and that my friend Ace is going to stay with her while we hunt after the monster who took her father?"

Aodh quickly spoke to the little girl, who dug her fingers into Harlow's back even tighter as she gripped her, but then suddenly let go, her face turning practically feral. "Please find my daddy."

Okay, Harlow definitely understood that.

It was clear Ace didn't want to stay behind, and while they'd originally planned to only hunt down the witch, everything else be damned, it was impossible to leave a scared kid with a dead nanny in her kitchen behind by herself. They simply couldn't do it.

"I'll finish looking through the rest of the homes for signs of life," Ace said.

"I can help you." The little girl's English was stilted and Harlow realized she must be twelve or so, older than she'd originally thought.

Harlow looked at her in surprise. "You speak English?"

"Ah...only a little human English and French. I'm better with French."

"If he orders you to run, you do it. Understand?" Harlow asked the girl.

She nodded.

"Let's go. We're not losing the trail." Aodh's voice mirrored her own impatience. They needed to get the hell out of here before they lost the scent trail forever.

CHAPTER THIRTY-FOUR

It took only minutes for the four of them to reach the edge of the forest with their supernatural speed. They'd raced after the witch's scent and it had led them outside the town toward the thick cluster of trees bordering the village to the west.

They'd left a clear path in the freshly fallen snow, so even if Ace couldn't catch their scents, he'd have no problem tracking them into the forest if necessary.

A swarm of bees buzzed through Aodh as they stepped past the border of the forest, his energy a pulsating live wire, his dragon ready to strike at any second. The moment they entered the forest, everything shifted before his eyes, a burst of color exploding everywhere, the grayness of the snowy day dissipating.

It was as if they'd walked into a Pollock painting, with color splashed everywhere, their surroundings almost canvas-like, as if they were in a 3-D watercolor image. He growled in frustration, automatically turning to Harlow.

She wasn't there.

None of them were.

His dragon wanted to roar out in rage, but he'd been fooled before, could see this for the illusion that it was. And he could feel his mate through their mating bond. His Harlow was close. And he could scent her, that unmistakable sunflowers scent somewhere nearby.

"Harlow!" he shouted as instinct took over. He shifted to his dragon form, his magic taking over in an angry burst dripping with power. As he did, his surroundings shifted again, and now that he was a dragon he could see the spell overlaying the forest. The faux bursts of color over the gray day.

"Aodh!" Harlow's voice came as if through a tunnel, and he could almost make out her shape fifty yards away.

Fear punched through him as he searched for the witch. "Shift! Change to your tiger form!" Harlow would be able to see through the magic better. It was more difficult to fool their animal side with magic, especially since they were aware of the spellwork happening.

Through the haze of the faux painting overlaying the reality of the forest, he saw a brief burst of sparks, then Harlow's beautiful tiger form.

She was still fuzzy, not completely clear, maybe even farther than he'd originally thought, but he could feel their link as he scanned around them, looking for the witch.

The monster had to be nearby, had clearly led them into this trap. Maybe that was why she'd taken that fae male? To lure them here, of course. Didn't matter.

They were here now and that bitch was too.

"Close your eyes when you shift and use your nose," Axel called out to them, his voice much farther away.

Something had happened when they'd entered the forest to separate them, divide them. A spell.

Following the lion's order, Aodh closed his eyes even as he flapped his wings, took to the air. He needed to get higher, try to get an aerial view below. But he inhaled deeply as he breached the treetops, got a lock on the scent of blood.

Metallic, fresh—and underneath it all was that putrid rot emanating from the witch herself.

It was so faint, but it didn't matter how much she tried to mask it with a beautiful shell. She couldn't hide her true nature. There was something very wrong with the female who only seemed to crave power for power's sake. Who had no respect for any life other than her own. And to what end? For more power?

What was the point of it all?

He opened his eyes as he swooped down toward the forest again, an icy wind rolling over his scales as he pulled his wings in tight, arrowing downward.

Through the thick trees he spotted two individuals. A prone male, and a standing female.

He called on his fire, let it out in a targeted burst, aiming right at the female.

She turned, held her hands up, blasted magic at him.

He barrel-rolled in the air, dodged the blow. Even though he had a spelled amulet, he wanted her to tire herself out, to waste all her stolen magic and drain her unnatural power.

As he dove straight for her, thunder cracked the air and a deluge of water fell from the sky, making it impossible to see.

He swerved upward, trying to see through the thick fall of— Wait, he wasn't getting wet. *Son of a...* He closed his eyes, focused on the witch's scent and dove back downward, ignoring the sound of thunder and rain falling. It wasn't real.

He opened his jaws, breathed out another blast of fire as the female's scent shifted directions. She had to be running. He aimed in her direction.

A screech rent the air and he opened his eyes as he felt treetops brushing his wings, pulled them in tight for a hard landing.

He slammed into the icy snow, felt the cold against his body as he sank into it. As he did, he realized that the painting-like overlay was gone, the spell likely broken.

The witch was on her back in the snow, her head at an odd angle as she lay motionless beneath a huge tree the size of a redwood.

There was no more rain, no thunder.

Aodh stayed in his dragon form, eyed the surrounding forest warily.

The fae male lay in the snow fifty yards away, his body unmoving. Harlow's tiger was creeping in behind the male, her movements that of the sleek, silent predator she was.

Body tense, he approached the unmoving witch. Crimson stained the snow around her, the scent of iron and rot strong.

But...she wasn't burned, he realized. Why the hell was there blood all around her? Another illusion?

He turned, saw Harlow approaching the male, and fear exploded inside him. His gut told him this was a trap. It had to be. Everything this witch had ever done had been based on illusions.

And this had been too easy.

~

CROUCHING BY THE INJURED MALE, Harlow shifted to her human form and felt for a pulse. It was thready, but at least he was alive.

"You're gonna be okay, buddy," she murmured, hoping it was true for that child's sake.

Out of the corner of her eye, she watched as Aodh approached the fallen witch, and moved in his direction. She could help the fae male later. Her mate needed her now and she'd always choose him first.

No matter what.

Behind her in the forest, she scented her twin and Axel moving in, was glad they'd all finally reunited. Somehow when they'd entered the forest, they'd been separated. Scattered from each other in a burst of magic that had scraped over her skin like little knives.

As she moved toward Aodh, ready to help him finish the witch if she wasn't already dead, a slight movement registered in her ears.

She turned, saw the male sitting up—and the glamour slid away as the beautiful blonde witch with soulless eyes smiled at her, her expression feral as she reached out inhumanly fast, ripped Harlow's necklace off with a quick jerk.

Just as fast, Harlow's claws extended and she slashed out, slamming her claws and fist into the witch's chest with a savage snarl.

Eyes wide, the witch screamed, and that was when Harlow saw the glint of the blade flash under the sunlight as the witch slashed at her.

Harlow released her other set of claws, swiped at the witch's face, slamming her paw at the female with brute force.

The witch dodged back even as blood poured from her chest and the slash marks on her cheek.

Energy glowed in the female's hand and she threw a ball of magic at Harlow.

Harlow ducked and rolled, felt heat sear across her hip as she hit the snow. As she moved, she called on her beast even though it'd make her a bigger target as a tiger.

It would also turn her into a seven-hundred-pound killing machine.

As she shifted back to tiger, she leapt at the witch, ready to rip her head off.

But Aodh was suddenly there, using his magic to transport himself behind the witch in a flash of a moment.

Harlow was fully extended, in mid-leap when the witch threw her blade. It sang through the air.

Harlow tried to move, but was a fraction too slow.

The razor-sharp edge slammed into her upper shoulder. Pain pierced her, hazed her vision as she fell to the snow.

Poison. She could feel it. Smell it.

Coursing through her veins, making it impossible to move as she stared at the witch's dark, gleaming eyes.

She shifted to her human form without thought, the pain lancing through her forcing the shift as her body tried to shove the poison out.

"Got you, bitch," the witch snarled, baring her teeth in a feral smile.

"Did you?" Harlow whispered as blackness crept in at the edge of her vision, her gaze on Aodh now.

Even if she died, this bitch was going down too. A small consolation that wasn't a consolation at all because it meant her mate would die with her.

Her mate was a silent beast behind the female, his dragon eyes gleaming as he opened his jaws and—clamped down hard, tearing the female completely in half in one savage rip.

Light burst from the female before the pieces of her charred body fell to the snow, burned everything beneath it away.

"Harlow!" Aodh crouched down next to her in human form, naked, fear in his amber-orange eyes as he cradled her close.

213

He was so damn powerful and beautiful. "I'm okay. Just...poisoned, I think."

"That bitch. You're not going out like this, I swear it." Brielle was on her other side, clasping her hands to her chest even as Axel hovered behind her, his hand on one of her calves in a comforting grip.

"You're going to be okay," Axel murmured.

"We need a healer," Aodh growled.

Harlow tried to speak, but couldn't make her vocal cords work as agony coursed through her veins. Oh goddess, was this what she'd stabbed Aodh with all those years ago?

"You're not dying on me! You don't get to leave me." Aodh's desperate voice was filled with pain as he pulled her in his lap.

"No one's dying!" Brielle released a claw, sliced over her own wrist and held it to Harlow's mouth.

As the sweet blood touched Harlow's tongue, rolled down her throat, the pain eased immediately and she sucked in a breath of crisp, fresh air. Tiger blood wasn't like phoenix blood, but it had healing qualities. And her twin had just bought her some time until she could find her backpack, get the vial of Aurora's blood they'd brought along.

"Goddess." Aodh buried his face against her neck and held her close.

"I'm...okay," she murmured, but clutched onto him tight, wrapping her arms around him as he stood, bringing her with him. She had to reassure him. Soothe him. "I'm totally good, see?" She stood, looked down at the thankfully healing wound on her shoulder and winced.

But as she did, everything went fuzzy, hazy, and she stumbled forward, lost her footing as pain ricocheted through her.

"I'll find you in the next life," she whispered, unsure what the hell was happening. But if she was dying, she needed him to know that she wasn't letting him go. Not even in death. She was a greedy bitch like that.

He screamed out in agony, fire erupting out of his mouth as he threw his head back. "No! You won't leave me! You're not allowed to!"

But blackness consumed her.

CHAPTER THIRTY-FIVE

A odh's entire world tilted on its axis as Harlow started to fall. He caught her as her eyes rolled back in her head, saving her from hitting the ground.

No. Goddess, no...

"Come on, Red." The old nickname slipped out as he eased her back to the snowy ground, feeling her pulse.

Steady.

Their link was still there, pulsing between them, but she wouldn't open her eyes. "Open your eyes!" She couldn't be gone. He couldn't lose her.

His only saving grace was that if she went, he did too. He'd been in prison before, and the thought of losing his Harlow was a thousand times worse than being imprisoned again. It would be a slow, eternal death without his other half.

"Jesus, Aodh, we need to find her backpack. It has Aurora's blood in it and—" Axel broke off as the ground rumbled beneath them.

When he looked up, all around them the forest was starting to blacken and disintegrate. A shot of adrenaline punched through him as reality set in. "Now that she's dead, her spells are collapsing on each other." He'd seen something similar in the past and they were already losing time. Hell, it might be too late. "Jump on me when I shift," he ordered, not waiting for a response.

They had to get the hell out of there now. Or they were all dead.

He called on his magic faster than he'd ever done, his dragon bursting free in moments. As he scooped Harlow up in his claws, he felt Brielle and Axel climbing up his scales with the quickness and surety of felines.

He launched straight up as the ground shook beneath them again, the witch's body parts bursting into flames as she fragmented, turning to ash.

This was her last "fuck you" to the world, he had no doubt. She would take them all with her if he didn't hurry.

Flapping hard, he flew toward the fallen fae male, scooping the stranger up in his other claws only because he knew Harlow would have wanted him to.

All he cared about now was his mate and his crew, the rest of the world be damned. But he did this for his mate.

He let out a roar that he hoped translated to "Hold on!" as he banked sharply upward.

The giant trees surrounding him were crumbling, turning to black ash as the ground continued to shake below.

Multicolored light burst up from a crack in the earth, then another. The earth groaned and creaked below them, caving in on itself.

Heart racing, he flew higher, higher, his lungs burning until ice crystals started to form on his scales and nose. He held Harlow close to his chest, trying to keep her as warm as possible.

Breathing hard, he finally shifted directions, evened out and looked down, far beneath them at the giant, blackened crater of what had once been a thick, beautiful forest.

It looked as if someone had dropped a JDAM and wiped out all life.

In his claws, he felt Harlow stirring and adrenaline punched through him. He needed to get her warm. And fast. This had been too quick of an ascent.

Far below, the last remnants of the witch's spell were falling away so he arrowed down toward the village. Even as he went in for a landing, he was thinking of the next step. He wanted to pick up Ace and get the hell out of here and get his mate the help she needed. Everything else could wait. Including this injured fae male in his other claws.

By the time he landed by the original bridge they'd crossed, Harlow was stirring in his claws and he was desperate to shift, to hold her in his arms.

Everything seemed to move in slow motion as he landed, waited for Axel and Brielle to slide off him. He set the fae male to the side then laid Harlow down gently in front of him and shifted. It all took moments, but it felt as if an eternity passed, longer than he'd been in that prison.

"Red." He knelt next to her, cupped her cheek, hating how cold her body was.

Little ice flecks were on her eyelashes, but they were moving slightly. "I'm good this time, promise. I can feel it," she rasped out, sitting up, blinking away the crystals.

He scooped her into his arms even as Brielle pulled a small blanket from her backpack, wrapped it around Harlow's shoulders. "What can you feel?"

"The poison or magic or whatever that was, it's gone. The witch is definitely dead." Relief rolled through Harlow's voice as she leaned into him. "She's really gone."

Aodh buried his face in her neck and breathed in deep as the remnants of his mind-numbing terror ebbed in small waves. Harlow was alive, in his arms. Safe. "You scared me," he choked out, holding her too tight but unable to ease his grip. He'd almost lost his love. His life. "I thought I was going to lose you." Was going to follow her into the after-life and find her again. Because that was the only option he'd allow. Not even the afterlife could keep them apart.

"Never. I would never leave you." Harlow leaned her head on his shoulder, cupped his cheek with one hand. Her gorgeous eyes were already drooping as she said, "I want to go home. Take a shower. Screw your brains out. Not necessarily in that order."

He barked out a laugh as he gathered her close, inhaled the scent of his mate. His female was alive and she wasn't going anywhere.

Except home with him.

In the distance he heard Ace making his way toward them, along with some villagers who'd managed to survive. And the fae male they'd saved was waking up as well, but Aodh ignored everything as he buried his face in Harlow's neck.

"Soon," was all he said.

Soon, they would be home. But they would start the rest of their lives together right now.

CHAPTER THIRTY-SIX

B rielle stood in the doorway of Vita's cottage, her heart happy to see her future mate again. The fae of this realm had a ton of shit to deal with after that witch's rampage of destruction, and the effects of it would be felt for years. That wasn't something Brielle or her crew had to deal with, however. They were ready to leave, to get home to their family.

And Brielle wasn't leaving alone.

She stepped inside, shut the door behind her as Vita retreated to the kitchen.

Brielle slid her boots off before following, knowing she'd chase this female anywhere. The way she felt was bananas; it should be too soon. But there was something about this fae that called to the core of her. It was like a part of her that had been locked had opened up when they'd started talking, when her tiger had gotten the scent of Vita.

"I've got to leave soon. My sister and her mate want to get home." It would be good for them. Besides, they probably all needed to get the hell out of this realm regardless. She was pretty sure someone had sent a message to the royal guard, and they didn't need to be here when those fae arrived.

"Ah, of course." Vita looked at a spot on Brielle's shoulder as she nodded slightly. She looked so delicate in her frilly sunshine yellow dress with fur at the collar, but Brielle knew better. This female was strong. "I appreciate you saying goodbye."

Uh, say what? Brielle straightened. "I'm not saying goodbye. I'm asking you to come with us."

Vita met her gaze for a moment, before looking away again. "This is my home."

"I know, but I'm asking you to make a new one. You wouldn't have to hide who you are, and there's a seer I'm friends with who I'm pretty sure you'd get along with."

"You don't know anything about me." She tapped her fingers on the kitchen table in a rhythmic succession.

"I know the important stuff." Like how intelligent she was. How brave she'd been when she'd gotten up in front of the town and defended Aodh. How her pretty cheeks flushed when she climaxed. Vita had a steel backbone, even if she didn't realize it.

"What if...things did not work out between us? Would you just discard me?" There was a wealth of pain in those softly spoken words.

And Brielle wanted to slay anyone who'd ever made this female feel less than.

"I don't know about the fae," Brielle said as she stalked forward, "but tigers mate for life. We're loyal till our dying breath. But I want one thing clear—even if you don't want to mate with me, if you just want to be friends...it'll break my heart, but I'm still inviting you to my realm. I think you would shine there. And honestly, I don't like that you've had to hide your light your entire life. It makes me want to claw shit up. So come to my realm because you deserve a better life with people who accept you and value you. Don't do it for me. Do it because you're worthy."

Vita sucked in a sharp breath and was silent for a long moment. "I enjoy your bluntness so I will be blunt in return. You could break my heart."

"And you can break mine." Brielle knew that without a doubt. But she was a tiger, a sneaky, sneaky cat. Though she knew that being sneaky with Vita would never have worked. This was a female who needed the truth not only shown to her, but told in words she'd understand. There would never be any games with this female. Not mind games, anyway. But she hoped for other, naked ones. "I'm willing to take that risk."

In her bones, she knew she and Vita had a chance at something wild and fun and *forever*. A different adventure than Brielle had ever imagined—with a brilliant, gorgeous female she'd never imagined. Goddess, this female brought her to her knees.

"I don't need you to save me," Vita whispered as she stopped tapping, took a small step forward.

Oh yeah, take another step, her tiger silently demanded. "Well maybe I need saving." Goddess, please save me, Brielle thought.

Vita smiled and the sight was a punch to Brielle's chest. This female lit up the entire room. Hell, the entire realm. "Then perhaps I will save you and...we can have an adventure." She crossed the rest of the way to Brielle.

And Brielle could finally breathe now that her female was close again. She'd been trying to give her some physical space so Vita wouldn't feel overwhelmed, even though the distance had been making her tiger cranky. Brielle clasped Vita's hands in her own, held tight. "An adventure that never ends."

Vita smiled again and Brielle pulled her into her arms. Even as Vita went up on tiptoe, Brielle covered her mouth with hers, ready to take this female home, and claim her forever.

CHAPTER THIRTY-SEVEN

One week later

With her fingers linked through Aodh's, Harlow and he stepped into their mansion's library downstairs as Bella spoke to someone via her laptop. They'd just finished dinner out on the back patio and Bella had called them in excitedly minutes ago.

Harlow knew that a lot of satellites had survived The Fall, as well as cell towers. But also knew that there was magic involved in keeping much of the communication up and running around the world.

"Hey guys," Bella said, smiling as she waved them over. "Meet my new best friend, Victoria. While you guys were gone, we dug into energy witches and she hacked some old databases using the information you gave us."

Harlow was surprised Lola hadn't hacked for Bella, but smiled at the pretty female with jet-black hair and emerald green eyes.

"Hey." The female half waved, a big smile on her face. Behind her appeared to be a large library of sorts, definitely bigger than their little one. "It's nice to put faces to your names. Bella told me you guys had quite the adventure."

That was putting it mildly. "You could say that."

"So, to jump right to it, I reached out to a lot of healers around the world. I think you might know this but I'm going to tell you anyway. We've created a linked database so we can work quickly when someone is injured with something we've never seen before. Or, whatever, you get the idea. I basically asked everyone I know about energy witches..." She cleared her throat. "And I might have hacked some old databases. Some of the security is outdated so don't be impressed. Anyway, a few healers got back to me and—"

"Just tell them!" Bella was practically wiggling in her seat like a toddler. "They don't need the details of how you got there."

"Oh my God, Bella!" Victoria said on a laugh and it was clear the two really had become friends. "Fine," she said, still smiling. "No details on how I 'made the baby.' What I've managed to put together—along with Bella, because I'm not taking all the credit for this—is that the witch you were hunting did indeed do work for hire years ago. Mostly for the Russian government, but she was truly a freelancer. It makes sense since the Cold War never really ended and...I'm rambling. Anyway," she said, giving Bella a pointed look. "Using the files you gave Bella and what I found on my own, I was able to create a map of her killings in this realm. I can't do anything about other realms, but there was definitely a pattern. She had hunting grounds, and this dates back to well before you were even born or in the Marine Corps. So like you suspected, she would have been killing regardless. She just liked to get paid for it."

"Was she part of a coven?" Aodh asked.

"Yeah, do we need to worry about her family coming after us?" Because bring it, Harlow thought. If there were going to be some revenge seekers, she wanted to know now and she'd bring the battle to their doorstep instead.

"No." Victoria shook her head, her dark braid falling back behind her shoulder. "What I've been able to research about energy witches is fascinating. They have a lot of similarities to snakes, which feels telling. And they're nothing like 'regular' witches. They don't create covens. They're quite asocial, prefer their own company, and usually only search out mages or other witches when they want to mate. Sometimes they kill their own children, which is horrifying, but more often than not they kick them out once they're old enough to take care of themselves. As far as loyalty, they have loyalty only to themselves and that's it, so I doubt you have to worry about any sort of revenge."

Harlow nodded, allowed a bit of relief to slide through her. She wanted this chapter of their lives closed so they could move on to the next, better one. "Thank you so much."

"No problem. Oh, and I found out her name. It was Flavia."

"What a stupid name," Aodh muttered.

"Sounds like a coffee flavor or something," Harlow agreed.

Victoria blinked. "My mate literally said the same thing. Okay, we're planning a visit because you guys are going to be my friends too."

"Hey," Bella interrupted. "You were my friend first."

"And that's not changing, bestie!"

Harlow eased out of the room with Aodh as the two women started talking about...something. Kinda sounded like they were plotting to take over the world, and Harlow figured these two could do it if they put their minds to it.

Once they were out in the hallway, Harlow wrapped her arms around Aodh, buried her face against his chest. "I didn't realize I was still carrying around any worry about her until now." Because now that she knew they weren't going to have to face a future threat related to the witch, she felt like she could take a full breath again.

"Same." Aodh kissed the top of her head, breathed deeply.

She breathed him in again, the sensation of everything being right in her world settling in deep. Goddess, she loved him. "I've been thinking about the offer from King and Aurora to run part of their territory." She'd been thinking about it since they'd returned home—in between the many bouts of sex with Aodh.

Aodh's grip around her loosened just a bit as she looked up at him. "You'll take it."

She blinked. "How are you so sure?"

"Because I know you. It's a challenge, will always *be* a challenge, which is something you love."

This male really did know her. "You're okay with it?" He looked surprised by her question, but they were a team now—she didn't make decisions in a vacuum.

"Of course. As long as I get to help with the security and we work the same hours. I want all our free time to be spent together."

Warmth infused her. "Same." They had a lot of lost years to make up for.

"So...you want to go upstairs?" he asked bluntly.

Aaaand back to the truly important stuff. She snickered. "You think we have time?" The mating need was still riding the two of them hard and wouldn't be letting up for weeks. Maybe longer.

"Your parents and Brielle and Vita are going to be gone for a while."

"True..." Their parents adored Vita as much as Aodh, and had been showering the fae female with affection the last week. The female had been soaking it up too.

"So?" Aodh's gaze landed on her mouth as he spoke.

And she felt that heated look all the way to her core. "Well," she murmured. Her parents were out looking at different living spaces, and she was pretty sure Brielle and Vita might be looking at a place for the two of them as well. They weren't officially mated yet, but it was heading that way. Harlow actually planned to ask all of them to move into a communal home with her and Aodh in the territory she'd be heading up, but that was something she'd deal with later tonight. "I don't know if you're up to the task of getting me off in that amount of time though."

His gaze narrowed. "I know what you're doing, but challenge accepted." Then he moved lightning quick, tossed her over his shoulder.

She yelped, slapping his butt as he raced for the stairs.

"Oh goddess, you two," Axel murmured as he passed them on the stairs. "I would say get a room but it's clear that you are."

As they reached the next floor, there was a cry of surprise from... Phoebe's room?

Before she could tell Aodh to put her down, he'd set her on her feet and thrown open the door. "What's wrong?" he demanded, looking for a threat, his dragon in his eyes.

Harlow did the same, sweeping into the room as Phoebe stood by her bedroom window, eyes wide. "Nothing."

"Damn it!" a male voice cried from outside.

Phoebe tried to shut the window, but Harlow moved quickly, peeked her head outside and...saw Micah, a teenage wolf shifter who'd only recently grown out of his gangly stage, tangled in a web of sorts.

"What's going on down there?" Harlow called out, trying to suppress her laughter.

Perfectly illuminated under the moonlight, Micah flailed against the netting, which flared a bright neon white every time he moved. Oh yeah, there was definitely some magic involved. "I don't know! Stupid net!"

Harlow drew back into the room, looked at Phoebe. "Has your boyfriend been sneaking in and out of your room?"

"Ah..." She cleared her throat, then crossed her arms over her chest, all defiant. "So what if he has?"

Harlow raised an eyebrow at the tone.

Phoebe dropped her arms. "Sorry," she muttered. "Yeah, we just wanted to spend more time together and...I didn't want to deal with everyone hassling him when he comes over. You guys are psychos sometimes and you know it. Asking him eight billion questions that he's already answered before, demanding to know his intentions with me. It's ridiculous!"

Harlow could actually understand that because they were a lot when they wanted to be, especially when it came to protecting their own.

"That's an impressive trap." Aodh had his head out the window now, nodding approvingly.

"A little help here!" Micah called up.

"We'll ease back," she said to Phoebe. *Probably.* "Legend!" she called out and moments later the little boy raced in, his expression serious.

"Yes?"

"Your trap worked. Can you let your sister's boyfriend go now?"

He pumped a fist in the air. "Yes! And yes, I'll release my prisoner." His grin was as feral as his twin's normally was as he raced away.

Phoebe blinked. "Legend set that up?" she murmured, even as she hurried after her brother, yelling at him for being "a tiny little monster."

Aodh slid an arm around Harlow's shoulders as they followed after them. By the time they made it outside, Legend had somehow untied the knots and neatly folded the spelled netting.

Harlow was pretty sure he'd used his own magic, since phoenixes had an inborn kind of magic, but wasn't going to question him. Well maybe later, because this trap was awesome and she wondered if he could make one for her.

"That was impressive, kid." Micah was pulling leaves out of his hair as Phoebe brushed some off his back.

Legend shot him a surprised look. "You're not mad?"

"Nah. I live with a bunch of wolves so I'm used to pranks. But you do know that this means payback, right?"

Legend grinned again, some of that normal seriousness fading away. "Bring it on," he said before running off.

"You're going to stop using the trellis and window to enter and exit the house, Micah." Harlow gave him what she thought of as her "big sister" look. "Just use the front door, okay?"

He rubbed a hand over his short curls and nodded sheepishly. Then he looked over at Phoebe as if she hung the moon.

"Am I in trouble?" Phoebe looked at Harlow with those big green eyes, her expression pleading.

And Harlow figured that one day these two were going to end up mated. So she vowed to ease back on them. A little. "No. Just...make smart choices, okay?"

"Okay." Phoebe grinned, her expression pure relief. "Since you're being so nice, I'm going to push my luck and ask if it would be okay if we met up with some people? Some of our friends are having a movie night and asked us to go."

"Yeah, go on." Maybe she should have punished her for sneaking her boyfriend in, but she didn't have the energy and Phoebe was a good kid. She needed the room to make mistakes.

"That was surprisingly lax." Aodh's deep voice wrapped around her, soothed her as he pulled her into his arms once the teens had run off.

"I know." She hugged her mate tight. Her *mate*—she would never tire of that word. "But I worry if we're too strict, she'll buck at the rules and not trust us. And she's right, we are kind of hard on her boyfriend. And he's a good kid." A hell of a lot better than she'd been at that age.

"He's a boy," Aodh grumbled.

Which just made Harlow laugh. Aodh had fit right into living here with ease, as if no time had passed. She knew they'd have issues to deal with in the future, but for now she was enjoying the pure bliss of being newly mated.

She'd been given two weeks off from work since they'd returned from the Domincary realm, to enjoy the newly mated period. And she didn't plan to waste one moment of it. "So...bedroom? Or do you want to fly into the outer territory for some privacy?"

They'd found privacy in the wild forests surrounding the territory and had used it to their full advantage. Because they could be as loud as they wanted, and sometimes a tiger just wanted to scream her mate's name as he was making her climax.

"Once in the bedroom, then we head out." He brushed his lips over hers, but it quickly turned into a hard claiming as he backed her up against the outer wall of the house. "Or," he said, breathing hard, his eyes darkening with need, "we leave now. Because I don't want to be quiet."

"We leave." Because she didn't either.

Her mate stripped with shocking speed before he shifted to the most beautiful creature she'd ever seen—her richly dark dragon with scales the color of midnight and eyes the color of her tiger. Fire rolled over his scales once, teasing the ends of them, before it retreated, his dark scales shimmering under the moonlight.

She raced up his back and settled in as he took to the air, inhaling the crisp scents of the fall evening of their home.

Home. Wherever Aodh was.

The End

Dear Readers,

Thank you for reading my latest book! If you'd like to stay in touch and be the first to learn about new releases you can:

- Check out my website for book news: https://www.katiereus.com
- Follow me on Bookbub: https://www.bookbub.com/profile/katie-reus
- Follow me on TikTok: https://www.tiktok.com/@katiereusauthor

Also, please consider leaving a review at one of your favorite online retailers. It's a great way to help other readers discover new books and I appreciate all reviews.

Happy reading,
Katie

ACKNOWLEDGMENTS

I owe a big thanks to you, my wonderful readers! Thank you for reading this series and asking for more. It's still going because of you. As always, I'm grateful to Kaylea Cross for all the things! I'm so thankful you're in my life. For Jaycee, thank you for another fabulous cover. Sarah, thank you for all the behind-the-scenes things you do. Julia, I'm incredibly grateful for your thorough edits and your help in keeping my Ancients Rising world organized. For my son, who is not allowed to read any of my books for many years (or maybe ever), thank you for being you. Your humor and the way you view life keeps me on my toes. For my mom, who doesn't like to read about 'all that paranormal stuff' and will likely never see this, you are another rock star in my life. Thank you for all you do that allows me to write more. And of course, to the best writer pups anyone could ask for—Piper and Jack, thank you for keeping me company every day.

ABOUT THE AUTHOR

Katie Reus is the *New York Times* and *USA Today* bestselling author of the Red Stone Security series, the Ancients Rising series and the MacArthur Family series. She fell in love with romance at a young age thanks to books she pilfered from her mom's stash. Years later she loves reading romance almost as much as she loves writing it.

However, she didn't always know she wanted to be a writer. After changing majors many times, she finally graduated summa cum laude with a degree in psychology. Not long after that she discovered a new love. Writing. She now spends her days writing paranormal romance and sexy romantic suspense.

COMPLETED BOOKLIST

Ancients Rising

Ancient Protector

Ancient Enemy

Ancient Enforcer

Ancient Vendetta

Ancient Retribution

Ancient Vengeance

Ancient Sentinel

Ancient Warrior

Ancient Guardian

Darkness Series

Darkness Awakened

Taste of Darkness

Beyond the Darkness

Hunted by Darkness

Into the Darkness

Saved by Darkness

Guardian of Darkness

Sentinel of Darkness

A Very Dragon Christmas

Darkness Rising

Non-series Romantic Suspense

Running From the Past

Dangerous Secrets

Killer Secrets

Deadly Obsession

Danger in Paradise

His Secret Past

Paranormal Romance

Destined Mate

Protector's Mate

A Jaguar's Kiss

Tempting the Jaguar

Enemy Mine

Heart of the Jaguar

CPSIA information can be obtained
at www.ICGtesting.com
Printed in the USA
LVHW031349120423
744161LV00001B/13